Doom With a View

Also available by Kate Kingsbury

MERRY GHOST INN MYSTERIES
Dead and Breakfast

PENNYFOOT HOTEL MYSTERIES
Mulled Murder
The Clue is in the Pudding
Ringing in Murder
Shrouds of Holly
Slay Bells
No Clue at the Inn
Maid to Murder
Dying Room Only
Death with Reservations
Ring for Tomb Service
Chivalry is Dead
Pay the Piper
Grounds for Murder
Check-Out Time
Eat, Drink, and Be Buried
Service for Two
Do Not Disturb
Room with a Clue

PENNYFOOT HOTEL CHRISTMAS SPECIAL MYSTERIES
Herald of Death
Mistletoe and Mayhem
Decked with Folly

MANOR HOUSE MYSTERIES
An Unmentionable Murder
Wedding Rows
Fire When Ready
Berried Alive
Paint by Murder
Dig Deep for Murder
For Whom Death Tolls
Death is in the Air
A Bicycle Built for Murder

For a complete list of titles,
visit doreenrobertshight.com

Doom With a View

A Merry Ghost Inn Mystery

Kate Kingsbury

CROOKED
LANE

NEW YORK

This is a work of fiction. All of the names, characters, organizations, places and events portrayed in this novel are either products of the author's imagination or are used fictitiously. Any resemblance to real or actual events, locales, or persons, living or dead, is entirely coincidental.

PUBLISHER'S NOTE: The recipes contained in this book are to be followed exactly as written. The publisher is not responsible for your specific health or allergy needs that may require medical supervision. The publisher is not responsible for any adverse reaction to the recipes contained in this book.

Copyright © 2017 by Doreen Roberts Hight

All rights reserved.

Published in the United States by Crooked Lane Books, an imprint of The Quick Brown Fox & Company LLC.

Crooked Lane Books and its logo are trademarks of The Quick Brown Fox & Company LLC.

Library of Congress Catalog-in-Publication data available upon request.

ISBN (paperback): 978-1-68331-776-0
ISBN (hardcover): 978-1-68331-235-2
ISBN (ePub): 978-1-68331-236-9
ISBN (ePDF): 978-1-68331-238-3

Cover illustration by Joe Burleson
Book design by Jennifer Canzone

Printed in the United States.

www.crookedlanebooks.com

Crooked Lane Books
34 West 27th St., 10th Floor
New York, NY 10001

Hardcover edition: September 2017
Paperback edition: September 2018

10 9 8 7 6 5 4 3 2 1

To Bill, for helping me to follow my dream, for encouraging me when I feel lost, and for celebrating with me when I succeed

Acknowledgments

To Michelle and Jessica, thank you for giving me such a pleasant place to research my books.

To the editors and staff of Crooked Lane Books, my thanks for your help and enthusiasm and for your genuine delight in my accomplishments. It's a pleasure to work with you.

To my agent, Paige Wheeler, for all your help and support. You and Ana-Maria Bonner are my anchors in this unpredictable and sometimes bewildering profession. Thank you both.

And to my readers, who keep me sustained and entertained with your lovely e-mails and posts. I write for you, and I thank you all for making it such a delightful and rewarding way to spend my time.

Chapter 1

"And now," the magician said, brandishing a red silk scarf at his inattentive audience, "I will make this egg completely disappear."

The elderly gentleman sitting a few feet in front of him uttered a coarse laugh. "What are you going to do? Eat it?"

Ignoring him, the magician draped the scarf over the egg in his other hand and waved his fingers over it. The handful of people in the living room watched in varying degrees of interest. Standing by the door, Melanie West smiled when she saw her assistant staring anxiously at the magician, who was apparently having difficulty getting rid of the object beneath the scarf.

When Cindi Metzger had first suggested Melanie and Liza Harris hire her boyfriend to entertain the guests at the grand opening of the Merry Ghost Inn, they had been less than enthusiastic. For one thing, they hardly knew their new employee, having hired her less than a month ago. In fact, when Melanie had told Liza that she had employed the young woman, her grandmother had tried to talk her out of it.

Liza had complained that they needed someone more mature. Melanie had argued that their new assistant was twenty-three and had work experience. Liza had grudgingly agreed to give Cindi a chance to prove herself.

Not that Melanie could blame her for being skeptical. Sometimes Cindi looked like a member of a punk rock band. One side of her head was shaved while jet-black hair covered the other side down to her chin, ending in pink streaks. She wore rings in her ears and studs in her nose and one eyebrow. Her eyes were ringed with black, and a string of tattoos cascaded down her arms.

Right now Cindi was dressed for the welcoming Halloween party, wearing her ever-present black tights and a black miniskirt. Her black boots reached her knees, and her black leather top had an emblem emblazed on the front of it. When Liza had asked her who she represented, she said she was a warrior huntress, which did nothing to enlighten Liza.

The impatient guest called out again. "Come on, you pathetic excuse for a magician. What are you waiting for?"

Up on the stage, Nick Hazelton appeared to ignore the heckler as he struggled to dispose of the egg. With a final flourish, he whipped the scarf away from his hand, revealing an empty palm to the audience.

Cindi applauded loudly while the disgruntled man seated on the couch snorted. "Call yourself a magician? You couldn't make a snowflake disappear."

The woman seated next to him gave him a hefty nudge with her elbow. "Shut up, Walter. You're spoiling it for everyone else."

Melanie could have hugged her. According to the information she'd received on their first group of guests, Gloria Olsen was in her early seventies, but she looked closer to her fifties. Her bleached hair swept upward in a sophisticated knot, her eyelashes were obviously false, and her Cleopatra costume was cut low enough to show some cleavage.

Seated next to her, Joe McAllister leaned over and whispered something in her ear. Judging from Gloria's smile, his words had bolstered her ego.

Joe had covered his bald head with a dazzling orange, blue, and green scarf, apparently borrowed from one of his female companions. Melanie assumed he was supposed to be a pirate, since he wore a black patch over one eye. It kept slipping down over his cheek, however, making him look like an aging clown instead of the dashing swashbuckler he was aiming to portray.

The twenties flappers seated behind him were sisters, both in their sixties and apparently enjoying a week without their husbands, who were on a hunting trip. Next to them, wearing a witch's outfit, Beatrice Carr sat dozing. She was the oldest of the group. All six guests were members of a book club and lived in the same retirement community in a Portland suburb. They were also the inaugural guests at the newly renovated Merry Ghost Inn.

Melanie and her grandmother had bought the centuries-old house on the northern Oregon coast six months earlier, intending to turn it into a bed-and-breakfast inn. But shortly after they had begun redecorating the rooms, a fire had destroyed a fair portion of the house.

Forced to delay their grand opening until now, they'd struggled to manage the renovations and finishing touches to the inn.

Melanie had been determined to preserve the old-world charm of the house, and both she and Liza were pleased with the results. The living room looked spectacular with its wall of books, dark-purple drapes, smoky-gray carpeting, and the sparkling marble fireplace.

They had replaced the brown leather couch and tweed armchairs with a lighter gray couch and chairs, accented with purple cushions. The grandfather clock in the corner had been a great find, thanks to a friend in the antique business, and added just the right accent to the room.

Now they were officially open, with six guests who had booked for the entire week. They had bookings after that all the way through the holidays. Things couldn't be better, Melanie thought as she turned her attention back to the magician. Except for Walter Dexter, who seemed determined to disrupt the poor magician's performance.

Nick had apparently given up on making things disappear. "I would like someone to help me with this next trick," he announced. He looked across the room and nodded at Cindi. "You, young lady. Will you help me?"

Walter snorted again. "What's the matter, can't find your egg?"

One of the flappers tittered, earning a frown from her sister. She leaned over and muttered something, making the younger woman hunch down on her chair.

Cindi had moved forward and now stood directly in front of Walter. She very slowly leaned down toward him until her face was inches from his.

Melanie caught her breath. Surely their new assistant wasn't about to yell at one of their first guests on the very first night of his visit? She was about to step forward to intervene when Cindi leaned in closer and whispered something in his ear.

Walter looked as if he would refuse whatever it was she'd asked of him, but when Cindi smiled at him, he shoved his hand in his pocket and withdrew something in his closed fist.

Cindi held out her hand, and after another moment of hesitation, he dropped something into her palm. Still with her back to Nick, she said loudly, "I have something in my hand, and you're not allowed to peek. Can you tell me what it is?"

Nick put his hand over his eyes and lifted his other hand in a theatrical gesture that brought another snort from the reluctant participant.

Cindi silenced Walter with a quick shake of her head, and the room grew quiet as Nick concentrated.

At that moment the door opened, and Liza appeared in the doorway. "Why is everyone so quiet in here?" she demanded just as Nick dropped his hand from his eyes.

Melanie grabbed her grandmother's arm, pulled her gently into the room, and closed the door behind her. Liza mouthed the word "sorry" at her and turned to look at Nick.

He seemed not to notice the interruption but stood staring at the back of Cindi's head as if trying to read her mind. Finally he stepped forward. "I see a shiny object with sharp edges. Ah, now I have it. The young lady is holding the gentleman's pocketknife."

Light flashed off the knife as Cindi waved it triumphantly in the air. "Nicholas the Magnificent has done it again," she called out amid a smattering of applause.

Walter stood up and grabbed the knife from her. "Magnificent, my ass. I saw better acts than that in kindergarten."

"Then maybe you should go back there," Cindi said sweetly.

"Yeah," Joe said, scowling at Walter. "Give it a rest, you miserable old codger. I don't know why you even came down here with us. Look at you. You couldn't even dress up for Halloween."

Walter's face turned red. "Some people have too much self-respect to make a spectacle of themselves."

Joe was about to speak again when Gloria put a hand on his arm. "Let it go, Joe. He's not worth making a scene."

"Let him make all the noise he wants. I'm going to bed." With that, Walter marched to the door and left the room.

"Well," Liza murmured, "that was awkward."

Melanie couldn't agree more. An ominous silence had settled over everyone, except for a faint snoring coming from Beatrice.

Cindi stood at Nick's side, helping him pack up his bag. Gloria sat patting Joe's hand, trying to calm him down, while the two sisters looked as if they would rather be anywhere else than in that room.

Melanie cleared her throat. "How about some more refreshments? There's plenty of food left over there." She nodded at the table where the remaining sandwiches, cheese and fruit, deviled eggs, and pastries still sat, waiting to be devoured.

"I'll have some!" Amy Parsons was a paler version of her older sister. Both women had white hair, but where Eileen Chapman's was permed with pale-blue highlights, Amy's hair hung gray and limp on either side of her face. Eileen wore makeup while Amy's face held very little color at all. In Melanie's opinion, Amy needed to stand up to her sister once in a while. From what Melanie had seen, Eileen treated Amy like her child instead of her sibling.

Right now Eileen was rolling her eyes at her sister. "You're still hungry after everything you ate earlier?"

Amy hesitated, then bravely moved over to the table and began piling up her plate.

Beatrice finally woke up. "What time is it?"

Joe got up from the couch and stretched his arms. "Time I was getting some shut-eye." He looked at Gloria. "How about you?"

She stared at him for a moment, then shook her head. "I'm going to have another glass of wine."

Joe looked disappointed as he left the room.

Melanie saw Nick folding up his table and walked over to him. "If you'll meet me in the kitchen, I'll give you a check," she told him.

"I'll start cleaning up," Cindi said, glancing over at the food table. She nodded at Amy, who now sat on the couch, balancing her plate on her knees. "She's the only one who went back for more."

Liza appeared at her side, saying, "I'll help you. You need to get home. You have an early start in the morning."

Melanie felt a little quiver in her stomach. Tomorrow would be the big test. Tomorrow they would be serving their first breakfast, and they really needed it all to go well. Good reviews were crucial if they were to make a success of the inn.

She could only hope that the little upset this evening wouldn't make a lasting impression on their guests. Or that Walter Dexter wouldn't antagonize anyone else, since he had all the signs of an agitator.

*   *   *

The following morning, the enticing aroma of banana nut muffins filled the kitchen as Melanie opened the oven door. She was almost afraid to look as she slid the tray out and sat it on the counter. There was so much depending on her new recipe. Relieved to see the muffins had browned evenly, she tipped them out onto the cooling rack.

Standing at the island counter, her grandmother sniffed the air, a look of bliss on her face. Above her head, the copper pots and pans gleamed in the new fluorescent lighting, adding a reddish glow to her hair. "Heavenly smell. How about a taste test?"

Melanie arranged the muffins in even rows. "If we keep tasting everything we cook, we'll both be fighting to get into our clothes."

"That's okay. I could use a new wardrobe." Liza tilted her head on one side, her brow creased in concentration. "Is that Max I hear?"

Listening to the faint barking of a dog outside, Melanie sighed. "He's probably chasing a squirrel."

"He sounds agitated."

"He's always agitated when he's chasing squirrels. How're the quiche crusts coming along?"

Liza finished flattening crescent dinner rolls onto a pie plate. "They're ready to bake. I can't believe we're finally cooking our first breakfast for our guests. Who would have thought when we bought this place in the spring that it would take until the end of October to have our grand opening?"

Melanie took the plate from her and sat it in the oven. "We're lucky to be open at all. Considering the house was on fire, it looks pretty good now that all the repairs are done."

Liza handed her another pie plate. "The Halloween party went well last night. The magician was a nice touch, though I wish we'd hired a piano player. The CDs were okay, but you can't beat live music."

Melanie slid the second plate into the oven and shut the door. "You could have played. I thought that was why you bought that beat-up old piano, so you could entertain the guests."

"Heavens, no. My creaky old hands can't tickle the ivories that well anymore. We need some young player who can jazz things up."

Melanie laughed. Liza had just had her hair cut and colored a pale gold. She wore cream linen slacks and a bright-orange sweater and looked nowhere near her seventy-six years. "All six of our guests are retired and probably wouldn't appreciate being jazzed up. And by the way, nothing about you is old. You put every one of our guests to shame. I'm betting you could out-jazz them all."

"I don't think my aching bones would agree with that." Liza moved over to the sink and turned on the faucet to rinse her hands. "As a matter of fact, I was going through my sheet music in the garage the other day. I'm thinking of selling it."

Melanie uttered a cry of dismay. "Oh, don't do that! You can still amuse yourself if you don't want to play for the guests. You know I always love to hear you play."

"I play mostly by ear nowadays, anyway." She paused, her head tilted on one side. "There goes Max, barking again. I hope he didn't catch that squirrel."

"He's much too afraid of them to actually get that close." Melanie listened for a moment. Max did sound a bit upset. Maybe she should go check on him.

"Okay, we have ninety minutes until serving time," Liza said, grabbing her attention again. "The fruit is cut up, and the bacon is cooked for the quiche. What's next?"

Melanie checked the list on the message board hanging on the wall. "The cereal and muffins will go on the tables right before we ring the gong. For now I just have to beat the eggs for the quiche and fill the crusts. We'll fry the potatoes while they're eating the cereal."

Liza nodded. "Bacon and garlic potatoes? You sure you want to deal with all that garlic breath?"

Melanie grinned. "It's only garlic pepper. Not enough to be a problem." She turned her head as she heard Max bark once more.

Liza frowned. "What is his problem? He doesn't usually make all that noise."

Melanie leaned over the sink and drew back the orange-checkered curtains at the window to catch a glimpse of the dog. The sky was still dark over the ocean, with streaks of purple and blue closer to the beach. It was already daylight on the shore, with the sun peeking over the mountains, though it was still too early for strollers. The sands were deserted, except for the sea gulls competing with the terns for food.

The sea looked calm, lapping around the towering, jagged rocks that stretched toward the sky. For a moment, Melanie was captured by the scene outside. Sully's Landing had to be the most beautiful spot on the Oregon coast.

Seconds later Max broke the spell, barking closer to the house. Now she could hear the urgency in his voice and hurried to the door. "It sounds like he's out in the front yard," she said, throwing the words over her shoulder. "He must have jumped the fence. I'd better bring him in. Something's got him riled up. Take the piecrusts out of the oven if I'm not back in five minutes."

Speeding down the narrow hallway, she prayed the barking hadn't woken up the guests. They had been lucky to get such a good booking for their opening. Their guests were staying the whole week in order to attend the Arts Festival that weekend. The last thing she needed was complaints about a barking dog on top of the unpleasant incident last night.

Opening up the front door, she was about to scold Max when she spotted him racing out of sight around the corner of the inn. Frowning, she followed him, hurrying as she heard him barking again.

She rounded the corner and started toward the driveway, where Max stood over what appeared to be a bundle of clothes. As she drew closer, she could see why the dog was so upset: one of her guests lay in the driveway, and judging by his chalk-white face, he was in serious trouble. His head lay at an odd angle, and he didn't seem to be moving.

Melanie stared down at the tortured features, then slowly bent down and felt for a pulse. Seconds later, she straightened her back. Whatever had happened to Walter Dexter, it seemed unlikely he would ever move again.

*   *   *

Liza looked up from the oven when Melanie charged back into the kitchen, an excited Max at her heels. "What on earth?"

"We've got a problem." Melanie grabbed her cell phone off the counter and started thumbing.

Anxiety lines creased Liza's forehead. "What's wrong?"

Melanie held up her hand as the voice of the emergency dispatcher spoke in her ear. Making an effort to speak calmly, she answered her. "This is the Merry Ghost Inn on Ocean Way. One of our guests is lying in the driveway." Her voice faltered a little. "I think he's dead."

Liza's cry of dismay almost drowned out the dispatcher's next words.

Melanie thanked her and ended the call.

Liza's green eyes widened with shock. "Who is it?"

"Walter Dexter." Melanie filled a mug with coffee from the percolator.

"What happened to him?"

"I don't know. We didn't exactly have a conversation." Her legs felt weak, and she sank down in the kitchen nook next to the corner window.

Liza sat as well and buried her face in her hands. "This is the last thing we need. Just when things have begun to pick up. *Bugger!*" Although Liza had lived in America for fifty years, she had not relinquished her English accent, which became more pronounced whenever she was upset.

Max, apparently satisfied that his job was done, had been gobbling down his breakfast, but Liza's outburst raised his head, and he stared at her with anxious eyes.

"They're sending an officer and an ambulance over," Melanie said, mournfully examining her mug. "They should be here any minute."

Liza shot up again. "The piecrusts!" She hurried over to the oven and pulled open the door. "They look okay, thank goodness." Grabbing an oven mitt, she muttered, "All this commotion is going to have our guests swarming all over us."

"Just hope they don't use the sirens, or we'll have the entire neighborhood over here."

"He must have had a heart attack or something." Liza pulled both pie plates from the oven and closed the door. "What was he doing out there so early in the morning?"

"Good question." Melanie got up and put her coffee down on the counter. "I have to make the filling for the quiches. We can't blow our first breakfast at the Merry Ghost Inn. We'd never live it down."

"Right. The show must go on. I'll get to work on the potatoes." Liza opened a drawer and took out a potato peeler. "What time is Cindi supposed to get here?" The words were barely out of her mouth when the door opened and the assistant sauntered in.

Cindi bent down to pat Max, who stretched up far enough to deposit a wet kiss on her chin. Grinning, she straightened up. "Did you know there's a guy lying out in the driveway?"

Melanie exchanged a rueful glance with Liza. "I did notice him, yes. Want some coffee?"

"Sure." Cindi slumped down on the chair. "So who's the guy? Is he dead?"

"I think so. The ambulance is on the way. It's Walter Dexter, the guest who stormed out of the magic show last night. We think he had a heart attack."

"Seriously? Poor dude."

Melanie took a mug down from the cabinet and filled it with coffee. When she'd told Liza she'd hired Cindi to help out at the inn, her grandmother had argued that they needed someone a bit more dignified to wait on tables and mingle with the guests. "That girl," she'd told Melanie, "will give our guests nightmares."

Melanie had countered her protests by promising her grandmother that Cindi seemed more enthusiastic than the other two applicants for the job, and her conduct was a lot calmer than her appearance.

Cindi had won Liza over her first day, proving she was willing and able to take on any task with a smile and efficiency—something Liza greatly admired.

"What about the other guests?" Cindi asked as Melanie put the mug down in front of her. "Do they know?"

"I don't think so." Melanie opened a cabinet door and took out a bowl. "We still have an hour or so until breakfast. They're probably all still in bed."

"I don't think they liked him much." Cindi took a sip from the mug. "He was, like, a bit of a grouch. He didn't even wear a costume for the party last night, and he took those mean shots at Nick."

"I thought Nick handled it well," Melanie said, opening the fridge door.

"So did I." Liza picked up a potato and began peeling it. "There's one thing I'm dying to know—how did he make that egg disappear, and what happened to it?"

Cindi grinned. "Sorry. I can't reveal Nicholas the Magnificent's secrets."

Liza sighed. "I was just hoping he didn't leave it somewhere to be trampled on. Broken eggs make such a mess."

"Don't worry. The egg is back in the fridge." Cindi yawned.

"Well, I'd like to know how he knew you had Walter's pocketknife," Melanie said.

Cindi peered at her for a moment. "Oh, all right. I guess I can tell you that. Just don't let on to Nick that I told you." She leaned forward and lowered her voice. "It's a code. We have one for just about anything someone would carry in their pocket. Like, I told Nick he wasn't allowed to peek.

That was the code word for pocketknife. Get it? Peek. PK. Pocketknife."

Liza gaped at her. "So that's how they do it."

"Yep. So now you know. Just don't tell anyone else."

Liza drew her fingers over her mouth. "My lips are sealed."

Melanie was about to add her own promise when the faint whine of a siren brought up Max's head. "Shoot. That's probably the ambulance." She started for the door.

Cindi got up, her mug still in her hand. "What do you want me to do?"

"How good are you at whipping eggs?"

She grinned. "I'm great at everything."

"Then you can make the filling for the quiches. Liza will give you the recipe."

Cindi lifted her hand in a salute. "No problem."

The siren whined louder, and Melanie hurried out the door with Max close behind her.

By the time she got outside, the ambulance was pulling into the driveway. As the medics jumped down, a black Tahoe pulled up at the curb, and a familiar figure in a cop's uniform stepped out.

Melanie felt a rush of relief as Ben Carter strode past the medics, who were now kneeling by Walter's still body. Happy to see a friendly face, she gave him a shaky smile.

"What happened?" He glanced at the medics.

"I don't know. I found him like that a few minutes ago. I think he's dead."

Max nudged Ben with his nose, and he bent down to pat the dog's head. "You okay?"

She gave him a brief nod as he straightened, then watched him walk over to the medics. She couldn't make out what they were saying to him, but she had no desire to get any closer to the dead man. Realizing she was shivering with cold, she turned to go back inside for a coat.

She'd taken a couple of steps when Ben called out to her.

Looking back at him, she hesitated. He must have understood her reluctance, as he said something to the medics and walked back to her.

One look at his face and she knew he had bad news. "What's wrong?"

As an answer, he looked up at the second-floor balcony.

She followed his gaze, and her spirits plummeted as she saw a jagged gap in the wooden railings, with splintered wood swinging in the breeze. "Oh, my God. He fell." Visions of lawsuits swept through her mind. They'd just had the railing renovated. How could it have broken?

"I have to go up there to take a look before we can remove the body." Ben's blue eyes were full of sympathy when he looked at her. "This doesn't look good."

"Tell me about it." She glanced at her watch. "I want to come with you. I have to stop by the kitchen first and make sure the quiches go in the oven."

Ben saluted her. "Lead the way."

Her heart still thumping with anxiety, Melanie called to Max, then darted back inside and practically ran down the hallway to the kitchen.

Liza stood at the sink, still peeling potatoes, and spun around when Melanie burst back into the kitchen. Max made a beeline for his bed and snuggled down in it.

Melanie paused to draw a deep breath. "He fell through the railings," she said, wincing when Liza dropped the peeler with a clatter on the floor.

Standing at the island counter, Cindi muttered, "Wow, that's a bummer."

Ben reached the door at that moment and stepped inside.

Cindi's eyes opened wide, and she looked at Ben as if she'd never seen a policeman before while Liza bent down to pick up the peeler and had to hang onto the sink to get up again.

In that moment of silence, a low gust of laughter echoed down the hallway outside.

Max barked, Cindi giggled, and Ben swung around and looked out into the hall.

"What the heck was that?" Ben's frown made him look stern. "There's no one out there. Is someone playing tricks?"

"That was Orville," Liza said quietly. "Our merry ghost."

Ben looked at Melanie. "Are you telling me the rumors about a ghost in this house are real?"

Melanie shrugged. "The sound of laughter is real. Where it comes from is up for debate. Liza's convinced it's the ghost; I'm more inclined to think there's a physical cause for the sound. I'll tell you the whole story later, but right now I have to get quiches in the oven."

"What are we going to do about the railings?" Liza sounded close to tears. "Will we be sued?"

Melanie dropped the piecrusts on the table, then rushed over and hugged her. "Let's not worry about that now. We're insured anyway, so we should be okay. Besides, the railings were repaired and painted by the contractor. He should be responsible. Right now we have to get this breakfast on the tables."

Liza visibly pulled herself together. "Right." She turned back to the sink and started viciously chopping at the potato in her hand with the peeler.

"I think I've got the mixture right," Cindi said when Melanie reached her side. "Eggs, whipping cream, bacon, cheese, salt, and pepper. Right?"

Melanie picked up the bowl. "Perfect." She poured the mixture into the two piecrusts, then put both pies in the oven. "Now I'm going to run upstairs to the balcony with Ben. I'll be back in a few minutes. Cindi, start laying the tables. Liza will tell you what you need."

Without waiting for an answer, she hurried to Ben's side. "Okay, let's go."

Climbing the stairs ahead of him, she tried not to panic at the thought of lawsuits and court cases. Apart from what it might cost them, the publicity would be disastrous for the inn. No matter how it came out, the fact that someone had fallen to his death through defective railings was sure to be perceived as negligence.

There was still more than half an hour to go before breakfast would be served, and Melanie was relieved to see the upstairs hallway was empty when they reached the top of the stairs. She hurried to the end and opened the door to the balcony.

Stepping outside, her stomach churned when she saw the splintered railings again. One of the planters lay in its side, the soil spilled out onto the floor. Seeing the roots of the juniper exposed, Melanie winced. When had this happened? Walter must have come out to get an early breath of fresh air, leaned against the railings, and . . . She shuddered, closing her eyes against the vision.

The pressure of a strong hand on her shoulder opened her eyes. Ben stood looking down at her, and his warm gaze went a long way to helping her feel better.

"You okay?" She nodded, and he gave her shoulder a gentle squeeze. "Wait here, and I'll take a look. Don't go any closer. It's not safe."

Shivering, she watched him walk over to the broken part of the railing. He squatted down, peering closely at the slats. After a few moments, he rose to his feet and walked back toward her.

She couldn't tell anything from his expression, and her heart started thumping again.

"Come on, let's go inside. You look cold."

He was right; her teeth were chattering, but she wasn't sure if it was from the cold or from anxiety. She followed him down the stairs and almost bumped into him when he halted at the bottom. Drawing her farther down the hallway, he said quietly, "Your railings were fine. It looks like somebody used a saw on them. Just enough to make sure that with enough pressure, they'd give way."

For a long moment, Melanie struggled to understand. "Sawed through our railings? Why would someone do that?"

Ben's face was a stern mask. "It appears that the death of your guest wasn't an accident after all. We're looking at a possible case of homicide."

Chapter 2

Staring up at Ben, Melanie's first surge of relief that it wasn't a case of negligence turned quickly to dismay. "Who would want to kill an old man like Walter?"

"That's what we'll have to find out." Ben's scowl softened. "I'm sorry, Melanie. This is going to mess up your opening."

Melanie was still trying to grasp the implications of his words. "You think someone here in the house killed him?"

"I think Detective Dutton will probably want to question everybody."

"But they're all old!"

"It doesn't take much to saw through a couple of railings." Ben's smile was cynical. "Anyone is capable of murder if the motive is strong enough."

Melanie tried to picture the remaining five guests. One man and four women. All senior citizens. None of them seemed remotely capable of murder. "Are you sure it wasn't something the contractors did? Like maybe they accidentally sawed through the railings without noticing?" Even as she spoke the words, she realized how unlikely that sounded.

"I'm sure Detective Dutton will figure out what happened." Ben fished his cell phone out of his pocket. "I have to call the medical examiner. He'll need to take a look at the body before we move it."

Melanie was about to answer when Cindi appeared in the hallway, looking a little frazzled. "Oh, there you are," she said, running a hand down the unshaved side of her head. "Liza's freaking out in there." She jerked a hand at the kitchen door. "It's time to get the guests down for breakfast. She sent me to ring the gong."

All thoughts of a murder investigation vanished as Melanie focused on the new crisis. "Fine. Go ring the gong. Are the tables all set?"

"Everything's out there. We just have to serve the quiche and potatoes."

Cindi dashed off, leaving Ben staring after her pink hair. "That's your new assistant?"

Melanie sighed. "She's had a tough time. She grew up in foster homes and hasn't had much security in her life. I felt she needed a break. Besides, I like her. She's very capable."

"Then I hope she works out for you." He thumbed a number into his phone while Melanie wondered why she'd felt it necessary to defend her new assistant.

The clanging of the gong jolted her into action. "Gotta run," she called out as she leapt for the kitchen door. "See you later."

Ben said something she didn't catch as she bounded into the kitchen, where the pungent aroma of garlic, onion, and bacon assured her the potatoes were cooking.

Liza was at the oven, pulling out the second quiche.

"How do they look?" Melanie rushed over to her.

"Perfect." Liza laid the pie plate on the counter. "We'll give them a moment or two to cool before Cindi serves them. The potatoes are just about ready."

Melanie took down plates from the cabinet and set them in the oven to warm. "I'm so sorry. I didn't mean to leave you alone to do all this."

"You didn't have much choice." Liza rinsed her hands under the faucet. "So are we looking at a case of negligence here?"

Looking at her grandmother's white face, Melanie rushed to reassure her. "The railings didn't break. Someone sawed through them."

Liza's eyes opened wide. "With a saw?"

"I guess. That's generally what you use to saw through wood."

"But why?"

"Ben says it looks like someone wanted to get rid of Walter Dexter and make it seem like an accident."

"Not one of our guests?"

"Ben says it's possible. It had to have happened in the last couple of days. We put those planters up there on Friday. We surely would have noticed if the railings had been cut." Melanie shook her head. "I just can't imagine any of our guests doing something so terrible."

"How could someone have sawed through the railings without us hearing it?"

Melanie thought about it. "It could have been sometime during the party. We were playing the music pretty loudly."

Liza opened her mouth to answer, but just then Cindi charged into the kitchen. "They're all down here, gobbling up the cereal and fruit. We can start serving now."

The next few minutes sped by as Melanie and her grandmother dished up the quiche and potatoes, handing the plates to Cindi, who whisked them into the dining room. Melanie slid bread slices into the two toasters while Liza refilled the coffeepots.

"They keep asking me where Walter is," Cindi said as she brought empty cereal bowls back to the kitchen. "I didn't know what to say. I just told them he'd probably overslept."

Melanie sighed. "I guess I'll have to tell them soon." She hesitated, then added, "We have something we need to tell you, Cindi. We didn't say anything before because we didn't want to worry you, but now you should know."

Cindi's expression was wary. "What is it?"

"It's about Walter. The police think someone intentionally caused his fall off the balcony."

Cindi sat down hard on a chair. "Jeez. Why would they think that?"

"The railings have been cut with a saw."

Cindi nodded. "I guess that would do it. Who cut them?"

"We don't know." Melanie glanced at Liza, who looked about ready to cry. "It's possible that it was one of our guests."

Cindi lowered her gaze to her sneakers. "So the cops will be coming around, questioning everybody?"

Not for the first time, Melanie wondered if the assistant had something to hide. "Yes. We wanted to warn you."

Cindi looked up. "I got no problem with that." She got to her feet. "I'd better take the coffee in." She grabbed a coffeepot and sauntered out the door.

Liza's expression was skeptical, and she shook her head. "I *hope* she doesn't have a problem."

"I guess we'll soon find out." Melanie started stacking the cereal bowls in the dishwasher. "The medical examiner is on his way, and Detective Dutton will probably be with him."

Liza groaned. "Grumpy Dutton? He wasn't too happy the last time we saw him. Remember? He was upset about us investigating our skeleton's murder."

"How can I forget? He blew up when I told him we had no choice because he was too busy solving other cases."

"You'd have thought he'd have jumped at the chance to solve ours. It isn't every day someone discovers a skeleton hidden behind a bedroom wall." She picked up an empty pie plate and carried it over to the sink.

"Detective Dutton doesn't strike me as the sort of guy who lets his personal feelings get in the way of his duties."

Liza pulled a face. "You've got that right. He's relentless."

"I guess he has to be in his line of work." Melanie looked up at the clock. "I'd better get into the dining room while the guests are all there."

"Want me to come with you?"

Melanie nodded. "It should come from both of us."

"Right." Liza dried her hands on a kitchen towel. "Let's get this over with."

Cindi met them in the hallway and held up the coffeepot. "This one's empty. I'd better make some more."

"There's a full one on the counter," Melanie told her. "There's plenty of quiche and potatoes left. Help yourself to whatever you want. We'll be back in a minute or two, after we've told everyone about Walter."

"Thanks. And good luck."

Cindi disappeared into the kitchen while Melanie and her grandmother walked down the hallway to the dining room. Taking a deep breath, Melanie pushed open the door.

This room was brighter than the rest of the house. Liza had decided that a breakfast room needed to sparkle with color to wake up everyone in the mornings. Melanie had graciously conceded to her ideas, and the insurance money from the fire had allowed Liza to indulge a little.

She had chosen yellow drapes dotted with little white daisies. Melanie had to admit that the pale-turquoise carpeting contrasted beautifully. They had bought the house partially furnished, and the antique buffet table that had come with the sale had escaped damage in the fire. Liza had had it refinished, and it now graced the floor next to one of the cream walls.

She'd covered the individual tables with white lace-edged tablecloths. Melanie had found yellow vases online and filled them with the last of the golden chrysanthemums from the garden. Brightly colored seascapes hung on the walls, and the mantle over the fireplace was covered with shells and blue and green glass balls—floats that had washed ashore from Japanese fishing boats. No matter the weather outside, inside the dining room of the Merry Ghost Inn, it was always sunny.

The guests sat at separate tables—the sisters together at one and the other two women at another while Joe McAllister, the sole man left in the group, sat alone. He'd apparently expected to share a table with Walter Dexter since a place had been set opposite him.

Eileen was talking, her strident voice overpowering the women at the next table, who were quietly chatting. Everyone looked up as Melanie walked into the room, followed closely by Liza.

"Good morning!" Melanie pasted on a wide smile as expectant faces turned in her direction. "I hope everyone enjoyed the breakfast."

Murmurs of appreciation answered her.

"Very nice," Eileen said. "The muffins were delicious, right, Amy?" She nudged her sister with her elbow.

Amy jumped. "Delicious!"

"But we're all wondering where Walter is," Eileen continued, staring hard at the others of her group as if ordering them to speak.

Gloria obediently spoke up. "He's probably still snoring in his bed."

Joe gave her a meaningful look. "Lucky for you."

Gloria batted her heavy eyelashes at him as if she understood what he meant.

Beatrice didn't seem to notice the interchange next to her. She sat quietly sipping her coffee, her gaze fixed on Melanie.

Liza cleared her throat. "Would anyone like more to drink?"

When no one took Liza up on the offer, Melanie said quietly, "I'm afraid I have some very bad news. I found Walter lying in the driveway this morning. He apparently fell from the upstairs balcony."

Her announcement was met with cries of shock and dismay.

Beatrice was the first to speak, her voice quavering with emotion. "Is he okay?"

"I'm afraid Walter has died." Melanie started forward as Beatrice burst into tears.

Eileen jumped up from her chair and rushed over to Beatrice, with Amy close behind her. Eileen hugged her frail shoulders, and Amy held one of Beatrice's hands.

"What was Walter doing on the balcony?" Eileen demanded, giving Melanie an accusing look.

Liza spoke up before Melanie could answer. "We don't know. Unfortunately, the railings seem to have been tampered with, and the police will be investigating the case. All of you will have to talk to the detective. In the meantime, the balcony is off-limits to everyone. The door will remain locked for your safety."

Once more shocked exclamations greeted her words. Joe stood up, his face turning red. "Are the cops saying one of us did it?"

Melanie held up a hand as Amy whimpered. "They are not saying anything right now. No one knows what happened, and until we do, I suggest you all try not to get too upset by all of this. I'm sure the police will get it all sorted out before long."

She could tell by their faces that no one was convinced.

"Come along, Beatrice," Eileen said in a voice that tolerated no argument. "We'll go outside and get a breath of fresh air. It will help you feel better." She tugged the weeping woman to her feet, tucked her hand under one elbow, and led her from the room with her sister following close behind.

"I don't know why she's crying," Joe said, pushing back his chair. "She never had much to do with Walter. Can't say I blame her. He was a miserable old goat—always had his nose in a book, and God help anyone who interrupted him."

Gloria shot to her feet. "You shouldn't speak ill of the dead, Joe. Walter might not have been the life and soul of the party, but he was one of us and deserves some respect."

"Respect?" Joe uttered a short laugh. "You know the only reason he joined the book group was because you belonged to it. He couldn't care less about discussing what we were reading. After what he did to you, I'd think you'd be glad to be rid of him."

Two red spots burned on Gloria's cheeks. "I think you've said far more than enough." She stalked past Melanie and headed out the door, closing it a little too firmly behind her.

"Sorry about that." Joe's smile was rueful. "Gloria's right. The old grouch is dead. May he rest in peace."

He left the room, and Liza walked over to his table to pick up his empty plate. "Well, it seems Mr. Dexter wasn't too popular with the crowd."

Melanie started clearing the other tables. "He did seem uncomfortable at the party last night. He was the only one not wearing a costume."

Liza reached for an empty coffee mug. "He looked like he was having fun insulting Nick, though."

Melanie stacked three plates on top of each other. "Obviously he didn't think much of Nick's magic tricks. What did you think of him?"

"Nick?" Liza carried her dishes to the door. "Okay, I guess. I didn't have a chance to talk to him much. He looks a bit old to be Cindi's boyfriend, but he seems harmless enough."

"I hope so. I worry about her."

Liza laughed. "I wouldn't worry too much about that girl. She's a tough little devil. I'm confident she can take care of herself."

Melanie followed her grandmother out the door, balancing dishes on her arms. "We should have brought a tray in with us."

"Well, normally this would be Cindi's job." Liza reached the kitchen and walked through the open doorway. Melanie followed her and put the plates in the sink.

Cindi sat next to the corner window with a plate of quiche, potatoes, and fruit in front of her. She looked guilty and shot up as Liza set her dishes on the counter. "I should be doing that," she said as Melanie opened up the dishwasher.

"Finish your breakfast." Melanie smiled at her. "You can get the rest of the dishes when you're done." She stacked dishes in the dishwasher, then moved over to the island counter and slid a slice of quiche onto a plate. Handing it to Liza, she added, "I don't have much of an appetite, but I guess we should eat something."

Liza took the plate from her and turned to the stove to scoop up some potatoes from the pan.

"How'd it go in there?" Cindi asked as both women sat down in the nook.

"They were all shocked, of course," Melanie said, reaching for the pepper shaker.

"I hate to say it," Liza added, "but I don't think anyone's heart was breaking. Except maybe that little woman. What's her name?"

"Beatrice." Melanie sprinkled pepper on her potatoes. "She actually cried, but that could have been the shock. Joe said she didn't have much to do with Walter."

Liza dug her fork into her quiche. "It didn't look as if anyone had much to do with him."

"Except Gloria. She was quick to come to his defense when Joe criticized him."

"Yes, I noticed that. I wonder what was going on there. What was it Joe said? Something about Walter doing something to upset Gloria?"

Melanie thought for a moment. "He said, 'After what he did to you, I'd think you'd be glad to be rid of him.'"

"Wow. Seems to me he was good at upsetting everyone," Cindi said, putting down her fork.

"Well, he won't be doing that anymore." Liza's face took on a look of bliss. "This is excellent quiche."

"You can thank Cindi for that." Melanie smiled at her new assistant. "She made the mixture for it."

"With your recipe," Cindi reminded her. "I couldn't have come up with it by myself."

"Well," Liza announced, "I proclaim our first breakfast a resounding success. It's just too bad it had to end on such a gloomy note."

Melanie sighed. "This will totally spoil the vacation for the rest of our guests. I wonder if they'll all go home."

Liza looked up in alarm. "We can't let that happen! I'll talk to Eileen—she seems to be the one in charge. She told me she drove them all down here from Portland in her SUV."

"She's definitely the bossy one. I think she likes ordering people around." Cindi dropped her fork on her plate with a clatter. "I'd better get going and clear the rest of the tables." She shot up and headed for the door.

Just as she reached it, the front doorbell chimed in the hallway. Max uttered a soft bark, and Cindi turned to look at Melanie. "I'll get that."

Cindi disappeared, and a few moments later, Ben appeared in the doorway. The man standing behind him was almost as tall, and his frown did nothing to ease Melanie's anxiety.

Her last encounter with Detective Tom Dutton had been uncomfortable. He'd scolded her and her grandmother in terms that left no doubt of his disapproval. Liza had argued with him, reminding him that they had solved the case, which only seemed to annoy him more.

"Detective Dutton would like to ask everyone a few questions," Ben said, giving Melanie a look that warned her not to protest.

The detective pushed past him into the kitchen. Max got out of his bed and walked over to him, sniffed his shoes, and then, apparently deciding the detective was harmless, padded back to his bed.

Detective Dutton appeared not to notice the dog as he nodded at Cindi. "You first." He looked at Melanie. "Is there somewhere we can talk in private?"

"Liza and I have things to do." Melanie took hold of her grandmother's arm. "We'll leave you alone in here. You won't be disturbed."

Dutton nodded while Cindi walked back to the chair and sat down, her lips tightly clamped together.

Melanie led Liza out into the hall, where Ben waited for them. Closing the door behind her, she asked quietly, "He thinks someone in the house killed Walter?"

"The ME says the victim's neck is broken. There's no doubt the fall killed him. And those railings didn't saw themselves. Someone wanted to commit murder and came up with a plan to achieve just that."

Liza shook her head. "Wonderful. Our grand opening week and we have another dead body before it's barely begun."

Ben looked uncomfortable. "This will probably mean your guests will have to stay in town for a while."

"What?"

"Bugger!"

Liza and Melanie had spoken in unison, and Ben shrugged. "You know how this goes. If all your guests are suspects, they'll be ordered not to leave town until they're cleared."

"And what are we supposed to do in the meantime?" Liza folded her arms and glared up at Ben. "We have more guests coming in next week."

"I'm sure some reasonable arrangements can be made." Ben looked at Melanie. "I have to get back to the station, but I'll let you know if I hear anything useful. Oh, by the way, the balcony is a crime scene now. We've taped it off, but Detective Dutton wants the door locked."

He took off, leaving both women staring after him.

"Reasonable arrangements," Liza muttered. "Why do cops always sound so vague? Does he talk like that when you have dinner with him?"

Melanie was still trying to absorb the impact of Ben's words. If the guests were forced to stay past their reserved date, that could cause a lot of complications. "I've only been out to dinner with him once," she reminded Liza.

She didn't add that it was a sore point with her that he hadn't asked her out again. Although she had ruled out an intimate relationship with him, she really liked the man and would have enjoyed his friendship. The one night she'd had dinner with him had gone well, she'd thought. They had kept it comfortable, without any of the underlying tension she'd anticipated. Afterward, although Ben had always been friendly when they'd bumped into each other, he hadn't suggested a second meeting. Apparently he hadn't enjoyed it as much as she had.

"Well, you need to go to dinner with him more often and soften him up." Liza started for the stairs. "We'd better alert the guests that they're going to be grilled by the cops."

Melanie sighed. Her grandmother had read so many mystery novels that she was beginning to talk like one. "I hope you're going to sound a bit more refined than that."

Liza waved a hand in response and started slowly climbing the stairs.

"I'll check out the living room first in case someone's in there," Melanie called after her. "I'll catch up with you in a minute."

Again Liza waved and vanished into the upstairs hallway.

There was no one in the living room when Melanie looked in there, and just to be sure, she checked the dining room. That was empty too. More than likely the guests were in their rooms, preparing to go outside and enjoy some fresh air.

She turned to leave and froze as she heard a familiar low chuckle echo throughout the room. "Okay, Orville," she muttered, "you might find another dead body funny, but we are not amused." She waited, but only silence answered her.

Annoyed with herself for talking to an imaginary ghost, she headed down the hallway to the stairs. She had almost reached them when the piercing ring of the doorbell made her jump.

Her first thought was that one of her neighbors, alerted by all the commotion, had come to find out what was going on. She was rehearsing what she would say as she opened the front door.

The young man standing on the porch grinned at her. "Hi, Mel! I see you'll be in the news again."

Melanie let out her breath. Josh Phillips was a local newspaper reporter—a friendly young man with spikey hair and warm brown eyes. She greeted him with a smile and looked out behind him, relieved to see that the ambulance and Ben's car had left.

"I know you're probably swamped, but I was wondering if you could spare me a few minutes." Josh looked over his shoulder. "I talked to the medics, but they couldn't tell me much about what happened."

Melanie opened the door wider. "Come in." It occurred to her as Josh stepped into the hallway that he'd be a good match for Cindi. Josh's easygoing temperament was much closer to Cindi's personality than the somewhat intense, enigmatic attitude of Nick Hazelton.

Realizing that she was beginning to copy Liza with her matchmaking efforts, Melanie banished the thought and led Josh to the living room. After closing the door, she waved him to a chair. "How did you hear about this already?"

"I know one of the assistants at the police station. She calls me when something's going down."

Melanie could tell by his expression that he was personally involved with his informant. So much for hooking him up with Cindi. "Well, I can't tell you much either," she said as he pulled out his phone and sat down.

"That's okay. Just tell me what you know so far." He held up his phone. "Mind if I record?"

"No, go ahead." She settled herself on the couch. "What do you want to know?"

"I heard that you discovered the body. Tell me about that."

Melanie shuddered at the memory. "There's not much to tell. Max was barking. I went to see why he was making so much noise and found Walter Dexter lying in the driveway. I couldn't feel a pulse, and I called for an ambulance."

"Did the medics tell you how he died?"

She hesitated, wondering how much she should tell him.

"I know the cops suspect it wasn't an accident," Josh said quietly. "I wasn't sure if you knew that. Judging from the look on your face, I'm guessing you did know."

Warning bells started ringing in Melanie's head. The last thing they needed was more bad publicity the very first week they opened. Eventually the news would get out, but the less Josh knew right now, the better. "You know what cops are like," she said lightly. "They don't tell you anything. It's all guesswork right now, anyway. Nobody really knows what happened."

Josh gave her a searching look. "I heard that Dutton is questioning everyone in the house."

"I guess that's the usual protocol when there's a death on the premises."

Apparently realizing she wasn't going to help him any further, he slipped his phone in his pocket. "Well, I hope you'll let me know if there are any developments in the case."

Melanie stood up as he unfolded himself from the chair. "I'm sorry, Josh. I really don't know much at this point."

He turned to look at her. "Would you tell me if you did?"

Again she hesitated. "Only if you would promise not to publish anything I tell you."

Josh rolled his eyes. "You're talking to a newspaperman."

She smiled. "Exactly."

"Okay." He moved to the door. "I guess I understand. I'll try not to pressure you, but I might come back with more questions later on."

She followed him down the hallway to the front door. "You're always welcome here. You know that."

He stepped outside, pausing a moment to sniff the air. "Winter's coming." He looked back at her. "I know this must be hard on you and Liza. Not what you had in mind for your grand opening."

"We'll get through it." She smiled at him. "I'm sorry I couldn't be more helpful."

He lifted a hand. "That's okay. Take care." With that he turned on his heel and marched down the driveway to his car.

Feeling a wet nose touch her hand, she looked down to find Max staring up at her. The detective must have finished questioning Cindi if he had gotten out of the kitchen. "Come on, buddy. We'll go and find Liza. Maybe we'll take you for a walk later."

Max's ears pricked up, and he trotted after her as she headed for the kitchen, just as Liza reached the bottom stair.

."He's upstairs, questioning the guests," Liza said, answering Melanie's unspoken question. "They're all on pins and needles, wondering what he's going to ask them."

"If they're innocent, they've got nothing to worry about." Melanie pushed open the door to the kitchen. Cindi had disappeared, hopefully to the dining room to finish clearing the tables.

Max loped across the floor to his bed and slumped down on it.

"I'm going to make a cup of tea." Liza walked over to the stove and picked up the kettle.

Melanie reached the island counter and picked up the empty pie plates. "Do you think one of them could have pushed Walter off that balcony?"

"I don't know. I guess if I had to pick one, I'd choose Joe. He sounded a little bitter when he made that crack about Walter only being in the group because of Gloria."

"I'd like to know what he meant when he said Walter had done something to her."

"I wonder about that too." Liza frowned. "Whatever it was, it certainly was enough to get Joe in a tizzy."

"You think Joe has a thing for Gloria?"

Liza shrugged. "She's attractive and available. What more does a man Joe's age need?"

"That sounds a bit cynical."

"I know. Sorry. Put it down to anxiety." Liza looked up at the clock on the wall. "I guess Grumpy will be questioning us when he's done with the guests."

"Don't let him hear you call him that. I don't think he has much of a sense of humor."

"You're right about that." Liza carried the kettle over to the sink and filled it with water. "Let's get cleaned up in here, and then we can relax with a nice cup of tea."

Melanie smiled. Liza had left her native England after marrying an American airman—Melanie's grandfather, Frank Harris. Although Liza had adopted many local customs and traditions, she still clung to a few of her British ways. Her remedy for all crises, big or small, was a cup of tea.

She walked over to the sink and started rinsing dishes. "I promised Max we'd take him for a walk this morning."

"Sounds good. We'll go after we get rid of Grumpy."

Cindi arrived with the last of the dishes a moment later. "I'll get these in the dishwasher," she said as she laid the tray on the island counter. "That grouchy detective is still upstairs asking his nosy questions."

"Leave them." Liza picked up a couple of the plates. "We'll do this. You go ahead and get the rooms cleaned. Don't let old Grumpy get in your way. We have a business to run."

Cindi grinned. "I'll tell him you said that."

Melanie took the plates from Liza and rinsed them under the faucet. "How did the questioning go?"

Cindi shrugged. "Okay. Like I told him, I got here after all the excitement. He asked me if I'd heard anyone threaten Walter. I said, 'No one seemed to like him much, but he didn't have any trouble,' and he goes, 'Let me know if you hear anything.'"

"So you didn't tell him about Walter's little outburst at the party last night?" Liza asked.

"I didn't think it was important." Cindi sauntered over to the door. "I'm going to clean the rooms now. If Grumpy gets in my way, I'll tell him you said to get lost."

The door closed behind her, leaving Liza staring after her with a mixture of admiration and alarm. "I hope she doesn't."

Melanie stacked a plate in the dishwasher. "That is pretty much what you told her to say." She reached for another plate. "I wonder why she didn't tell Dutton about Walter's attack of insults on Nick last night."

"She's protecting her boyfriend, that's why. She's probably worried that Grumpy will think it's a motive for murder."

Melanie turned to look at her. "Do you think Nick has a motive?"

Liza stared back at her. "Not until just now."

"We're probably overreacting." Melanie slid the plate into the dishwasher. "After all, Nick didn't seem too upset about the heckling. We have to be careful not to jump to conclusions."

"I agree." The kettle started whistling, and Liza hurried over to the stove. "So let's try to forget all of this for now and enjoy our cup of tea."

Minutes later they were sitting in the nook with steaming mugs of tea in front of them.

"We need to do something about your birthday," Liza said. "It's three days away, and I haven't bought your gift yet. With all the scrambling to get the inn opened on time, I'm afraid your birthday was the last thing on my mind. I need to do some shopping."

"You already bought my birthday gift. That lovely scarf you got for me in Sharon Sutton's dress shop. Remember? I wore it the last time we went out to dinner."

"I bought that scarf for you six months ago."

"I know. You said it was an early birthday gift. And I love it, so please don't buy me anything else."

Liza sighed. "I can at least take you out to dinner on Wednesday night at your favorite restaurant."

Melanie felt a rush of pleasure. "The Seafarer? I'd love that!"

"Good. I'll make reservations. It will be good for us to have a night out." Liza sipped her tea. "Oh, which reminds me—they're holding a bingo game at the town hall on Tuesday night. I know you want to go to the museum that night to see the presentation about settlers on the Oregon coast, so I thought I'd go to the bingo game."

Melanie looked at her in surprise. "I didn't know you played bingo."

Liza leaned back on her chair, her mug clasped between both hands. "I've played a few times. I just don't want to sit around here on my own, worrying about a killer living in our house."

Now Melanie felt guilty. Of course her grandmother wouldn't want to be alone after finding out they were quite possibly entertaining a murderer. "I'm sorry. I can go to the bingo game with you if you'd like. Or we can just stay here, since we'll be going out the next night. I'm sure they'll be having that presentation at the museum again sometime."

"Nonsense." Liza leaned forward and put her mug down on the table. "I'm quite happy playing bingo on my own. I've always found someone to talk to when I go. You've been looking forward to that presentation, and I'm not going to deprive you of it now."

Still doubtful, Melanie gave her a searching look. "Are you sure?"

"Positive. I can promise you, if I were that desperate for your company, I'd go with you to the museum, but frankly I'd be bored stiff. I'd much rather be sitting at a table, frittering away my hard-earned money on a bingo game."

Reassured, Melanie relaxed. "Then I'll just look forward to your company on Wednesday night at the Seafarer. I can't think of a better way to spend my birthday."

A vision of her one date with Ben flashed through her mind, and she quickly suppressed it.

"Then it's settled." Liza got up. "And now I'm going to pour myself another cup of tea."

Chapter 3

It was more than an hour later when Detective Dutton finally finished interrogating the guests. Melanie was alone in the kitchen when he came looking for her. "I need to ask you a few questions," he said, shaking his head when she offered him coffee.

She sat down with him in the nook, feeling uneasy and worried that she'd say the wrong thing. What was it about Dutton that always made her feel as if she'd committed a crime?

His face wore the usual rigid expression as he took out his phone. "I'm going to record this conversation." He laid the phone on the table between them.

It would have been nice if he'd asked her permission, she thought, but then he was a detective and apparently didn't have to stand on ceremony. She tried not to think about the phone as she waited for his first question.

"When was the last time you looked at your balcony railings?"

She hesitated for a moment. "If you mean checked them out, that was about two months ago, after the contractors left, but we've been out there several times since then."

A look of impatience crossed Dutton's face. "So when was the last time you were on the balcony?"

"Two days ago. Liza and I put planters out there."

"So you would have noticed if the railings had been cut?"

Melanie thought about it. "Yes, I'm pretty sure we would have noticed. There was a planter right about where the railings were cut. I saw it on its side this morning."

"About what time did your guests retire to their rooms last night?"

Melanie frowned. "Walter left the party early, around ten thirty. Everyone else had left by eleven. As far as I know, they all went to their rooms right after that."

Dutton nodded and stared at his phone, as if hoping it would give him some answers. Finally, he said quietly, "The ME has put Walter's death at somewhere between midnight and four AM. It seems unlikely that one of your guests would be wandering out on the balcony at that hour, unless he had a specific reason. Can you think of any reason Mr. Dexter would be on the balcony after midnight?"

"I have no idea."

"Do you have any idea who might have wanted to hurt him?"

After what he did to you . . . She shut out Joe's voice. It was just hearsay and probably didn't mean anything. "No, I don't. Our guests arrived yesterday. We've never met any of them before this, and we know nothing about them."

"What about last night? Did you hear or see anything out of the ordinary? Anything that seemed out of place?"

For a moment, she struggled with the memory of Walter hurling insults at Nick. "No," she said carefully. "We had a nice party, and everyone seemed to enjoy it." *Everyone except Walter*, she added inwardly. Again, it didn't seem relevant enough to tell the detective that. The last thing she wanted to do was make unnecessary trouble for Cindi's boyfriend.

"So tell me how you found him. What time was that?"

She told him how she'd heard Max barking and found the dog standing over Walter's dead body. "I felt for his pulse," she said, "but I could tell he was dead. I thought he'd had a heart attack or something, so I called for an ambulance. It wasn't until Ben . . . Officer Carter told me that the railings were broken that I knew he'd fallen from the balcony."

"How did your guests react when you told them the news?"

"Pretty much as you'd expect them to react. They were shocked, upset. One of them actually broke down and cried."

"No one cheered or looked relieved?"

She stared at him, wondering if he was joking. His expression remained inflexible, and she said sharply, "No. No one cheered."

He nodded, then picked up his phone and slipped it into his pocket. "Keep your eyes and ears open, and if you hear or see anything suspicious, give me a call." He turned to leave, then looked back at her. "That doesn't mean to go around asking questions or interfering with our investigation. Leave that to the people who know what they're doing. Understood?"

She felt like saluting. "Got it."

"Good." He gave her a hard look and left.

Letting out her breath, she headed for the fridge and took out a can of soda. Thank heavens that was over. Hopefully she wouldn't have to deal with him again.

Comparing notes with Liza later, her grandmother had apparently answered the same questions.

"It's pretty obvious he suspects one of our guests of shoving Walter off that balcony," Liza said as she pulled on a black leather jacket. "Did he warn you not to get involved?"

Melanie zipped up her windcheater. "Yes, he did."

"What did you tell him?"

"I didn't give him a real answer."

"Good. Neither did I."

Melanie followed her grandmother down the hallway while Max trotted alongside her. "That doesn't mean we are going to get involved."

"Of course not." Liza reached the front door and pulled it open. "Unless we have to."

The moment she pulled the door open wide enough to get through, Max bounded outside and stood with his legs braced, ears twitching with excitement.

Melanie followed him and clipped his leash to his collar. "Come on, buddy, let's go take a walk on the beach."

Max leapt forward, nearly dragging her off her feet.

Liza laughed. "Who's taking who for a walk?"

Melanie gave a warning tug on the leash. "He knows who's boss."

They set off down the street, with Max darting back and forth ahead of them. Dark clouds had begun to gather over the Coast Range, threatening a change in the weather. The sides of the mountains wore splashes of brown, red, and yellow mixed in with the evergreens, reminding Melanie that winter was on the way. Before long the peaks could be covered in snow.

"Wait." Liza halted. "Isn't that Beatrice Carr coming up the street?"

Melanie followed her grandmother's gaze to where a petite, elderly woman walked slowly toward them. She must have caught sight of them at the same time, as she waved and quickened her step.

Melanie was surprised Liza had recognized Beatrice, since she had a thick gray scarf wrapped around her head. She wore a heavy coat and leather gloves, and her shoulders were hunched against the wind.

"I thought I'd take a walk," she said when they reached each other. "I was going to go down to the beach, but the ocean breeze is a little too biting for me. I grew up in California, and I've never gotten used to the cold up here." She shivered, emphasizing her words. "I'm going inside where it's warm to read my book." She looked up at Melanie, her eyes anxious behind her oversized glasses. "Has that detective left yet?"

"Yes, he's gone," Melanie assured her. "I'm so sorry you've all had such a horrible start to your vacation."

Beatrice's face looked pinched, and she hunched up even more. "It was a terrible shock. As we get older, we hear of friends dying, but this was so unexpected. So tragic." She moved closer to Melanie and peered up at her, dropping her voice to a whisper. "I think that detective believes someone pushed Walter off that balcony. I don't trust him. I think he has a hidden agenda. I didn't answer any of his questions; I just kept saying I didn't know. And I didn't tell him anything about the skeleton."

Melanie blinked. "Skeleton?"

Liza groaned. "Not another one."

Beatrice nodded. "Yes, at the party last night. Someone wearing a skeleton mask. I thought it was another guest, but he didn't want to talk to anyone, and he left before the magician arrived. I didn't see him after that."

Melanie looked at Liza. "Did you see a skeleton last night?"

Liza looked just as confused as Melanie felt. "I did not." She looked back at Beatrice. "Are you sure about this?"

Beatrice raised her chin. "I didn't imagine it, if that's what you're thinking. Ask the others. We all saw him." She lowered her voice again. "Some of us think the skeleton pushed Walter off the balcony. We're all scared now, wondering who he is and if he'll come back."

It took Melanie a moment to gather her senses. An intruder at the party? She could see the apprehension on her grandmother's face, and it mirrored her own. Beatrice was looking at each of them, obviously searching for reassurance.

Melanie puffed out her breath. "Well, you can stop worrying about that," she said firmly. "We'll find out who he is and why he was at the party. I promise you, he won't be back."

Beatrice's face expressed her doubts about that. With a quick nod, she scurried up the driveway to the porch.

Max tugged at the leash, impatient to be on his way, and once more Melanie set off down the street.

"What on earth was Beatrice talking about?" Liza sounded out of breath, and Melanie slowed her step. "I thought we were done with skeletons."

"I have no idea." Melanie replayed Beatrice's words in her mind. "She said he left before Nick's performance, and neither one of us got there until after the magic show had started, so if there really was a skeleton there last night, we wouldn't have seen him."

"I don't know. Beatrice sounded a bit paranoid with that comment about Dutton having an ulterior motive for his questions. I think she may have imagined the whole skeleton thing."

"You're saying she's got some kind of mental disorder?"

Liza shrugged. "I guess we could ask the other guests if they saw a skeleton. Just to be sure."

"I think we should ask Cindi first. She was at the party from the beginning. There's no point in upsetting the other guests if it's all in Beatrice's mind."

Liza shook her head. "I just can't believe someone would take the trouble to dress up and crash our little party. It doesn't make sense."

"Unless," Melanie said slowly, "that someone was there to push Walter off the balcony."

Liza stopped in her tracks. "We have to report this."

Melanie looked back at her. "We will, if the skeleton is real. You're right. It could be Beatrice's mind playing tricks. I'm sure Cindi would have told us if there was a stranger at the party."

"Maybe it was our merry ghost enjoying the festivities."

"I thought Orville was invisible."

"Not if he's wearing a costume and a mask." Liza frowned. "We should probably tell Detective Dutton."

"And listen to him yell at us again for interfering in his case? I don't think so."

"Well, then we need to tell Ben."

"Once we know for sure there was a skeleton." They had reached the end of the lane that led to the sands, and Max was straining at the leash. "Anyway," Melanie added as she let the dog tug her down the slope, "right now I don't even want to think about strangers or murders. I need to clear my head, and I can't think of anything better to do that than an ocean wind and the smell of sand and seaweed."

Liza sniffed the air. "Agreed. Let's hit the beach."

In spite of the chill in the wind, several people were strolling along the water's edge. The tide was in, putting a stretch of water between the sand and the massive rocks rising out of the waves. Sprays of foam chased the sea gulls from the lower edges, and they circled the jagged peaks, looking for a spot to land.

Melanie unclipped Max's leash and watched him bound toward the ocean, only to halt as a wave swept in, covering his feet. He danced away, then sniffed at something in the sand, before racing off again to join a couple of other dogs farther down the beach.

"Your mother loved the beach," Liza said, shading her eyes to watch the dogs play.

Startled, Melanie stared at her. Liza very rarely mentioned her daughter.

Janice had been a widow just a few short weeks when she had left for an extended stay with relatives in England, leaving a four-year-old Melanie with her parents. She had never arrived at her destination. With no knowledge of what had happened to her, Liza and her husband, Frank, had raised Melanie while doing their best to keep the memory of her mother alive.

When Frank died, Liza had bought the house at the coast with the intention of turning it into a bed-and-breakfast and had offered Melanie a partnership in the business. Recently divorced and tired of her job as an analyst for a stockbroker, Melanie had jumped at the opportunity.

With more time on her hands, she started a search for her missing mother, mostly on the Internet, but so far had no success in finding out if she was dead or alive. Since then Liza had been careful not to mention Janice's name too much.

Melanie wasn't sure if her grandmother was protecting herself or her granddaughter. Or maybe she was just afraid to hope for too much.

Right now, Liza seemed intent on watching Max romp around in the sand. Melanie cleared her throat. "Did you bring her here to this beach?"

"Yes, I did." Liza turned her head to stare out to sea. "She thought the rocks were castles where mermaids lived."

Melanie smiled. "I like that."

"She brought you here when you were about two years old." Liza looked back at her with misty green eyes. "You hated the water and screamed when she carried you too close to the edge."

"Really? I wish I could remember that. I love the water now. If it wasn't so cold all the time, I'd go swimming in it."

"Do you remember anything about her?"

Melanie struggled for a moment to catch hold of a fleeting memory. "Not really. I remember someone holding me and making me laugh, but I can't picture her at all. If it wasn't for your photos, I'd never even know what she looked like."

"Just look in the mirror. Although you have your father's lovely hazel eyes, you have your mother's thick, dark hair and creamy skin. You even have her freckles across your nose, and when you laugh, you sound like her."

Melanie felt a stab of pain. Her grandmother had told her the same things before, but although she had held up the photos of her mother next to her reflection in the mirror, she still couldn't see the likeness.

A sudden barrage of barking turned both their heads. Max was chasing a sea gull that swooped low over the sand, apparently looking for food and ignoring the noisy dog charging behind it.

Melanie called out to him, and he reluctantly gave up the chase, loping back toward them with his tongue hanging out the side of his mouth.

"Come on, buddy. Time to go home." Melanie clipped the leash to his collar again.

Liza was quiet on the way home, and Melanie missed her usual chatter. She wondered if her grandmother was reliving memories of her daughter.

In a way Melanie was thankful she couldn't remember that time in her life. It made the loss easier to bear.

The inn was quiet when they walked in a few minutes later. The guests were either in their rooms or outside, enjoying the fresh air. Cindi had left, apparently having finished making the beds and cleaning the bathrooms.

Although Melanie was convinced Beatrice had imagined the skeleton at the party, she called Cindi's cell phone right away. The assistant's voice mail picked up, but rather than leave a message, she decided to try again later.

Liza settled herself in the living room with one of her favorite mystery novels, and Melanie seized the opportunity to sit at her computer and catch up on the accounts.

The moment she logged on to her e-mail, she noticed a message from Vivian Adams, her friend in England who had been helping her with the search for her mother.

With a spark of excitement, Melanie opened the file. Vivian's note was short and to the point. She'd met someone who thought he might know Melanie's mother. Vivian had worked with him and had told him the story of how Janice had disappeared on her way to visit British relatives. He lived close to the neighborhood where Liza's cousin had once lived. He'd told Vivian that he had a neighbor who suffered from amnesia and was about the same age as Melanie's mother.

I don't know how reliable he is, Vivian wrote, *but he's promised to take a pic of her next time he sees her, and when he sends it to me, I'll forward it on to you. So keep your fingers crossed!*

Melanie stared at the words until they blurred in front of her eyes. Had her mother had some kind of accident, leaving her with no memory of who she was and what had happened to her? It was a question she'd asked herself many times before. Was it really possible that her mother had been living in a neighborhood so close to Liza's cousin without the woman bumping into her? Then again, Janice had grown up in Oregon. The cousin might not have known what she looked like.

Struggling to suppress her mounting hope, Melanie dashed off a note to Vivian, thanking her for her help. She would not tell Liza yet, she decided. Better to wait until she'd actually seen the photo.

After working for an hour on the accounts, she realized she was hungry. A quick glance at the clock told her it was way past her usual lunchtime. The detective had interrupted her breakfast, which she'd barely touched. After shutting down the computer, she tried calling Cindi again, but once more the call went to voice mail. Sighing, she went in search of Liza.

Her grandmother was in the kitchen, piling ham, cheese, lettuce, and tomato onto slices of bread. "Oh, there you are," she said when Melanie walked in. "I was just coming to look for you. We're late for lunch."

"I know." Melanie opened the fridge and took out a can of soda. "We'll have to get better organized than this."

"Hey, it's our first day. We'll soon settle into a routine." She wrinkled her nose as Melanie popped open the can. "That stuff will put pounds on you."

"Not likely, with all the exercise I'm getting." Melanie took the sandwich Liza handed her. "Thanks. Do you have any big plans for the afternoon?"

"Not unless you call reading my book a big plan. Did you have something in mind?"

"I thought I'd run over to the RV park and ask Cindi about the skeleton. I called her a couple of times, but her phone went to voice mail. I guess she turned it off. I don't want to wait until tomorrow to talk to her. We need to find out whether Beatrice imagined a stranger crashing our party. If she was actually telling the truth, the police should know as soon as possible."

"Good thinking. I'll come with you." Liza sat down in the nook. "I feel sorry for that girl, living in a trailer. Those things are so cramped. I'd die of claustrophobia."

Melanie smiled. "She's young, and she probably doesn't spend a lot of time in it. She's here for half of the day, and she helps out a lot at the campground."

"Oh, right. I forgot about that." Liza took a bite out of her sandwich. "Did she ever tell you what happened to her parents?"

"No, and I didn't ask. All I know is that she grew up in foster homes, and from the little she told me, I got the idea she had a pretty miserable childhood. She's a tough young woman and seems quite capable of taking care of herself. I like that."

"Me too." Liza put down her sandwich and reached for her iced tea. "Though I have to admit, when I first saw her, my thought was that we were inviting trouble by hiring her. But she's turning out to be a really good worker and is so cheerful all the time. The guests really seem to like her. Just goes to show, you can't judge people by their appearance."

For some reason, a vision of Ben popped into Melanie's mind. Her first impression of him had been a stern cop with little patience and steely eyes that saw too much. The few times she'd seen him since then had softened her opinion of him.

He'd worried about her and Liza when they'd faced danger earlier this year, and the night she'd had dinner with him, she'd sensed a sadness inside him that he was determined to keep hidden. That edge of vulnerability in such a seemingly invincible man had deepened her attraction to him, much to her dismay. Fortunately he had kept the conversation on an impersonal level, avoiding any awkwardness.

"What are you stewing about?"

Melanie jerked her mind back to the present. Liza was watching her with intent eyes, a frown creasing her forehead.

"I was just thinking about what you said—that you can't judge people by appearances. It reminded me of something

Ben said when I said that our guests were too old to be suspects. He said that everyone is capable of murder. It's a sobering thought."

"Aha." Liza pointed a finger in triumph. "I knew you were thinking about Ben. You had that look on your face you get whenever he's around."

Melanie scowled at her. "As usual, you're imagining something that's not there. I've told you a million times, Ben is a friend. Nothing more."

"Uh-huh. And I'm the next Miss America. You can't fool an old woman. I've been around you long enough to know what you're thinking."

"Really? Well, if you know what I'm thinking now, you'll know to quit yakking and finish your lunch."

Liza grinned. "Spoken like a true Harris. You remind me of your grandfather."

Unnerved by her grandmother's insight, Melanie sought to change the subject. "I wish Cindi had answered her phone. I don't like to drop in on people uninvited."

"It's better to talk to her face-to-face. It's easier to tell if someone is lying."

Surprised, Melanie stared at her grandmother. "You think she's hiding something? You were singing her praises just now."

"As far as her work goes. Who knows what she does in her private life."

"You don't trust her."

"I don't trust anyone I don't know well. Even then, I have my reservations."

Melanie leaned back against her chair. "You've become a bit cynical since you started devouring those mystery novels."

Liza stood up and reached for Melanie's empty plate. "I've always been cynical. Just not out loud. Old age has its advantages."

Melanie got up too. "You could live to be a hundred and you'd still never be old."

Liza smiled. "You, my dear Mel, are prejudiced. But thank you. Now let's get down to the RV park and talk to Cindi. But first, I need to stop in the living room and pick up my book. I left it lying on the table, and I don't want someone else to pick it up and take off with it."

Following her grandmother down the hallway to the living room, Liza's reluctance to trust the assistant lingered in Melanie's mind. Maybe it would be better to surprise the girl and see what her reaction was to their question.

Disgusted with herself for being so mistrustful of someone she really liked, she had to remind herself of the last time somebody had fooled her, making her believe he was someone completely different to his true self. She'd made the mistake of marrying him, and it had ended badly. Which was why she was no longer married to him.

Liza had reached the door of the living room and stepped inside, stopping so suddenly that Melanie bumped into her. Looking past her grandmother's shoulder, Melanie saw the sisters seated on the couch, each with a book in her hand.

A quick glance at the coffee table assured her Liza's book was still lying where she'd left it.

Liza must have seen it at the same time, as she hurried forward to pick it up.

Eileen smiled up at her as Liza bent over to reach the book. "I've read that one," she said, "and you'll never guess how it ends."

"I sincerely hope you're not going to tell me," Liza said crisply.

Melanie winced, but Eileen seemed unfazed by Liza's bluntness. "I wouldn't dream of it. Did the detective find out who did it?"

Liza blinked. "What?"

"The detective." Eileen waved a hand at the door. "The one who was asking all those questions about Walter. Did he find out who threw Walter off the balcony? I hope so, because all of us are scared to death wondering who could have done such a thing. The killer could still be in this house."

Amy uttered a soft whimper, and Melanie decided it was time to intervene. "We really don't know what the detective found out," she said, moving closer to her grandmother. "He didn't say anything to us before he left. I'm sure, though, that whoever killed Walter is far away by now."

Eileen's forehead wrinkled in distaste. "Well, I hope that detective catches him soon and quits asking us questions. I didn't like the man. He acted as if we were criminals." She looked at her sister. "Amy was so upset after he left, I had trouble calming her down."

Amy opened her mouth to speak, but Eileen continued in her forceful voice, "None of us answered any of his questions. We're a close-knit group and watch out for each other. We're not about to take the chance of making trouble for someone, so we all agreed to keep our mouths shut."

"But—" Amy began, but once more her sister drowned her out.

"No one really liked Walter, you know. He was always upsetting everyone. Especially Gloria. He was always hitting on her. Can you imagine?"

She leaned forward and dropped her voice to a hoarse whisper. "I heard her going off at him once. She was accusing him of breaking up her relationship with her boyfriend. He kept denying it, but she obviously didn't believe him. She actually threatened to cut off his equipment if he didn't leave her alone." She straightened up again and continued in her normal tone. "But then one shouldn't speak badly of someone who's passed. Whatever he was, Walter didn't deserve to die like that."

"Who—"

Amy barely got the word out before her sister cut her off again. "Joe's always standing up for Gloria, you know." Eileen nodded, as if confirming her own words. "He's the protective type. Though I do think he's fond of Gloria, if you know what I mean." She gave Liza a lewd wink. "Not that he'd ever tell her that. I think he's afraid he'll get brushed off like Walter was."

Melanie decided it was time to halt the harsh flow of words. "Well, Granny," she said, giving Liza nudge, "we should get going. We have errands to run."

Liza seemed a little dazed by the nonstop barrage of one-sided conversation. She looked at Amy, then back at Eileen. "There's something we wanted to ask you ladies. Did either of you see a skeleton at the party last night?"

Eileen exchanged an odd look with her sister. "Yes, we did. We were wondering who he was. Was he another guest? We didn't see him at breakfast this morning."

Melanie caught her breath. "You actually saw the skeleton?"

"Everyone saw him. He was fooling around, pretending to be drunk and making us all laugh." Eileen sighed. "Everyone except Walter, of course."

Liza gave her a sharp look. "Did he and Walter speak to each other?"

Eileen raised her eyebrows. "I didn't notice. Why? Who was he, anyway? The skeleton, I mean." A look of dread crept over her face, and she lowered her voice. "Was he the one who killed Walter?"

Amy's face looked pinched as she exchanged another look with her sister.

Wary of frightening the sisters any further, Melanie blurted out the first thing that came to mind. "He was just a friend playing a joke on everyone. There's nothing to worry about. Now we really must go." She took a firm hold of Liza's arm and led her from the room.

"A *friend*?" Liza shook her head as they walked down the hallway.

"I had to tell them something. They were so scared. Now we really need to talk to Cindi. I can't believe she let a stranger fool around with our guests. She must have known he didn't belong there."

"I'm wondering why she didn't mention him to us." Liza paused to take her coat from the closet. "She has to be hiding something."

Worried now, Melanie hurried out to the car with Max hot on her heels.

A few minutes later, they drove into the wide parking lot of the RV park. A motor home was parked in the waiting lane, and another sat at the side of the gas pump, filling up with fuel.

Melanie drove slowly past them and up the winding lane, where a few travel trailers, a couple of massive fifth wheels, an elegant motor home, and a tiny pop-up camper sheltered beneath the trees. In the summer, every space in the park would be taken, but now, with winter approaching, empty spaces abounded.

Cindi's trailer was at the very back of the park. Melanie left Max in the car in the guest spot and walked Liza toward the thick stand of trees, hoping their new assistant would be home. The air felt damp and smelled of wood smoke as they approached the trailer.

They had almost reached it when Cindi appeared in the doorway, waving at them. She looked worried, and when they got closer, she asked anxiously, "Is something wrong?"

"No, not really." Melanie smiled up at her. "We just wanted to ask you about something. I tried calling you, but your voice mail was on."

"I left my phone charging in the office." Cindi sent a doubtful glance over her shoulder. "I'd let you in, but it's a bit jammed in here." She stepped down onto the tarmac. "What did you want to ask me?"

Melanie glanced over her shoulder. Although the campsite seemed deserted, she would have preferred talking to Cindi somewhere more private.

Liza, however, apparently had no such problem. "We heard there was a man dressed as a skeleton at the party last night." She frowned at Cindi. "Do you have any idea who he was and why he was there?"

Cindi looked uncomfortable. She flicked a glance at Melanie and back again at Liza. "It was Nick. We thought it would be fun for him to dress up and entertain the guests before the magic show. I didn't tell you because I wanted to surprise you, but then you didn't get there before he had to change into his magician's outfit, and after that, with everything happening, I forgot about it. I'm sorry. We should have told you."

"Yes, you should have." Liza folded her arms—never a good sign. "All the guests are scared to death thinking the mysterious skeleton killed Walter."

Cindi's eyes grew wider. "Nick? He wouldn't hurt a fly."

"I'd like a dollar for every time I've heard that one," Liza said grimly.

Melanie jumped in quickly as Cindi's expression darkened. "There's no harm done," she said, pinching Liza's arm. "I already told the sisters it was a friend playing a joke, which is more or less the truth. I'm sure they'll pass it along to the rest of the guests."

"I'll tell them myself tomorrow," Cindi said, stepping back up into the doorway of her trailer. "We never meant to scare anyone. And just so we're clear about this, Nick didn't kill anyone. I'd bet my life on that. I'll see you tomorrow."

Before either of them could answer, she'd firmly closed the door.

"Whatever got into you?" Melanie demanded as they walked back to the car. "You really upset Cindi, suggesting that Nick might be a murderer. Didn't we agree not to jump to conclusions?"

Liza shrugged. "I know, but it wouldn't be the first time an entertainer has sought revenge for being publicly humiliated."

Melanie rolled her eyes. "Well, whatever we think, we can't go around accusing people without good cause. We're talking about an amateur magician at a senior citizen party, not an opera star at the Met."

"And if you'd read as many detective novels as I have, you'd know not to leave one stone unturned."

"Well, I just hope your stone turning hasn't cost us a good assistant." Melanie reached the car and opened the passenger door for her grandmother. "Cindi was telling the truth. Now that I think about it, I paid Nick myself when he left, and everyone else was still at the party."

"Nick could have come back later."

Shaking her head, Melanie shut the door and walked around the car to the driver's side. Much as she hated to admit it, her grandmother was right. Everyone connected to Walter Dexter was a suspect, which included their entire guest list. Any one of them could have pushed Walter off the balcony. Until the murder was solved, everyone in the Merry Ghost Inn could be living with a killer. It was not the way she'd envisioned their grand opening would go.

All she could hope was that this latest catastrophe wouldn't put an end to the Merry Ghost Inn's future before it had barely begun.

Chapter 4

The following morning breakfast went much more smoothly in the kitchen. Along with the lemon poppy seed muffins and toasted walnut bread, Cindi served large slices of spinach and tomato frittatas with hash browns and sautéed mushrooms.

"They're real quiet in there," Cindi said when she returned to the kitchen later with empty plates, "but they must have enjoyed their breakfast." She placed the almost-clean plates on the counter. "They were so busy stuffing their faces, they didn't have time to talk."

Melanie looked up from the sink, where she was rinsing off a frying pan. "Did you explain to them about the skeleton?"

"I did." Cindi sat down in the nook. "I told them it was my boyfriend entertaining them, just like he did with the magic show."

Liza took the brimming coffeepot off the percolator and replaced it with an empty one. "Did they seem relieved?"

Cindi shrugged. "They didn't seem anything. They just kind of looked at me as if they already knew."

"The sisters must have told them what Melanie said yester-day." Liza carried the coffeepot over to Cindi. "Here you go. They'll be needing a refill by now."

Cindi got up again. "Nick didn't kill Walter," she said quietly. "He would never do anything like that. He's the sweetest guy you'll ever meet."

Melanie held her breath when her grandmother looked as if she'd disagree, then exhaled when Liza said just as softly, "I'm sure you're right. I just hope the police find out who did it so we can all breathe easier."

"Me too." For the first time that morning, Melanie saw Cindi smile. She took the coffeepot from Liza and left the room.

Melanie dried the frying pan and tucked it onto a shelf in the cabinet. "Do you really believe her?"

"I don't know what to believe." Liza sat down by the window and stared at the storm clouds gathering over the gray ocean. "I just can't imagine one of our guests being that vicious. If one of them did kill Walter, he or she had to have a really good reason to hate him."

"More so than being humiliated in front of an audience?"

"Exactly. So far, Nick is the only one with a motive."

"What about Gloria? Eileen said Walter broke up Gloria's relationship with her boyfriend. I'd think that would be a good reason to hate him."

"Enough to kill him? I don't know." Liza turned her head slowly to look at her. "Maybe we should talk to everyone and find out if anyone else had an ax to grind."

Melanie picked up the second frying pan and plunged it into the soapy water. "That's exactly what got us into trouble with Detective Dutton the last time. He wouldn't be too thrilled to find out we were interfering in his police business again."

"He can't say too much to us if we're simply having a pleasant conversation with our guests. Besides, they're not talking to him. I think they're afraid of him. So maybe they'll talk to us. Someone must know something that could help find out who killed Walter."

Melanie swished a sponge around the pan and rinsed it under the faucet. She wanted to solve the murder as badly as Liza did, but the memory of Tom Dutton's resentment earlier that year still resonated in her mind.

His face had burned with annoyance when he'd scolded them. *My job is tough enough without a couple of amateur snoops to worry about. In the future, I'd appreciate it if you'd stay out of my way and mind your own damn business.*

She still shuddered when she thought about it. "We'd have to be careful not to make it sound like we're questioning them."

Liza flapped a hand at her. "Oh, don't worry about that grumpy old detective. It's not a crime to talk to people. What can he do to us, anyway?"

"Put us in jail for obstruction of justice?"

Liza threw up her hands. "We're not obstructing. We're helping."

"I don't think he sees it that way."

"Who cares?" Liza got up from the chair. "Look, if this case isn't solved by the end of the week, our guests can't leave, not to mention our balcony will still be a crime scene. So where would we put next week's guests? We need to find out who killed Walter. No one is talking to the detective, so we have to get them to talk to us."

Melanie sighed. "Maybe you're right. Okay, I'm in. Just don't get too carried away."

Liza raised her eyebrows. "Who, me? This is your grandmother you're talking to. I never get carried away."

"Uh-huh. I seem to remember you running all over town earlier this year, questioning everyone you met about a murder."

Liza grinned. "You had to admit, it was exciting."

Remembering the fire that had almost cost them the inn, Melanie shook her head. "That kind of excitement I can do without."

"All right, so maybe things did get a little hairy at times, but we solved the murder, and I think if we do this right, we can solve this one. We just need to act casual with the whole thing and make it sound like we're just talking about Walter and what happened to him."

Melanie put the second pan in the cabinet. "Well, right now I'm going to take Max for his walk. Want to come with us?"

Liza glanced at the window again. "I would, but I'm on the last chapter of my book, and I really want to find out who did it before someone spills the beans."

Having heard the word "walk," Max was already panting at the door. Melanie took down his leash from the hook and clipped it to his collar. "We won't be long. It looks like a storm brewing out there."

She left the kitchen just as Cindi appeared in the hallway holding the empty coffeepot. "That bunch in there gulp coffee down like it's water," Cindi said as she pushed open the door to the kitchen. "They'll be wired all day." She disappeared inside, leaving Melanie to follow an impatient Max to the front door.

Once outside, the crisp wind bit into Melanie's ears, and she pulled up the collar of her jacket. Spots of rain hit her nose, and Max shook his body all the way from his tail up to his head. "It's a little too windy to go on the beach today, buddy." She tugged on his leash. "Come on, we'll take a walk around the backyard."

He seemed to understand and obediently trotted by her side as she walked around the garage and through the gate that led to the backyard. A wide expanse of grass spread out to the white picket fence lining the edge of the cliffs.

Melanie unclipped the dog's leash, and he bounded over to the railings to stare down at the sand below. The beach was almost deserted, with just a half dozen or so people wandering along the shore. Max spotted another dog prancing along the water's edge and barked at it, then turned away in disgust when it ignored him.

Farther out to sea, Melanie could see a couple of ships anchored, sheltering from the approaching storm. As she watched, they disappeared in the mist of rain. Angry waves dashed against the rocks, sending spray high into the air.

The wind tossed her hair, and she pulled it back from her face, turning her back to the stinging blast. The salty air was heavy with the smell of seaweed and pine, and needles flew from the trees bending to the wind's onslaught.

Max had lost interest in the view and was wandering around the flowerbeds, his nose almost touching the ground. She hoped he'd soon take care of business so she could get back inside the inn before the heavy rain arrived.

After examining yet another flowerbed, Max finally wandered onto the grass and squatted down. The raindrops were larger now and coming faster. Melanie hurried over to pick up after Max, then started back toward the gate. The dog seemed engrossed in another flowerbed, and growing impatient, she sternly called his name.

Max ignored her and kept sniffing at something in the dirt. He seemed so intent, Melanie wondered if he'd found a mouse or, worse, an injured bird. Anxious now, she hurried over to him.

"Max, what in the world are you doing?" She stared down at the bark dust and noticed at once that part of it rose in a little pile. "Did you do that?" She stretched out her foot to smooth it out, and as she did so, the toe of her shoe struck something hard.

Thankful that she was wearing gloves, she bent down and brushed away the pile of bark dust, revealing a piece of bright metal. Carefully she took hold of it and pulled. It came up easily, shedding lumps of damp soil as she slowly straightened up.

Her breath caught in her throat as she stared at the saw in her hand. There was no doubt in her mind why it had been buried in the backyard of the inn. This had to be the saw that had sliced through the railings of the balcony, sending Walter Dexter to his death.

The rain fell in earnest now, beating on her head and soaking Max's coat. She ran for the gate, and Max dove through it, then stopped to shake the moisture from his fur. Melanie ran down the path, around the garage, and across the driveway to the front porch.

The dog leapt up the steps with her, and together they burst through the front door, nearly colliding with Cindi, who was pulling on her jacket.

The assistant's eyes opened wide when she caught sight of the saw in Melanie's hand. "Is that—?" She cut off the rest of the sentence, sending a wary glance over her shoulder at the empty hallway.

"I think so." Melanie stepped back as once more Max violently shook his entire body, sending drops of water in the air. "Are you leaving?"

"Yeah, everything is done." She looked anxious. "Unless there's something else you need me to do." She nodded at the saw. "What are you going to do with that?"

"Give it to the police, I guess." Melanie looked down at it, shuddering at the thought that it had been in a killer's hands. "It might have prints on it or something."

"If the rain hasn't washed it all off." Cindi zipped up her jacket. "Let me know what the cops have to say about it."

"I will. Do you know where Liza is?"

"She's in the living room reading."

"Okay, you can go ahead and leave. We'll see you in the morning."

Cindi nodded and headed for the front door while Melanie hurried down the hallway to the kitchen. Max headed straight for his bed and curled up inside.

After spreading a couple of kitchen towels on the island counter, Melanie laid the saw down on them and picked up her cell phone.

The assistant who answered her call to the police department assured her that Ben was in the office and transferred her to his phone. His deep voice went a long way to settling her nerves, and she sounded calmer than she felt when she said, "I think I found the saw that the killer used on the railings."

Ben's voice sharpened. "Where did you find it?"

"It was buried in the backyard. Max was sniffing at something. I went to look and saw the bark dust had been disturbed, and when I smoothed it out, the saw stuck out from the dirt."

"Did you leave it there?"

"No, I didn't know what it was until I pulled it all the way out, so I brought it back to the house." She felt a pang of dismay. "Did I do something wrong?"

"No, it's okay. I'll be right over to get it. Just don't let anyone touch it, okay?"

"I won't." She hung up, worried now that she'd messed up a chance to find the killer. She should have just left the saw in the flowerbed.

The kitchen door opened, and Liza poked her head in the gap. "I thought I heard you in the hallway." She walked in and closed the door. "What have you got there?"

"I think it's the saw used to cut through the railings. It was buried in the yard."

Liza's eyes widened. "Goodness. How did you find it?"

"Max was sniffing around there, and I saw it sticking out of the ground." She sighed. "I should have left it there. I've probably destroyed evidence."

"Did you call Grumpy Dutton?"

"No, I called Ben. He's coming over to get it."

Liza grinned. "There you go!"

"Don't go getting any ideas." Melanie crossed over to the counter and picked up the coffeepot. "I need coffee. That wind is frigid."

Liza glanced at the window, where the rain beat against the glass in a loud tattoo. "Definitely not a day for strolling on the beach. That's why everyone's in the living room in front of the gas fire. They're watching the soaps on TV. Everyone except Joe. When I left he had his nose buried in the sports page of the newspaper."

"Did you finish your book?"

"I did." Liza walked over to the fridge and opened it. "It's time for lunch. How about an apple bacon grilled cheese sandwich?" She pulled a pack of bacon out of the fridge. "This won't take long. You go ahead and make the coffee."

Minutes later they were seated in the nook, enjoying the sandwiches, while Max waited patiently for a morsel to drop to the floor.

They had barely finished before the doorbell rang, bringing Melanie to her feet. "That's probably Ben."

Ignoring Liza's smug smile, she rushed out into the hallway and down to the front door, with Max barking behind her. Laying one hand on his collar, she shushed him and opened the door.

Ben had his back to her, watching the tree branches being tossed around in the wind. He wore his uniform cap pulled low over his eyes, and when he turned to look at her, he gave her just a glimmer of a smile.

He had on what Melanie called his official face. The night she'd had dinner with him, he'd looked so much more relaxed. Although he'd made it clear that he just wanted to talk to her about the events that had brought him to the inn, he'd soon loosened up, and the conversation had become more personal.

He'd actually laughed when she'd told him stories about her grandmother, and although he'd been guarded about his private life, he had talked a lot about his life as a cop. She'd had a whole new respect for people in law enforcement after that night.

"Come in." She stepped back to let him pass her. "The saw is in the kitchen. Liza and I have just finished lunch, but I can offer you a cup of coffee."

"I'm fine. Thanks." He followed her down the hallway to the kitchen, with Max padding alongside him. The dog really liked Ben, which told her a lot about the kind of man he was.

Liza was at the sink when Melanie led Ben into the kitchen. Her grandmother turned to smile at him, water dripping from the plate in her hand. "You should have got here earlier. You could have had lunch with us."

Ben took off his cap. "Sorry I missed that." He glanced at the saw on the island counter. "Is that it?"

"Yes." Melanie watched him pull on a pair of plastic gloves. "I'm sorry I didn't leave it out there, but I didn't realize what it was until I had it in my hand. I was wearing gloves, though. I hope I didn't mess things up."

He flicked a glance at her. "It's okay. Don't worry. You did the right thing by calling me and keeping this away from everyone." He pulled a large plastic bag from his pocket and dropped the saw into it. "I'll get this back to the lab, and we'll see what we can find."

"If you find prints on it," Liza said, "I guess we'll all have to be fingerprinted."

Melanie looked at Ben in alarm. "Seriously? Our guests won't be too happy about that."

"We'll only do that if it's absolutely necessary." Ben moved to the door. "Chances are that any evidence was lost when the saw was buried, but you never know, we may get lucky. I'll be in touch." He pulled on his cap and opened the door.

"I'll show you out," Melanie said, obeying a frantic nudge from Liza. She followed the cop down the hallway to the front door. "Thanks for coming over. I wasn't sure if I should have called Detective Dutton."

"Oh, he'll be interested in seeing this." Ben held up the saw. "I imagine he'll be back here before long to question everyone again."

"I was afraid of that."

Ben touched her shoulder. "Hang in there. Hopefully this will all be over soon."

"I hope so." She managed a smile. "You take care."

"You too."

She watched him walk to his car, just a little too fascinated by his long-legged stride. She quickly shut the door. The last thing she needed right then was another complication in her life.

Detective Dutton arrived at the inn less than an hour later. Everyone was still in the living room, watching TV or reading. The detective took the guests into the dining room to question them while Melanie and Liza did their best to reassure everyone it was just a routine part of the investigation.

Gloria was the last one to be questioned, and she looked a little frazzled when she walked in to the living room later. "I don't like that man," she said as she arranged herself on a chair.

"He asks too many personal questions." She stretched out a leg and pinched the crease in her black pants, then crossed her knees. "I just kept saying 'I don't know' to everything. He got a little peevish."

"He didn't get anything out of me," Joe said, giving Gloria an approving smile.

"Nor us," Eileen declared while Amy nodded.

Beatrice didn't say anything. She sat on the edge of the couch, biting her lip.

"He wants to see you next," Gloria said, looking at Melanie. "He told me to send you in there."

With a twist of apprehension, Melanie got up. "I don't know what else I can tell him," she said, looking at Liza for some sign of reassurance.

"Just tell him that," Liza said. "It'll be fine."

Wishing she could be sure of that, Melanie walked into the dining room.

The detective sat at one of the tables, a laptop in front of him. His fingers were flying across the keyboard, and Melanie waited for him to quit. It seemed an eternity before he finally looked up. "Sit," he said, waving a hand at the chair opposite him. "I'll be with you in a minute."

Melanie sat and stared at the freshly painted walls. The fire in the spring had ruined the wallpaper that had been on there for the last fifty years or so, and the room seemed bigger now with the painted cream walls. Dutton had chosen the table next to the window to conduct his investigation. He sat with his back to the view outside, but Melanie could see the ocean. The water looked a little calmer, and the sky was lighter on the horizon. It looked as if the storm was passing over.

"Tell me how you found the saw," Detective Dutton commanded, making her jump.

Looking at his rigid features, she wished she were still outside with Max instead of facing this grim interrogator. Carefully she recounted the story of Max sniffing in the dirt and finding the saw sticking out of the ground.

"You should have left it there," Dutton said, giving her an accusing glare. "Any time you find evidence of a crime, you don't touch it. You call us instead."

"I didn't know what it was until I'd pulled it out of the ground." Melanie made an effort to curb her resentment. "I called as soon as I had put it down in a safe place."

"You didn't call me."

"I called the police station." She hoped the assistant hadn't told him she'd asked for Ben.

"Have any of the guests given you the impression they were angry with Walter Dexter?"

"Angry? No, not really. Though I don't think any of them liked him much."

He gave her a sharp glance. "Why do you say that?"

Melanie shrugged. "He didn't seem to be very sociable."

"Anyone give you a specific reason?"

A vision of Gloria popped into her mind. What was it Eileen had said? *I heard her going off at him once. She actually threatened to cut off his equipment if he didn't leave her alone.*

"Mrs. West?"

Melanie winced. How she hated that name. It wasn't so much the name as the fact that it reminded her of her ex-husband every time she heard it. Gary had been responsible for the worst tragedy of her life, and the last thing she needed was a reminder every time someone used her last name. She should get it changed back to her maiden name.

"Is there something you want to tell me?"

She dragged her gaze back to the detective and found him staring at her with intense brown eyes. He had a receding hairline, which made his wrinkled frown all the more formidable. "No, I was just thinking about what you asked."

She wondered for a brief moment if she should mention Gloria's problem with Walter, then decided it wasn't enough to accuse the woman of murder. Dutton would probably find out about it sooner or later, and if he wanted to make something of it, that was up to him. She wasn't about to make trouble for one of her guests.

"Well?"

His impatience annoyed her. "Well nothing. Nobody has said anything specific. I suggest you ask them yourself."

"I have." He snapped the lid of his laptop down. "Nobody's talking, which usually means they all have something to hide."

Melanie raised her eyebrows. "All of them? You think Walter's death was the result of a conspiracy?"

"I don't think anything, Mrs. West. I question and deduce. That's what detectives do." He stood up. "Now show me where you found the saw."

The possibility that the rest of the reading group had conspired to kill Walter disturbed Melanie as she led the detective out into the hallway. Pulling on a hoodie, she thought about the detective's words. *Nobody's talking, which usually means they all have something to hide.* What were they dealing with here? How dangerous was this group of guests?

By the time they reached the flowerbed where she'd found the saw, reason had returned. Envisioning each of her visitors, Melanie just couldn't see them sitting around plotting a murder. Then again, she couldn't imagine any of them pushing the poor man to his death. Which left only two possibilities—the only other two people in the house that night. Cindi and her boyfriend, Nick Hazelton.

The rain had tapered off to a few sprinkles, but the wind still tossed the branches of the pines. The detective had been poking around the flowerbed and the surrounding grass verge, but now he straightened up. "Your assistant, Cindi Metzger. You've just hired her, right?"

Uneasy that he'd read her mind, Melanie answered reluctantly, "Yes, she's been working for us for less than a month."

"So you don't know her that well."

Melanie raised her chin. "I know her well enough to know that she wouldn't push an old man to his death."

"Did you know she has a record?"

Shock kept Melanie speechless for a moment or two. "What kind of record?"

"The kind that puts you in jail. I suggest you ask her yourself if you want to know more."

His parody of her earlier comment ticked her off. "I will. Now if you're quite done, I need to get back to the inn. I have work to do."

She'd managed to make it sound as though he were wasting her time. The gleam of battle in his eyes gave her a lot of satisfaction.

She was turning away when he said sharply, "One more question. What do you know about Nick Hazelton?"

"I know he's the maintenance manager at the Happy Haven campground."

"He was at the inn last night."

"Yes, he did a magic show for our guests."

"Did you see him leave?"

"He left in his car right after I paid him." She turned away again. "I'll be in the house if you need to know anything else." She walked off before he had a chance to reply.

Liza was waiting for her in the kitchen when she returned to the inn. "Where have you been? I looked in the dining room, but Grumpy was gone. I was getting worried about you. I thought he might have carted you off to jail or something."

Melanie laughed. "You would have heard me kicking and screaming if he'd tried."

Liza's eyes widened. "Good for you! I take it the questioning didn't go well."

Melanie sat down in the nook. "There was a certain amount of tension, yes."

"What did he ask?" Liza gazed up at the ceiling. "I wonder why he didn't question me. It must be my look of pure innocence."

Melanie managed to keep a straight face. "Yes, that must be it."

Liza looked back at her. "So what did you find out?"

"Nothing. Nor did Detective Dutton. Like he said, nobody's talking. He wanted me to show him where the saw was buried, so I took him out there. I don't think he found anything significant." She hesitated, then added, "He did tell me something disturbing."

Liza sat down next to her. "Go on. What was it?"

"He said that Cindi has a record."

Liza's face changed from expectancy to dejection. "That doesn't surprise me."

"It surprised me."

"Did he tell you what she'd done?"

"No, he told me to ask her."

"Then I guess we'll have to ask her." Liza shook her head. "I thought she was too good to be true."

"I'm not going to give up on her until we know what she's done," Melanie said, prepared to argue, if necessary.

To her relief, Liza nodded. "You're right. We shouldn't condemn her without giving her a chance to explain." She stood up. "But first thing tomorrow, we ask. Okay?"

Melanie sighed. "Okay." She stood up too. "The detective asked me if I knew if anyone was angry with Walter."

"What did you tell him?" Liza walked over to the fridge and opened it.

"I didn't tell him anything. But I did think about Eileen telling us Gloria threatened him."

Liza closed the door with a snap. "You still think Gloria had something to do with Walter's murder?" She turned to face Melanie, her eyes wide. "Seriously?"

"I don't know what to think." Melanie reached into the cabinet for a glass. "I have a problem imagining any of the guests deliberately shoving an old man off our balcony. It just doesn't seem feasible."

"So you think maybe Cindi or Nick did it?"

Melanie crossed over to the fridge. "I don't know. I'm just confused and upset and a little scared."

"I know what you mean." Liza opened the fridge again, took a can of soda out, and handed it to her granddaughter. "It's an uncomfortable feeling knowing we could be living with a murderer in the house."

"It's bad enough living with a ghost without having a killer to worry about. Speaking of whom, we haven't heard him lately. Maybe he doesn't want to hang out with a killer either."

"Well, we don't know that it's someone in the house."

Melanie flipped the tab open. "Which brings us back to Cindi or her boyfriend."

"Or a complete stranger."

"That's highly unlikely. Someone went to a lot of trouble to saw through those railings, bury the saw, and then lure Walter out to the balcony in the middle of the night to push him off. Someone hated him enough to want him dead."

Liza frowned. "What if someone from Portland followed him down here?"

"How would he get into the house? Only you, Cindi, the guests, and I can open the entry system."

"He could have climbed up a drainpipe or something to the balcony."

"I guess that's possible." Melanie poured soda into her glass. "Maybe someone in the group can tell us if Walter had any enemies back home."

"Well, we have some time before we make dinner. Let's talk to someone. Like Gloria, for instance. After all, she supposedly threatened Walter. She should be our number-one suspect."

Melanie pushed Cindi out of her mind. "Right. We'll talk to Gloria." She took a few gulps from the glass, then placed it in the fridge. "Let's go."

Max jumped up from his bed and padded to the door, his tail wagging back and forth.

"I guess we should take the dog for a walk first." Melanie glanced at the window. "I think it's stopped raining, and his walk earlier was cut a bit short."

"Good idea. I could use some fresh air. All this talk of murder is boggling my mind." Liza trotted to the door and nearly tripped over Max, who seemed determined to beat her into the hallway.

Melanie followed her grandmother to the front door, the dog's leash in her hand. Just as Liza was about to open the door, Max growled.

Looking down at him, Melanie could see the fur rising in a ridge at the back of his neck. "What is it, buddy?" She looked over her shoulder, but the hallway behind her was empty.

Liza paused with her hand on the doorknob. "Is he seeing something we can't?"

Melanie frowned. "Like what?"

"Like Orville?"

Max growled again, staring toward the foot of the stairs with his tail rigid behind him.

"Well, let's go and look. Come on, Max." Melanie started down the hallway while the dog stayed where he was, feet planted firmly on the floor, his head low and a menacing growl rumbling in his throat.

"Max?" Melanie looked over her shoulder at him. "It's all right, there's nothing here." She took another step toward the stairs, then halted as a soft chuckle drifted down from above.

Chapter 5

"I told you it was Orville," Liza said, sounding smug while Max uttered a low growl.

Losing patience, Melanie leapt for the stairs and stared up them. Shadows from the trees outside the window danced on the walls, giving her a jolt. For a second or two, she thought she'd seen someone—or something—moving about up there.

"Is something wrong?"

The grating voice behind her almost stopped her heart. She swung around to see Joe staring at her with anxious gray eyes.

He must have stepped out of the dining room without her noticing. "No," she said hastily and gave him a shaky smile. "I was just going to take my dog for a walk." She hurried away from him, back to where Max now sat at Liza's feet. "Let's get out of here. I need some air."

Liza opened the door, and Max shot out onto the porch and down the steps. "Looks like you're not the only one who needs air," Liza said, following the dog outside.

Melanie stepped out into the wind and shut the door behind her. "We have to do something about that noise."

"You say that every time we hear it." Liza tilted her head on one side. "Know what I think? I think you're afraid to have someone inspect the house, because if he didn't find anything, you'd have to accept that Orville is real."

"That's crazy." Melanie whistled to Max, who raced back to her. Bending over to fasten his leash, she tried to convince herself that there was no vestige of truth in Liza's words.

"Practically the entire house was renovated after the fire," Liza said as they walked down the road, past twisted pines and towering Western Hemlock competing for space with the mighty Douglas firs. "If something tangible was making that noise, I think it would have been discovered or repaired in the process."

"Maybe." Sheltered from the ocean breezes, the air felt balmy, and Melanie felt her tension relaxing. The argument over whether or not the ghost actually existed had been ongoing ever since they had moved into the inn.

Much as she wanted to believe that the sound of ghostly laughter was nothing more than a structural defect somewhere in the house, she had to admit that some things were difficult to comprehend. It wasn't just the laughter. Objects in the house appeared to have been moved without any logical explanation in spite of her struggle to find a reason for it all.

Right now, however, with the sun warm on her face and the salty air filling her lungs, she wanted to forget all about ghosts, murders, and a crabby detective. She could see the ocean sparkling in the sunlight, and the near empty beach beckoned. Her problems could wait for the time being.

An hour or so later, tired and hungry, they returned to the inn, where Max immediately headed for his bed in the kitchen and promptly fell asleep.

Liza peered into the living room on the way to the kitchen and reported that it was empty. Either their guests were in their rooms or the pleasant change in the weather had lured them outside.

Melanie put a lasagna in the oven, then switched on the small TV on the island counter to watch the local news. There had been only a brief mention of the murder the night before, when the solemn-faced news anchor had announced that the police suspected foul play and were investigating the circumstances of a death at the inn.

Liza walked into the kitchen just as the anchor announced that there were no new developments in the case. He assured the viewers that the newsroom was on top of it and that he would report any news about the suspected murder as soon as it became available.

"I guess Grumpy didn't tell anyone about finding the saw yet," Liza said, opening the fridge door. "Want some wine?" She took a bottle of Chardonnay from the shelf and waved it at her granddaughter.

"I'd love some wine." Melanie got up and turned off the TV.

"We have to figure out a way to get Gloria alone so we can talk to her," Liza said, pouring wine into two glasses. "Though if she did push Walter off that balcony, she'd not likely to admit it."

"No, but she might let something slip that could help find out what happened. We will have to wait until tomorrow, though." Melanie took a sip of wine and then carried it back to the nook. "Everyone will probably be in the living room tonight watching TV."

"Or reading."

"We'll try to catch her before she leaves the house after breakfast tomorrow."

"Sounds good." Liza sniffed the air. "That lasagna smells delicious."

Max must have agreed, as he sat up, yawned, then raised his nose to sniff before heading for his water bowl.

*   *   *

After enjoying the lasagna and salad, Liza retired to her room to read while Melanie headed for her computer with Max following close behind. After checking her e-mail and finding nothing from Vivian, she opened the day's edition of the *Oregonian*. The account of Walter's death was buried in the middle of the webpage, and it took her a while to find it.

Again, it was just a brief paragraph saying that a dead body had been found in the driveway of the inn, the apparent victim of an assault.

At least they hadn't made the headlines. She closed out the site, feeling more than a little depressed. Things were not going well for their first week.

She slept badly that night, disturbed by confusing dreams where she was searching for something without knowing what she was supposed to find. Then she was on the beach, her feet sinking into the sand as the ocean roared toward her. She struggled to escape, but her feet were trapped . . .

She awoke with a start to find Max's fifty-pound weight sprawled across her legs, his snores echoing in her ears. A quick glance at her alarm clock assured her she hadn't overslept, and half an hour later, she was in the kitchen—showered, dressed, and feeling a little more optimistic.

After plugging in the percolator, she let Max out into the backyard, then picked up the local paper from the front doorstep.

Back in the kitchen, the stimulating aroma of coffee filled the room. It must have permeated the hallway, as moments later Liza sauntered in, her flowered robe swirling around her ankles.

"You're showered already," she said as she headed for the percolator. "I need my coffee before I can face a deluge of water."

Melanie watched her grandmother pour coffee into a mug. "How come you don't drink tea first thing in the mornings anymore?"

Liza sat down in the nook, cradling the mug in her hands. "I don't know. I still enjoy my tea, but now I need that cup of coffee to start my day. I guess, after your grandfather died, some of the old habits died with him. It was easier to accept he was gone if there weren't constant reminders of our life together."

"I'm sorry." Melanie sat down opposite her. "I know you still miss him."

"I do." Liza sipped from the mug. "But it's been easier since we bought this house." She swept her gaze around the kitchen, lingering on the copper pots above the island counter. "Your grandfather bought those for me the first year we were married. He had them shipped from England. He knew I was homesick, and my mother had copper pots just like those. He said they would remind me of home." She smiled. "I can't believe that was more than fifty years ago."

"Neither can I." Melanie studied her grandmother. "You don't look a day over fifty."

"Thank you, dear, but my body is constantly reminding me of my age. I'd like to replace a few parts of it with a newer model."

"You know that's possible, right? People are getting hip and knee replacements every day."

Liza shuddered. "Don't remind me. This is depressing. Let's change the subject."

Melanie held up the newspaper. "Want to read the local news?"

"Are we in it?"

"I don't know. I haven't looked yet." She took out a section and handed it to her grandmother.

"Thanks." Liza opened the paper and fished for her glasses in her pocket.

Melanie scanned the front page and found the report tucked in a corner at the bottom. "Here it is." She began reading out loud. "*The owners of the Merry Ghost Inn were dismayed to find the body of one of their guests, apparently having fallen from the balcony during the night. The police are investigating the case as a possible homicide. The victim, Walter Dexter, was staying at the inn with a group of book lovers from Portland. Mrs. Elizabeth Harris and Ms. Melanie West, owners of the inn, are holding their grand opening this week and are understandably distraught over this unfortunate incident.*"

"That's putting it mildly," Liza said, lifting her mug again.

She turned her head as the kitchen door opened and Cindi rushed in, her nose in the air. "Coffee! Just what I need." She rushed over to the counter and grabbed a mug from the cabinet. "It's freaking freezing out there."

Looking at Liza's outfit, Melanie could see why her assistant was cold. The woman wore a white tank top with black tights and a black lacy sweater that had flowing sleeves, a jagged hem, and no substance.

"I hope you were wearing a jacket," Liza said, reading Melanie's mind.

"It's in the hallway." Cindi brought the coffee back to the table and sat down. "So any news about the murder?"

Melanie exchanged a quick glance with her grandmother. "Not really. Detective Dutton came and questioned everyone again. He took a look at where I found the saw, but I don't think he found anything significant."

She looked back at Liza, who was switching her eyes back and forth in an attempt to urge her granddaughter to get to the point.

Melanie took a deep breath. "Cindi, the detective mentioned something that I think we should talk about."

Cindi's face grew wary. "Oh? What's up?"

"He said that you have a record."

A long moment of silence followed. Max raised his head and whined, and Cindi cleared her throat. "I spent a month in juvenile for shoplifting. I didn't tell you because it was a long time ago, and I was a different person then, and . . . and . . ."

Liza leaned forward. "It's okay. Just take your time and tell us what happened."

"There's not a lot to tell." Cindi raised her chin. "I was fourteen. I'd run away from my foster home because I was afraid of my father. He had a mean temper when he was drunk, which was a lot. I was on the street and hungry, so I, like, stole what I could to eat. It started with an apple or banana, but the people I met on the street were hungry too, and I was good at stealing, so I took more stuff and shared it around. I got caught and put back in foster care, but I always left again, until they finally put me in juvenile."

Liza clicked her tongue. "That must have been a nightmare for you."

Cindi shivered. "It, like, turned me around. I never wanted to see that place again. Any foster home was better than that. I never stole another thing, and I stayed where they put me until I was sixteen. That's when a friend of my foster family offered me a job waitressing at the restaurant he was managing."

"Yes," Melanie said, "you told me about the restaurant when I interviewed you."

Cindi nodded. "I'd still be there if they hadn't closed it down. That was a couple of months ago. I was going to Seaside to find another restaurant job when I saw your ad in the paper." Her face filled with anxiety. "I'm sorry I didn't tell you about the shoplifting. I wanted this job so badly, and I know I should have said something, but—"

Liza patted her arm and let go. "I think we can live with that. Right, Melanie?"

Relieved that she and her grandmother were on the same page, Melanie smiled. "I agree. Your previous boss gave you a good reference, and that's good enough for me. Let's put all this behind us and get to work on today's breakfast."

Cindi let out a sigh of relief. "Thanks. Both of you. I wanted to tell you, but I was afraid it would lose me this job."

Liza got up from the chair, wincing as she edged her way around the table. "You can't go wrong if you always tell the truth." She gave Cindi a hard look. "Remember that."

Cindi nodded. "Right." She jumped up and took her mug over to the sink. "Okay, I'll go lay the tables." She rinsed out her mug and put it in the dishwasher. "See you later."

Liza waited until the door closed behind the assistant before asking quietly, "So what do you think?"

"I think we should give her the benefit of the doubt." Melanie rinsed out her own mug. "So far she's given us no cause to be concerned about her, and as I said, her last boss gave her an excellent reference. I really don't want to look for another assistant now, do you?"

"No." Liza joined her at the sink. "I just hope we can trust the one we've got."

Melanie tried to ignore the stab of uneasiness. She liked Cindi, and she hoped with all her heart that the young woman didn't have a hand in what happened to Walter Dexter.

The breakfast servings went smoothly, and Cindi reported that everyone loved the sausage casserole and fruit. Declaring that she was starving, their assistant sat down at the nook table with a large helping of the casserole. "The best part of this job is the food," she said as she dug into the mound on her plate.

Melanie laughed. "I'm glad you're enjoying it so much."

"When you've spent time on the street like I did, everything you eat tastes good." She popped a forkful into her mouth, chewed, and swallowed. "But this is truly awesome."

Sobering, Melanie tried to imagine the fragile-looking woman at fourteen, alone, hungry, and afraid in the dangerous environment among the homeless. Her heart went out to her, and she dismissed any lingering suspicions she might have had about her. As far as she was concerned, Cindi was family, and she would protect and take care of her to the best of her ability.

Despite their best efforts, Melanie and Liza had no luck in having a conversation with Gloria. When Melanie approached the woman as she was leaving the dining room, she excused herself, saying she needed to use the bathroom. When Liza met her in the hallway, she said she wanted to take the shuttle bus into town and had only a few minutes to get to the bus stop.

Frustrated, Melanie suggested they drive into town and try to encounter Gloria there. "It's only a few blocks," she said when Liza expressed some doubt. "It's possible we can catch sight of her, and it will be easier to talk to her outside of the house. We can pick up a few supplies at Martin's grocery store while we're out."

"We could stop by the hardware store for lunch," Liza said, her eyes brightening.

Remembering her grandmother's fascination with the owner of the hardware store, Melanie smiled. "So you can flap your eyelashes at Doug again?"

Liza snorted. "I've got better things to do with my time. I like the food there, and they carry a really nice selection of wines, which doesn't hurt."

"I still can't get used to the idea of a bar and restaurant inside a hardware store."

"It's more like an English pub, which is why I like it." She headed for the kitchen door. "I'm going to get my coat. I'll meet you out front."

Noticing her grandmother's limp, Melanie frowned. Liza's hip must be bothering her again. Although her grandmother appeared to be in excellent health, there were times when her arthritis slowed her down. Sometimes Melanie worried that running a B and B, even a small one like the Merry Ghost, might be too much for Liza.

In the next instant, she reminded herself that no matter what might ail her grandmother, Liza invariably bounced back. Sometimes Melanie envied Liza's energy and enthusiasm. Having spent most of her own working life behind a desk, there were times when she fell into bed at the end of the day, aching and exhausted.

Liza was waiting for her in the driveway when she followed Max outside. Excited to be going for a ride, the big dog ran back and forth until Melanie opened the back door and allowed him to jump in.

The ride into town took only five minutes, and Melanie parked the car behind the grocery store. In the summertime, when the town was packed with visitors, she would have had a hard time finding a spot, but today, with the chill wind whipping the trees and dark clouds scudding across the sky, there were few cars in the parking lot.

"I'd like to visit the bakery first," Melanie said as she switched off the engine.

"Good idea." Liza licked her lips. "I can load up on pastries."

Melanie rolled her eyes. "It will give us an excuse to walk down Main Street. We should be able to spot Gloria if she's window-shopping."

"Well, we can take a quick look in some of the stores too."
Liza climbed stiffly out of the car. "It's not very warm out. I
should have brought a scarf."

Melanie gave her an anxious look. "Do you want to go
back and get one?"

"No! I'll be fine." Liza patted her arm. "You worry too
much."

"Are you okay to walk?"

"Of course. It will help loosen up the old bones. Besides, it
will give me an appetite for lunch."

"As if you need one." Melanie closed the car door and waited
a moment for Max to settle down on the back seat before turning away. "I don't know how you manage to stay so slim. I'd be
as big as a house if I ate half what you eat."

"As you say, not with all the exercise we get running the
inn."

Melanie started walking toward the street. "Does it ever
feel like it's too much for you?"

"What? No!" Liza sounded defensive. "Does it to you?"

Melanie laughed. "No, but I'm a lot younger than you."

"But you've always been used to sitting at a desk behind a
computer, analyzing finances all day. This is a whole different
kettle of fish."

"And I'm loving it." She gave her grandmother a warm
smile. "I wouldn't change what we're doing for anything in the
world."

"Well, okay." Liza still looked worried. "I just feel sometimes that I may have taken you away from what could have
been a lucrative career. I was the one who persuaded you to
give up all that and go into partnership with me."

"And I jumped at it. You know how miserable I was after the divorce, living in that crummy apartment in Portland and spending weekends alone in front of the TV." They had reached the street, and she swept an arm out in front of her. "Look at what I got in exchange."

A scattering of people strolled along both sides of the street, peering into little shop windows that were crammed with everything from antiques and souvenirs to clothes, toys, and candy.

At the end of the side streets, the ocean beckoned with frothy waves, craggy rocks, and the salty smell of seaweed. On the other side of Main Street, beyond the grocery store and the parking lot, fields stretched to the highway, and beyond that, the forest flowed to the soaring mountain range.

Melanie's voice grew a little husky. "I'd say it was well worth it. Wouldn't you?"

Beaming, Liza took her arm. "I'm glad you love it as much as I do."

"I wouldn't want to live anywhere else." Catching sight of a bright red coat ahead of them, she caught her breath. "Isn't that Gloria up there?"

Liza squinted into the distance. "Where? I can't see her."

"That red coat. She was wearing it when she arrived at the inn."

Liza narrowed her eyes. "Oh, yes. I remember. Are you sure it's her?"

"No, but it looks like her, and she's going into the bakery. Come on!" Melanie quickened her step, then slowed again when she realized her grandmother wasn't keeping up with her.

"You go ahead," Liza said, sounding out of breath. "I'll catch up with you."

"No, we have plenty of time." Melanie peered at her face. "Are you okay?"

"I'm fine. It's just one of my slow days, that's all. I get them once in a while. It's nature's way of reminding me not to push too hard."

Melanie made a face. "We could all use reminders of that."

By the time they reached the bakery, the enticing aroma of baking bread made Melanie's stomach growl. She had barely eaten anything for breakfast, making do with a handful of grapes and an orange muffin. Now she was hungry, which meant it was a mistake to visit the bakery before lunch.

Inside the shop, the tantalizing smell was even sweeter. Two women stood at the counter, and Melanie instantly recognized the tightly coiled blonde hair of the woman in the red coat. She waited for Gloria to be served while Liza gazed greedily at the rows of French and Danish pastries, muffins, scones, and donuts.

Finally Gloria paid her bill, took the white bag of treats from the assistant, and turned around. Her eyes widened when she saw Melanie smiling at her. "Mrs. West! What are you doing in here?"

Liza popped up next to her granddaughter. "She didn't buy the muffins from here, if that's what you're thinking. Everything at the Merry Ghost Inn is made from scratch."

Gloria looked startled at first, then said a little tightly, "I didn't think any such thing." She shook the bag. "I'm quite sure these won't taste anywhere near as good as your home-baked muffins."

Aware that the bakery assistant could hear every word and was staring at them, Melanie cleared her throat. "Er . . . thank

you, Mrs. Olsen. That's sweet of you to say. And it's Melanie."
Liza gave her a nudge. "And Liza."

"Then please, call me Gloria. Everyone does." She looked
at the window. "Do you think it's going to rain? I'd hate for
these to get wet." Again she shook the bag.

"We'll be happy to drive you back to the inn. Our car is
just up the road." Only Melanie could have heard Liza's quiet
grunt of protest. "I'll just buy a couple of rolls for lunch." She
stepped up to the counter and met the assistant's raised eyebrows. "Hi, Jenna. Got a couple of haystack rolls left?"

Jenna nodded, turned around, and slipped two of the puffy
rolls into a bag. Handing it over to Melanie, she said sweetly,
"Hope they taste better than my muffins."

Melanie's cheeks warmed as she hurried to reassure her,
"Your rolls are wonderful. Everything in this shop tastes
incredible." Relieved to see Jenna smile, she paid for the rolls
and led the other two women out into the street.

"I hope you won't mind sharing your seat with a large hairy
dog," Liza said as they started back toward the parking lot.

Glancing at Gloria's immaculate black slacks, Melanie
cringed. The woman had a look of pure horror on her face.

"You can sit in the back with Max," Melanie told Liza,
ignoring the black look her grandmother gave her. "He'll like
that."

Gloria still appeared shaken. "It's very kind of you to offer
me a ride," she said, gazing up the street with the air of a hunted
animal, "but I can wait for the bus. I'm sure it won't be long."

At that moment, large drops of rain began to hit the side-
walk. "You'll get drenched." Melanie wished now she'd brought
an umbrella. "We're almost at the car."

Gloria seemed torn between risking a soaking and riding with a furry animal. As the drops fell faster, it seemed the furry animal won. She quickened her step, shielding the bag with her purse. "I'll ride with you. Thank you."

They reached the car just as the rain began in earnest. Gloria dived onto the front passenger seat as soon as Melanie opened the door for her while Liza climbed into the back, ordering Max to move over and give her room.

Max seemed delighted to have someone share his seat and tried to lick Liza's face as she did her best to fend him off.

Melanie slid behind the wheel, commanding, "Max! Behave!"

The dog answered with a soft bark, making Gloria squeal.

"I'm sorry," she said, sliding as close to the door as she could get. "I'm not used to being this close to a dog. My nerves haven't been the same since poor Walter died."

Grabbing the opening, Melanie said quietly, "I'm sorry. That must have been such a huge shock for all of you."

"Oh, it was! You have no idea." Gloria opened her purse and took out a tissue. After blowing her nose, she looked all around her, apparently seeking a trash bag. After a moment, she shrugged and tucked the tissue into the pocket of her coat.

"You knew Walter quite well, didn't you?" Melanie caught sight of Liza's face reflected in the rearview mirror. Her grandmother was mouthing something, but Melanie couldn't take her eyes off the road long enough to decipher what she was trying to say.

"Not as well as some of them. All the group members are neighbors, except for me. I live quite a few blocks from where the rest of them live."

Remembering Joe's remark about Walter joining the group to be close to Gloria, Melanie murmured, "But you knew Walter before he joined the group, right?"

Gloria hesitated before answering. "Yes, I did. How did you know that?"

Melanie could feel her staring at her. "I heard Joe mention it."

"Oh, yes." Gloria's tone turned caustic. "Joe the Protector. Sometimes he gets a bit too meticulous about things. I don't know how many times I've told him I'm quite capable of taking care of myself."

"He seemed to think that Walter had upset you," Liza said from the back seat.

Gloria sniffed. "I had to put him in his place once or twice. The man was no angel, but I don't want to speak ill of the dead. He's gone, and there's nothing any of us can do about it now."

"Did Walter have any problems with anyone in Portland?"

Melanie had tried to sound casual, but Gloria gave her a sharp look. "The detective asked me the same thing. Are you working for him?"

"No, just curious. I can't imagine who would want to kill him."

"Neither can I." Gloria slumped back. "As I told the detective, Walter wasn't a sociable man, but I don't know anyone who would want to kill him." After a moment or two of silence, she added, "I woke up the night he died. I keep thinking that I might have been able to prevent what happened if I had investigated a little further."

Melanie's pulse quickened. "Do you know what woke you up?"

"Yes." Gloria took another tissue out of her purse. "I heard someone laughing. A man. I thought it was either Walter or Joe, so I went out into the hallway to see what they were laughing at." She shook her head. "It wasn't either of them. No one was there. Then I remembered the stories about the ghost, and I beat a hasty retreat to my room. I've heard the inn is haunted. Everyone knows about it, but I don't think any of us really believed it. Now I'm beginning to wonder if your merry ghost is real."

Melanie exchanged a glance with her grandmother in the mirror. "You didn't see anyone in the hallway that night?"

"I didn't say that." Gloria dropped her voice, as if reluctant to say the words. "I wasn't the only one who got up that night. I saw Amy Parsons going back into her room."

Amy. Melanie tried to envision the fussy little woman shoving the hefty Walter off the balcony. "You didn't hear anything after that?"

"No, I didn't. I pulled the covers over my ears and went back to sleep. But I did find something weird the next morning."

"Oh? What was that?" Melanie stopped at a crosswalk to allow a young couple to pass. They looked totally enthralled with each other, oblivious to the rest of the world. Melanie ignored a pang of envy and focused on Gloria, whose voice had turned a little breathless.

"I found my gloves lying at the end of the hallway. I thought I'd put them into a drawer in my room, yet there they were, lying out there on the floor." She sighed. "I must have dropped them the day before without noticing. My eyesight isn't what it used to be."

"Nothing is what it used to be when you get to our age," Liza said tartly.

Melanie sent her a warning glance in the mirror. "They probably fell out of your coat pocket."

"I guess so. They are quite nice, don't you think?" She held up her hand, displaying a red leather glove. "Terribly expensive, but worth every penny." She uttered a hollow laugh. "I must be getting old. I was so sure I remembered putting them in that drawer." She paused, then added slowly, "I hope someone didn't come into my room to steal them."

Melanie shut out an image of Cindi pocketing the gloves. "I'm sure you just dropped them."

"Probably. I do have a habit of tucking them into the pocket of my coat." Gloria sighed. "Still, it's odd that nobody saw them there until I found them the next morning." She leaned back. "I'm just happy that nobody picked them up. They're brand new, and I'd hate to have to buy another pair."

Arriving back at the inn, Gloria thanked them for the ride and scrambled out of the car, brushing imaginary dog hairs from her coat.

Melanie let Max out of the car and waited for Liza to climb out. By then Gloria had disappeared into the inn.

"She was in a hurry to leave," Liza said as she climbed the steps to the porch.

"She's probably rushing to enjoy her pastries." Melanie called out to Max, who had found something interesting to sniff at the edge of the road.

Liza looked disgruntled. "And I didn't get any."

"I'm sorry," Melanie said, feeling guilty. "I was in a hurry to get out of the bakery before Gloria changed her mind about riding with us."

"And you did me out of my lunch at the hardware store."

"Yes, I did. I owe you a lunch. We can go tomorrow." Melanie looked at her watch. "Or we can go back there now, if you like?"

"No, I'm tired." Liza slid her card into the entry system, unlocking the door. "Let's have a sandwich for lunch and finish up the rest of the orange muffins." She stepped inside the hallway and looked back at Melanie over her shoulder. "Gloria was right about one thing—the bakery muffins aren't half as good as yours."

Smiling, Melanie slipped off her jacket and hung it in the hall closet.

"I wonder what Amy was doing wandering around in the middle of the night." Liza took off her coat. "Can you imagine her heaving Walter off the balcony?"

"No, I can't." Melanie took the coat from her grandmother and hung it in the closet. "But then I have a problem imagining any of the group getting that physical."

"Well, we should at least ask her about it, don't you think?"

"I guess so." Melanie followed her grandmother down the hallway to the kitchen, wondering what kind of review they would get if any of their visitors decided to write one. Faced with the probable murder of a group member, forbidden to go home, and constantly being questioned by the police and their hosts—it didn't exactly add up to a relaxing and pleasurable vacation.

"So what do you think happened with Gloria's gloves?" Liza asked as they sat in the nook later. "Do you think she dropped them?"

Melanie picked up the last tiny piece of her muffin and dropped it into Max's open jaws. "Probably. It's hard to imagine someone breaking into her room and taking gloves instead of jewelry. That makes no sense."

"Well, I have another theory. I think Orville took them. I think that's who Gloria heard laughing in the hallway."

Melanie sighed. "You think our ghost took Gloria's gloves and laid them in the hallway? Why?"

"I have no idea. But you know how he loves to move things around. Just the other day, I found my umbrella hanging from the shower head. I'm pretty sure I didn't put it there. Who uses an umbrella in the shower?" She grinned. "Orville does have a sense of humor, which is why he laughs all the time."

Talking about the ghost made Melanie uncomfortable. She hated that there were so many instances that didn't have a logical explanation—the objects that moved from one place to another, the laughter all over the house, the icy cold draft even on the warmest days—all things for which she could find no reason. No matter how hard she tried.

Max whined at that moment, reminding her that it was time for his walk. Grateful for the interruption, she stood up. "I'm taking Max out. Want to come?"

Liza thought for a moment, then nodded. "As long as it's not raining."

Melanie peered out the window. The ocean looked calm, brushing the sand with soft waves. There were more people this afternoon wandering along the water's edge, though a heavy mist hid the rugged line of cliffs in the distance. "It's not raining right now." She peered up at the dark sky. "If we go now, we might miss the next downpour."

"I'll get my coat." Liza pushed herself up from the chair. "Are you going on the beach?"

"Just down to the water and back."

Liza nodded and left, leaving Melanie to pick up plates and glasses and take them to the sink. She turned on the faucet to rinse them just as Max uttered a low growl. At the same moment, a quiet chuckle sounded from right behind her.

Max barked, and she swung around, fully expecting to see someone standing behind her. There was no one there. A cold breeze touched her cheek, and for a moment, she found it hard to breathe. Then Max whined, and the chill disappeared.

Shaken, she laid a hand on Max's neck, where the fur still bristled. "It's okay, buddy. He's gone." She immediately felt stupid, talking about a ghost as if he were real.

The door opened, and Liza poked her head in the gap. "Are you coming?"

"I'm right there." Picking up Max's leash, she decided not to mention the incident to Liza. The last thing she needed right now was a long discussion about Orville and his antics.

Chapter 6

The air smelled of newly washed pine and wet sand as they started down the street toward the lane that led to the beach. They had gone barely a block when the sisters appeared at the end of the lane.

"Here's our opportunity," Liza muttered as the women walked slowly toward them.

Eileen's shoulders were hunched, and Amy clutched the collar of her jacket as they approached. "That wind cuts right through you," Eileen said, shivering. "We should have known better than to go down on the beach in November."

"It isn't always cold this time of year," Liza said, sounding defensive again. "When the wind drops, it can be quite warm, even in January."

Eileen gave her a skeptical look. "Really. Well, you're probably used to it, living down here all the time."

Melanie decided it was time to intervene. She smiled at Amy. "I hope you're sleeping better now?"

Amy looked startled. "Sorry?"

"Gloria said she saw you in the hallway late on the night Walter died."

Amy opened her mouth to speak, but Eileen forestalled her. "Gloria talks too much," she said, drowning out whatever her sister had begun to say. "I wouldn't pay too much attention to what she says."

Liza had a look of battle in her eyes. "Gloria was quite sure she saw Amy at the end of the hallway that night."

"Well, I—" Amy began, but again Eileen cut her off.

"We really should be getting back to the house. Amy catches a cold so easily, and we really don't want her sick on top of everything else. It's not like she can go home and rest." She glared at Liza as if it were her fault they were confined.

"We'd just like to know what it was that disturbed you," Liza said, ignoring Eileen's baleful stare. "Something had woken up Gloria that night as well."

Amy started talking rapidly, ignoring Eileen's attempts to hush her up. "Yes, I did wake up that night. It was really late. I heard a man laughing in the hallway, and I went out to see what was going on."

"So what did you see?" Melanie could see Eileen's face slowly turning red from tension.

"I saw Beatrice going into her room, and I saw Joe disappearing down the stairs. I figured they had been laughing about something, so I went back to bed."

"She didn't kill Walter, if that's what you're thinking!"

Eileen had shouted the words, startling a jay sitting in the tree above her head. He flew off with a loud flapping of wings that made Max growl deep in his throat.

Melanie laid a hand on his neck. "It's okay, Max."

Amy looked as if she were about to throw up. "Surely . . . you don't think I . . . I couldn't do such a thing . . . I . . . would never hurt someone like that."

"Of course she wouldn't!" Eileen grabbed Amy's arm. "We're going back to the house. Come on, Amy."

She rudely pushed past Melanie and stalked off, dragging her complaining sister with her.

"Well," Liza said, "that went well."

"We're going to upset all our guests if we go around questioning everyone." Melanie started forward, and Max leapt ahead, eager to get to the beach.

"I know, but we have to get to the bottom of this." Liza glanced back at the inn. "If they won't talk to the police, they'll have to talk to us, or we'll be stuck with them, and we have more guests coming next week."

Melanie tucked a hand under her grandmother's elbow. "It's okay. We'll work it out. We'll talk to Beatrice and ask her if she was laughing with Joe in the hallway, and we'll talk to Joe and ask him why he was going down the stairs in the middle of the night. Maybe one of them can give us a clue we can pass on to Detective Dutton and get this investigation moving again."

"And if Beatrice says she wasn't laughing with Joe, then we'll know it was Orville."

Melanie wisely decided not to argue with that.

"You know," Liza said as they walked down the lane toward the beach, "we never asked Josh for the name of that artist who is supposed to be our ghost. I'd love to know his real name."

"Josh will probably be back for another story on the murder before too long. I can ask him then, though we don't know for sure if the ghost is the artist."

"He has to be the artist. Remember what Josh told us about him?"

"Well, I guess I can do some research online. Maybe I can find out who he was."

"Good idea." They had reached the beach, and Melanie unclipped Max's leash. He took off in a flurry of sand, heading straight for the water.

"That dog has no sense of feeling," Liza said, watching him splash along the edge of the waves. "That water is freezing."

"He won't stay in there long." Melanie turned her head as the wind whipped the words from her mouth. "I'm not staying down here long, either. Eileen was right—that wind could cut through your bones."

Liza pulled her white woolen scarf tighter around her head. "Just think how healthy your lungs are, filled with clean sea air."

"If it doesn't kill me first."

The ocean must have been cold, because Max came loping back toward them, his feet matted with wet fur and sand.

Melanie bent down to fasten his leash. "Come on, buddy, time to go home."

Arriving back at the inn, she brushed the sand from Max's paws and coat on the porch while Liza went inside to put the kettle on for a cup of tea.

The kitchen felt wonderfully warm when Melanie walked in a few minutes later. Liza had already filled two mugs with tea. "I'm going to take this back to my room and read for a while," she said, holding up her mug.

Melanie washed her hands and dried them on a kitchen towel. "I have some work to do on the computer. I'll see you later."

Max followed her to her room and immediately jumped onto the bed, where he instantly fell asleep. Envying his ability to do that, Melanie opened her laptop. Logging onto her e-mail, she eagerly scanned the messages and once more was disappointed to find nothing from Vivian. Her friend's coworker must not be having much luck taking a picture of the mysterious woman with amnesia.

For a long moment, she sat staring at the screen. She had exhausted so many avenues searching for any news of her missing mother. This was probably one more dead end. How could someone disappear so completely without a trace?

The conclusion that she fought so often and so hard to ignore surfaced once more to torment her. *Her mother couldn't be found because she didn't want to be found.*

It broke her heart to think that—to believe her mother had abandoned her only child to live a new life without her. She quickly shut down her e-mail. She didn't want to think about that now; it was too painful. She needed to concentrate on something else.

Her conversation with her grandmother popped into her head. Now would be a good time to look for the name of the artist who supposedly was haunting the inn.

On the other hand, she could just call Josh and ask him for the name. Picking up her cell phone, she stabbed out his number. His voice mail picked up, and she ended the call without leaving a message. If Josh had found the artist, then so could she.

She opened up the search engine and started looking for the history of Sully's Landing. Just then, Max uttered a low growl. She swung around to look at him. He'd raised his head and was staring at a corner of the room. She could see the ruffle of hair standing up on his neck, and her own neck muscles tensed. "What is it, Max?"

The dog looked at her, then back at the corner, then slowly lowered his chin on his paws.

Reassured, she turned back to the computer. To her surprise, her computer had shut down and she was staring at a black screen. Frowning, she started it up again and once more opened the search engine. She started to type, but almost immediately the computer shut down again.

Max sat up with a soft bark.

Irritated now, she picked up her charger and plugged it into the laptop. Her battery had to be dying—but she'd charged the computer just last night.

She barely started to type when the laptop shut off again.

She sat staring at the black screen, trying not let Max's growls unnerve her. There had to be something wrong with the computer. Just to be sure, she started it up again and typed her own name in the search engine.

A website popped up with numerous phone numbers and addresses for the name, Melanie West. She typed Liza's name in the search engine, and again the website popped up.

Very carefully, she began typing the search for the town's history again.

Her screen immediately turned black.

Max barked again, making her jump. She shoved back her chair and walked over to the bed. Sitting down next to him, she hugged his quivering body. "It's all right, buddy. For some reason, Orville doesn't want me looking up his past. We'll have to ask Josh if we want to know his real name."

Max whined and licked her nose.

She hugged him again, unnerved by the realization that she was beginning to accept that Orville was real, that she was actually willing to believe in the existence of a ghost.

"I think we need some fresh air," she told Max, getting off the bed. "Want to go out?"

The dog's ears pricked up, and he jumped off the bed and headed for the door.

Melanie pulled a blue sweater on over her T-shirt and followed Max out into the hallway. After stopping to grab her jacket from the hall closet, she led him through the kitchen and out the back door.

The rain had held off, and the skies were beginning to clear over the ocean. A thin sliver of blue lined the horizon, promising a dry evening. Even the wind had died down, softening to a light breeze that carried the salty smell of the ocean.

Melanie watched Max race over to the fence and peer down at the beach below. When she'd first brought him home from the dog shelter, she'd been afraid he would jump over the fence in his eagerness to get to the beach. Luckily he seemed to have enough good sense not to attempt to be Wonder Dog.

She was about to join him at the fence when she spotted someone moving among the trees. The figure emerged onto the lawn, and she realized it was Beatrice, wrapped up in a fur coat with her hands tucked in her pockets and a pink scarf wound around her head.

For a moment it seemed as if the petite woman was trying to avoid her, but then Beatrice changed direction and plodded across the grass toward her. "I needed a breath of fresh air," she told Melanie when she reached her. "It was too windy earlier." She swept an arm at the ocean. "The view is lovely from here."

"It is." Melanie followed Beatrice's gaze. "You can see so much of the coastline on a clear day."

"All those rocks jutting out of the water are so picturesque. So different from the beach where I grew up." Her face had a wistful look to it as she stared out to sea. "My grandchildren would love it here."

"You have grandchildren? That's so great. How many? How old are they?"

If Beatrice noticed Melanie's eagerness, she gave no sign. She seemed willing to talk about her family and spent the next few minutes relating stories about the grandchildren. "I miss them," she said, turning back to the ocean. "They are all in California. I don't get to see them too often anymore."

"I'm sorry. That must be hard."

When Beatrice turned back, her eyes were wet with tears. "It is. But that's life. It isn't always what we'd like it to be."

Melanie could certainly relate to that. "I hope you're sleeping well? Amy mentioned that she saw you in the hallway late the night Walter died."

Beatrice sighed. "I sleep well, but like a lot of people my age, I have to get up at night to use the bathroom. My room doesn't have one, so I have to use the one at the end of the hallway."

Guilt made Melanie's cheeks warm. "Oh, goodness. I had forgotten that. Maybe I can ask one of the other guests to change rooms with you. We were hoping to put a bathroom in that room, but the cost was so excessive, we just couldn't manage it this year."

Beatrice smiled. "It's quite all right. The bathroom is right next door to my room, and I don't usually run into anyone late at night."

"You didn't see Amy?"

"No, I didn't. I must have had my back to her."

"Did you hear someone laughing?"

Beatrice frowned. "Laughing? In the middle of the night? No, I didn't. Was someone having a party or something?" Her expression changed to one of horror. "The merry ghost? It was in the hallway?"

Melanie rushed to reassure her. "We think it was Joe. Amy also said she saw him going down the stairs."

"Is that right? What was he doing downstairs in the middle of the night?"

That, Melanie told herself, was something she intended to find out. "You didn't see him?"

Beatrice shook her head. "I didn't see or hear anything. I used the bathroom and went straight back to bed and fell asleep." She tucked the end of her scarf into the neck of her coat, the diamond on her finger flashing in the sun that was now peeking behind the clouds. "I didn't tell the detective I got up that night. I was too embarrassed to tell him I went to the bathroom. Should I have said something about it?"

Melanie smiled. "No, I don't see how that could help anything."

Beatrice nodded. "There were a lot of things I didn't tell that detective. I didn't want to get anyone in trouble with the police. I wonder if I should have told him about Walter blackmailing Amy Parsons."

Melanie stared at her. "Walter blackmailed Amy?"

Beatrice looked over her shoulder, as if worried someone would hear her. "I'm not supposed to know this, so please don't tell anyone I told you. I happened to overhear Walter talking to Amy one day. Her husband doesn't know it, but he isn't the father of their daughter. Walter found out somehow, and he made Amy buy him all kinds of expensive things so he wouldn't tell. He had her running all over the place doing errands for him."

That was definitely something Beatrice should have told the detective, Melanie thought, worried now that she would have to pass on that information. It gave Amy a motive for killing Walter, though it was still impossible to visualize the nervous little woman committing cold-blooded murder.

"You know," Beatrice added, "one other person at the party that night had a good reason to be angry with Walter."

Melanie's pulse quickened. "Oh? Who was that?"

"The magician. Walter insulted him. Quite badly." Beatrice dug her hands in her pockets and hunched her shoulders. "If I were that young man, I would be deeply offended." She shivered. "It's still so cold out here. I think I'll go back into the warm house." She looked at Max, who was busily sniffing the grass. "That's a nice dog."

"He is." Melanie sent him a quick glance, her mind still grappling with what she'd just heard. "I rescued him from a shelter."

"That's nice." Beatrice turned toward the house. "He's a lucky dog."

Melanie watched her trudge across the lawn, wondering just how much she could rely on Beatrice's revelations. Was she telling the truth about Walter blackmailing Amy, or was it just a huge misunderstanding in an aging mind?

If she told Detective Dutton what she'd heard, he would question both Beatrice and Amy quite aggressively, upsetting them both, perhaps needlessly. They were both fragile women. Yet if she said nothing, could she be accused of withholding evidence? Was hearsay considered evidence?

She needed advice, and the best person to give her that was Ben. In the meantime, she would discuss the whole thing with Liza and get her take on the matter.

Whistling to Max, she headed for the house, anxious now to talk to her grandmother.

She found Liza in the kitchen, making yet another pot of tea.

"It looks like the rain has left us for a while," Liza said as she poured a cup for Melanie. "Did you enjoy your walk?"

"We just went out in the backyard." Melanie glanced at Max, who was already asleep in his bed. "We saw Beatrice out there. She told me a story about Amy, but I'm not really sure if she was telling the truth or if she misunderstood what was going on."

Liza put both mugs on the nook table and sat down. "Well now you have my complete attention. What did Beatrice tell you?"

Melanie sat and closed her hands around the mug. "She said Walter was blackmailing Amy. She said that Amy's husband wasn't the father of their daughter and Walter found out about it."

Liza's eyes widened. "Oh, my. If that's true, Amy had a strong motive to get rid of the old boy."

"If it's true." Melanie sighed. "I don't know what to do now."

"You have to tell Detective Dutton."

"I know, but what if Beatrice got things all wrong? You know how Dutton is—he'll devastate them both with his questioning. All possibly for nothing."

"But if Amy did kill Walter, and you knew something that could implicate her and didn't tell anyone . . ."

"I'd be guilty of withholding evidence," Melanie finished for her. "I know. I've already thought of that."

"You have to talk to Amy again."

"I will. But I thought I'd also talk to Ben and sound out my options."

Liza's face lit up. "Great idea!"

"There's something else Beatrice said that bothered me. She told me that Walter gave Nick a hard time that night at the party. I got to thinking about what you said—that Nick could have come back later. I saw him leave, but Cindi was still here until much later, cleaning up after the party. She could have let him in. I hate to think that either one of them had anything to do with Walter's death, but we don't know them very well. They could be capable of anything."

Liza shook her head. "That's the problem when a disaster like this happens. You start suspecting everyone. You're right, though, we can't completely rule out Cindi or her boyfriend, no matter how much we may like her. The best thing you can do is talk to Ben. Tell him everything Beatrice said and let him deal with Grumpy Dutton."

"I'll call him tomorrow." Melanie looked at the clock. "Right now we have to get dinner if we're going out this evening."

"You're right." Liza climbed to her feet. "I'm looking forward to the bingo game. I have a feeling I'm going to win tonight."

An hour or so later, Melanie dropped her grandmother off at the town hall with a promise to pick her up when the game was over. The museum was just a few blocks away, and when she arrived there, she soon found a parking spot close to the street.

The presentation fascinated her, and the next hour or so passed quickly as she listened to the narrator and watched faded and grainy pictures of the past. Oregon looked pretty much like a wilderness in the middle of the nineteenth century when the first settlers built their homesteads.

Melanie tried to visualize living in a one-room log house with only a vegetable garden and a few acres of wheat. The harvested wheat, the narrator informed his audience, was used for money, since there was little actual currency available. Most of the settlers were completely isolated, he said. It wasn't until gold was discovered in Southern Oregon in the early 1850s that roads were built for stagecoaches and the land opened up.

It all sounded insane. Thinking about the lack of roads, towns, and neighborhoods, much less telephones, TV, and the Internet, it seemed that life was much simpler back then, but it wasn't a life she'd want. Having seen how the pioneers lived, she could really appreciate the conveniences and assets of the twenty-first century.

After being immersed in such a primitive past for the better part of two hours, walking outside to civilization was a bit of a culture shock. Melanie stood for a minute in the darkness outside the museum, just savoring the lights of the town and the cars passing by. Checking her watch, she saw that she had at least an hour and a half before the bingo game would be over.

She would go home and enjoy a glass of wine in front of the TV, she decided. Then she could go back and pick up Liza. She wondered if they should get another car, since they only had the SUV. But then they so rarely went to different places at the same time. It wasn't worth buying another car for it to sit in the garage, even if they had room for it, which they didn't.

Having settled that argument with herself, Melanie waited until most of the vehicles had left the parking lot before walking over to her SUV. She had just reached it when a pair of headlights swept into the parking lot behind her.

Startled, she sent a quick glance at the black car that had parked two spots away. The museum was closed now. Who would be parking there at this time of night? Images of Walter's dead body floated into her mind, and she grabbed the door handle.

As she pulled the door open, she heard a familiar voice behind her. "Hey! What's your hurry?"

Heart thumping, she turned around to see Ben smiling at her.

She wasn't sure if it was relief or pleasure at seeing him that made her heart so active. "Hi! How did you know I was here?"

"I didn't." He jabbed a thumb over his shoulder. "I was driving by and saw you standing over there. I thought you were lost or something."

Melanie laughed. "I was adjusting to the twenty-first century again."

"Ah." He looked over at the museum. "You went to the presentation. How was it?"

"It was fascinating. It made me realize how good we have it, compared to the dreadful conditions some of those people endured."

"Sounds like you enjoyed it."

"I did." She peered up at him. He had his back to a streetlight, and his face was shadowed, but he looked relaxed. This might not be a good time to talk to him about the murder. After all, he was off duty, and she knew what it was like to have work interrupt her leisure time.

He must have sensed her indecision because he moved closer. "Is something wrong?"

"No, I . . ." She hesitated, then added quickly, "I need to talk to you, but this is probably not the time."

"Any time is good enough for me. What is it?"

Still reluctant to ruin his evening, she said slowly, "Well, actually, it's about Walter's murder, but I know you're off duty. It can wait until tomorrow."

He looked down at her for a long moment while she made a feeble attempt to calm her racing pulse. "Okay, how about this—I was just on my way to have a nightcap at the Brewery. Come with me, and we can talk about it there."

She was tempted. No doubt about that. "I'd like that, but I have to pick up Liza from her bingo game," she told him, wondering why she was putting up barriers to something she badly wanted to do.

"What time does the game end?"

"Around eleven."

"That gives us more than an hour, and the Brewery is just down the road." He took hold of her arm. "Come on. I'll take you in my car and bring you back here afterward. Okay?"

It was more than okay. Telling herself it was just a casual drink, she went with him, prepared to enjoy the next hour in spite of the somewhat depressing subject of their conversation.

She found it hard to concentrate on anything but the fact that she was alone with him in his car and was relieved when they reached the Brewery a couple of minutes later. Although she had passed by the building numerous times, she had never been inside.

She wasn't sure if it was seeing it for the first time or the company she was with that made the place so appealing. The bar took up the center of the room, where several people sat watching a TV. Comfortable booths lined the windows with brass lamps hanging low over the tables, suspended from the high ceilings. Colorful striped benches provided more seating at individual tables, and a huge mural portraying the Oregon coastline lined one of the walls.

Ben led her over to a table in the corner, far enough from the bar to be reasonably quiet. "We should be able to talk here without being overheard," he said as she sat down.

He seemed about to say something else, but just then a server wandered over to them. The woman obviously knew Ben, as she gave him a familiar pat on his shoulder. "Okay, hon. What can I get for you lovely people tonight?"

"Hi, Terry." He looked at Melanie. "I'm guessing wine."

Melanie smiled. "Right." She looked up at the server. "Chardonnay, please."

"You got it, hon." She looked at Ben. "The usual?"

He nodded, and she turned back to Melanie. "I haven't seen you in here before."

There was no mistaking the curiosity in her voice, and Melanie hesitated, not sure how to answer her.

Before she could speak, however, Ben came to the rescue. "Melanie's the owner of the Merry Ghost Inn."

"Part owner," Melanie corrected him.

Terry's brown eyes gleamed behind her glasses. "No kidding! I've heard about you guys. You've had quite some trouble with that inn. First the fire last spring and now that poor man falling to his death. Some say that house is cursed." She leaned forward. "Is there really a ghost haunting the inn? You hear so many stories in this town, you never know what's true and what isn't."

Melanie struggled for an answer as Ben watched her with keen interest. "I guess it all depends on whether or not you believe in ghosts," she said at last.

Terry looked disappointed. "You've never seen it?"

"I've never seen it," Melanie said truthfully.

"Ah, well, you can't believe everything you hear." She looked at Ben. "So did you guys find out who killed that poor man?"

Ben raised his eyebrows. "Who said someone killed him?"

"It was in the paper. Possible homicide, it said."

"Yeah, well, you can't believe everything you read in the paper, either."

Terry sighed and gave Melanie a soulful look. "He never tells me anything. So do you guys want anything else?"

Melanie shook her head, and Ben said, "How about peanuts and chips?"

"Coming right up." Terry tucked her pad into her pocket and smiled at Melanie. "Welcome to Sully's Landing and the Brewery. I hope you get your mess cleared up real soon."

"Thank you." Unsettled by the exchange, Melanie watched her walk away.

"It was only a matter of time before the news spread all over town," Ben said. "I saw that report in the local paper."

"It was on TV as well."

"At least you're getting publicity for the inn."

"Not the kind we want." Melanie forced her shoulders to relax. There were bound to be questions from the locals about the murder. Sully's Landing was a small town. She and Liza had dealt with it once before, when they'd discovered the skeleton behind a wall and set off a chain of disturbing events.

Terry's words echoed in her head. *I hope you get your mess cleared up real soon.* She fervently seconded that.

"So tell me the story about the ghost," Ben said, leaning his elbows on the table.

Melanie made an effort to focus. "Well, this is really all just an assumption, though Liza is convinced it's all true. You probably know the Sullivan family once owned the house."

Ben nodded. "Most people around here know Paul and Brooke Sullivan. I know that Paul's family first settled here during the late 1800s and pretty much built the town. That's how Sully's Landing got its name, right?"

"Right. The house was built in 1905, and twenty years later, a young artist fell in love with one of the Sullivans' daughters. She played him along until he proposed to her, then laughed in his face. She told him he was crazy to think she'd marry a penniless bum, or words to that effect."

Ben winced. "Ouch. That was cutting."

"It was." Melanie looked down at her hands. "It hurt him badly enough that he killed himself, leaving a suicide note vowing that he would have the last laugh."

"Ah, I get it. Your ghost is the laughing artist."

"Right. The laughter supposedly started shortly after he died. The problem was that only the woman who had betrayed him could hear him. No one would believe her when she complained, and eventually her family was convinced she was insane. Or maybe she actually did lose her mind. Either way, she ended up in an institution and eventually died there."

"Depressing story. How did you find out all that?"

"You know Josh Phillips, the newspaper reporter?"

Ben nodded. "Yeah, I know him."

"Well, he heard rumors about the ghost when the Morellis still owned the house. They're the people we bought the house from last spring."

"Yeah, I knew them, too." Ben's expression suggested he disliked the couple, but Melanie decided not to pursue that.

"Well, Josh interviewed them, and they told him the story. They must have heard it from the Sullivans when they bought the house. Anyway, Josh checked out the story and found evidence of an artist's suicide around that time and that one of the Sullivans' daughters had been sent to a mental institution, but he wasn't able to prove any connection between them. So the whole thing could be just coincidence."

"Maybe, but in my line of work, we're suspicious of coincidences."

Melanie smiled. "I imagine you are. As for the ghost, like I told you, I personally believe there's a physical cause for that sound of laughter. There could be something wrong with the water pipes or a faulty vent or something."

She looked up as Terry arrived at the table with a glass of Chardonnay for Melanie and a beer for Ben, as well as peanuts and an assortment of chips and pretzels.

After she left, Melanie raised her glass. "To solving crimes and laying ghosts."

Ben answered her by lifting his own glass. "To pleasant company and good times. I hope we can do this again sometime."

She touched her glass to his. "I'll drink to that."

He held her gaze for a moment, then thankfully broke the spell by saying, "You wanted to tell me something about the murder."

It took her a second or two to come down to earth. Now that she was given the opportunity, she actually felt reluctant to tell him everything she'd heard. It seemed disloyal, somehow. Her guests had told her things in confidence—things they hadn't been willing to tell the police. And now, here she was, about to repeat to a police officer everything they'd told her. It made her feel like a traitor.

Chapter 7

Ben was watching her with an intensity that made her uncomfortable. "What's wrong?" He leaned forward and lowered his voice. "Did something happen? Is everyone okay?"

"Everyone's fine." She took a long sip of her wine. "It's just . . . some of the guests have been talking, but I don't know what is real and what is imagined."

He sat back, and she couldn't read his expression. "Why don't you tell me, and I'll decide if it's worth following up."

He'd sounded officious again, like the cop that he was.

Saddened to have lost the warm connection between them, Melanie swallowed. "Well, mostly it was Beatrice, and I'm not sure she really knows what's going on. She told me that Walter had been blackmailing Amy."

Ben pursed his lips. "Did she say why?"

"She said that Amy's husband didn't know that he wasn't the father of their daughter and Walter found out about it. He made her buy him things and run errands for him." Now that she was saying it out loud, it seemed ridiculous.

Ben, however, seemed to take it seriously. "Anything else?"

"It seems that most of them were wandering around the house after everyone had gone to bed on the night Walter was killed. Gloria said she got up because she heard someone laughing and saw Amy in the hallway, and Amy said she heard the laughing and thought it was Joe because she saw him going downstairs, and she saw Beatrice going into her room."

"Wait. They heard someone laughing? You're not telling me they heard the ghost?"

"I think they heard whatever is making that noise. Yes."

He sighed. "You realize how that's going to sound when I report it to Detective Dutton?"

"I know. I told you, I don't know how much of this is real. We just thought you should know. About the blackmail, anyway."

"That does bring up a few questions. Tom might want to look into that."

"There's something else, but it's just a suspicion, that's all."

"Go on."

Keeping her voice low, she told him how Walter had insulted Nick's performance at the party. "Not that I think Nick had anything to do with Walter's murder," she said while Ben listened without showing any emotion. "But it does give him a motive. He could have come back to the house later."

"What's your impression of him?"

Melanie hesitated, wary of condemning someone she didn't know well. "He seemed okay enough—a little ambiguous, I guess, but not dangerous or anything."

"But you don't like him."

Unsettled that he'd read her so well, she shrugged. "I don't dislike him."

"What did your assistant say about all this? Did she tell you what her boyfriend's reaction was to all that abuse?"

"She hasn't said too much about it. She's very defensive about the whole thing."

"Well, I'll pass all this along to Tom and let him decide what he wants to do. He's already questioned everyone a couple of times. I don't think he can do much without some kind of evidence."

"What about the saw? Didn't he get anything from that? Fingerprints?"

Ben gave her a wry smile. "You know I can't discuss the details of an ongoing investigation. It's a tough case when you have this many suspects all in the same place and nobody's talking. Tom will probably want to do another search of the inn, and he'll look into this blackmail business."

Melanie felt depressed. "That's what I was afraid he'd do. My guests are upset enough already. And like I said, Beatrice might have it all wrong."

"I know." His features softened. "It's a tough deal all around. Just be careful, okay? I'm not comfortable with you asking questions. These people may seem harmless, but one of them is probably a killer and right there in the house with you."

She nodded, still not convinced any of her guests would hurt her or anyone else. Then again, she'd been wrong before. Looking at her watch, she gasped. "I need to go. Liza's game should be ending right about now."

"No problem. We'll pick her up on the way back to your car." Ben took out some bills from his wallet and laid them on the table.

"Oh, that's okay. I'll have time to get there." Flustered, Melanie rose to her feet. The last thing she needed was an inquisition from her grandmother, wanting to know all the details of her evening rendezvous with the engaging cop.

Ben gave her an odd look. "You don't want your grand-mother to know we met tonight?"

Totally unnerved now by his ability to read her mind, she started to stutter. "No, it's not . . . of course not . . . I . . ."

Ben grinned. "She might get the wrong idea?"

Melanie sighed. "She always gets the wrong idea."

"Don't worry. I'll set her straight. Better than leaving her waiting all alone at the town hall for you."

He was right, and Melanie followed him out to his car, pray-ing her grandmother wouldn't say anything to embarrass her.

Liza was just walking out the door when Melanie climbed out of Ben's car. Liza looked worried as she hurried toward them. "Is something wrong?" She took hold of Melanie's arm when she reached her. "Are you okay?"

"I'm fine," Melanie assured her. "I bumped into Ben as I was coming out of the museum, and we had a drink at the Brewery while I waited until it was time to pick you up. I wanted to tell him about everything we've been hearing from our guests. I thought he should know what's been going on in case it might be useful and could maybe help find out who killed Walter and . . ." Her voice trailed off as she caught her grandmother's odd look.

Glancing up at Ben, she saw him grinning and realized she'd been explaining far too much for far too long.

"It sounds as if you had a really nice time," Liza said, managing to sound smug.

Melanie could feel her cheeks warming. "Ben's going to take us back to my car, so why don't you get in."

She'd put a note of warning in her voice, and to her relief, Liza got the message. She scrambled into the back seat of Ben's car without another word.

Determined to keep the conversation on a comfortable topic, Melanie slid in next to her, ignoring her grandmother's raised eyebrows. "So how was the bingo game? Did you win anything?"

"Not a penny." Liza leaned back and let out an exaggerated sigh. "My luck was out tonight."

Ben started the engine and pulled out of the parking lot without a word, and Melanie wondered if he was upset because she wasn't sitting up front with him. In the next instant, she decided that was a totally immature assumption and he was probably concentrating on the driving.

"I did enjoy the evening, though," Liza said, raising her voice a little. "I'm looking forward to tomorrow night too."

Apparently realizing she was including him in the conversation, Ben answered her. "You're playing bingo again tomorrow?"

"Oh, no. I'm taking my granddaughter out to dinner. Did she tell you it's her birthday tomorrow?"

Ben sounded amused when he answered. "No, she didn't."

Melanie had a bad feeling that Liza was about to embarrass her. She frowned at her, but Liza's attention was on the man in the front seat.

"We're going to the Seafarer to celebrate," she said. "It's one of Mel's favorite restaurants."

"It's a great restaurant," Ben agreed.

"Wait!" Liza leaned forward. "I have an idea. Why don't you join us and help us celebrate. We don't know too many people down here, and it would be nice to have some company. Right, Mel?"

Melanie was frantically shaking her head until she realized Ben could see her in the rearview mirror. Afraid she'd offended him, she said hurriedly, "I'm sure Ben is much too busy." She met his brief gaze in the mirror. "You must have a million things to do."

"Nonsense." Liza gave her a hefty nudge in the arm. "He's got to eat, doesn't he?"

Ben laughed. "I do, and I'd be honored to join you. That's if it's okay with the birthday girl."

Melanie winced as her grandmother's bony elbow dug into her arm again. There didn't seem to be any way out of it now without sounding ungracious. "Of course it's okay. We'd enjoy your company."

Liza beamed and looked out the window as Ben pulled into the parking lot of the museum. "Oh, there's our car. It looks lonely, sitting there all by itself."

Melanie was still trying to deal with what had just happened and didn't answer her.

Ben jumped out and opened the door for Liza while Melanie scrambled out the other side.

"I'll pick you both up tomorrow night," Ben said. "What's a good time?"

"We have reservations for seven," Liza told him. "I'm sure it won't be a problem to add another one to the table."

"I'll be at your place by six forty-five." He looked at Melanie. "Sure it's okay with you?"

She smiled at him. "I'm looking forward to it."

"Me too." He bid them both good night and turned back to his car.

"Thanks for the lift," Liza called out.

"And for the wine," Melanie added.

"My pleasure on both counts." He waved at them, then climbed into his car and took off.

"He's such a nice man," Liza said, gazing after him.

Melanie waited until her grandmother was seated next to her before demanding, "What were you thinking, inviting him to dinner?"

Liza widened her eyes. "I thought it would be polite to invite him along. He doesn't seem to have much of a social life. Besides, it was about time you had dinner with him again. It's been way too long."

"And I'm not having dinner with him now." Melanie drove out of the parking lot. "Thanks to you, he felt obligated to join us tomorrow night."

"He didn't look obligated to me." Liza sighed. "Relax, Mel. It's just dinner. And I'll be there to chaperone. You're making this into something a lot more complicated than it needs to be."

Her grandmother was right, Melanie told herself as she drove back to the inn. She always seemed to overreact when Ben Carter was around. She needed to get things into perspective. Her relationship with Ben was friendship, pure and simple. She should relax and enjoy it.

The truth was, no matter how much she tried to deny it, she was enjoying it entirely too much.

The inn was in darkness when they arrived back a few minutes later, except for the outside lamps and the light Liza always left on in the downstairs hallway.

"I think I'm going straight to bed," Liza said as they walked toward the kitchen. "I'm a little tired."

"I'm not surprised." Melanie paused at the kitchen door. "It's been a long day."

"Every day is a long day at the Merry Ghost Inn." Liza leaned in to plant a kiss on her granddaughter's cheek. "But I love every moment of it." She shivered, as if remembering their current problem. "Most moments, anyway."

Melanie gave her a swift hug. "We'll get through this. Get some sleep. You'll feel better in the morning. Have a good night."

"You too."

Melanie watched her disappear around the corner, then opened the door and braced for Max's enthusiastic welcome.

To her surprise, there was no dog lunging up to greet her. One swift glance at his bed told her he wasn't sleeping there, either. With a twinge of anxiety, she walked into the room. "Max? Where are you?"

A muffled bark answered her.

Frowning, she looked around the room, then under the table. Was he outside? No, that was impossible. She'd left him in the kitchen with both doors closed. Just to make sure, she checked the back door. It was still locked.

Someone must have come into the kitchen and let him out.

She called out to him, softly, just in case Liza heard her. The last thing she wanted to do was disturb her grandmother now. "Max!"

Again the muffled bark answered her.

It seemed to be coming from outside the room. She went back to the hallway and walked the length of it back and forth. Was he upstairs? As far as she knew, he never went up there. Unless he was chasing after someone.

Her stomach started performing its uncomfortable dance again. Had Max heard Orville laughing and gone up there to investigate?

She called out again, barely above a whisper: "Max?"

Nothing but silence. Max had sharp ears. He must have heard her and Liza come through the front door. Why wasn't he waiting there for them to come home? Was he hurt? Lying helpless somewhere?

Seriously worried now, Melanie went back into the kitchen. She'd have to go upstairs and as quietly as possible look for her dog. As she reached for the drawer where she kept the flashlight, she heard the bark again—more urgent this time and definitely closer than upstairs.

She stared at the cellar door. The key still sat in the lock, left there for Cindi to go down for supplies. "Max?"

His bark answered her.

She dashed over to the cellar door and pulled it open. "Max? Are you down there?"

A mix of barking and yelping galvanized her into action. All that noise was bound to wake up Liza as well as the entire household. "I'm coming, Max! Quiet down!"

She snapped the light switch on, gasping in dismay when the stairs remained in darkness. The bulb had to be burned out. For one second she considered going back for the flashlight, but Max's barking resounded throughout the cellar and, no doubt, up the stairs.

She could see the first steps in the light from the kitchen. Envisioning her dog lying wounded and in pain, she started down them.

As she reached the fourth step, her foot rolled on something. Her ankle twisted, and with a sickening stab of fear, she felt herself falling to the concrete floor below.

She flung out a hand and grabbed at the rail, snagging a nail as she made contact. By some miracle, her fingers briefly closed around it, slowing her down and toppling her upright. She slid down the rest of the stairs on her back and landed on her feet, her knees buckling as she hit the floor.

Max sounded frantic in a frenzy of barks and yelps, and she called out to him, trying to steady her shaking voice. "I'm all right, Max. Quiet down!"

"What in the world?"

Her grandmother's voice from above her made her heart sink. Between them, she and Max had probably woken up everyone in the house. "I'm okay. I fell down the stairs." She scrambled to her feet, wincing as pain shot through her ankle.

Liza's voice was sharp with concern. "Are you okay? Why is the light out?"

"I'm fine. Can you get the flashlight for me? It's in the drawer." Without waiting for her grandmother to answer,

Melanie limped over to the dark corner where Max was now whimpering.

Her eyes were adjusting to the dark, and she could just make out his shape in the faint glow from the kitchen. Reassured to see him standing on all four feet, she crouched down and reached out to him. He seemed to be attached to the wall. She stuck her fingers in his collar and found it caught on a nail.

He started to struggle, whining as the collar tightened around his neck. "Hold still, buddy. I'll have you free in a minute."

A stab of light almost blinded her. "What happened to him?" Liza demanded from behind her. "How in heaven's name did he get down here?"

"I don't know. He got caught on a nail somehow." Now that Melanie could see, it took her only a second or two to free Max's collar. He lunged at her, tail wagging, almost knocking her over. "He seems to be okay," she said, fending off his wet tongue on her face.

"How did he get through the door? And what happened to the light?"

Liza sounded shaken, and now that the immediate crisis was over, Melanie had some serious questions herself. "I don't know," she said again. She stood up, testing her ankle. The pain didn't feel quite as bad now. "The door was closed when I came into the kitchen."

Apparently eager to be out of there, Max bounded up the stairs.

Looking up after him, Liza murmured, "I'm going to make a cup of tea."

Following her grandmother up the steps, Melanie tried to avoid putting all her weight on her ankle. There had to be some rational explanation, she told herself. They just had to figure it out.

Reaching the kitchen, she shut the cellar door and locked it.

Liza stood at the stove in her pink robe and slippers, lighting the gas under a kettle of water. Max made a beeline for his bed and snuggled down in it. Everything looked so normal, yet there was no doubt in Melanie's mind that something odd was going on.

Liza waited until she'd poured the hot tea into two mugs and carried them to the nook before saying, "What do you think happened?"

Melanie leaned back on her chair. "Someone must have come into the kitchen and opened the door to the cellar. Maybe he or she heard a noise, like Orville laughing down there."

Liza looked unconvinced. "Then why shut the door again, knowing the dog was down there? Besides, who would come into the kitchen while we were gone?"

"Maybe it was Cindi."

Liza shook her head. "Cindi would never have left Max in the cellar. She would have gone down after him. In any case, why would she come back at night? Her workday here is over by lunchtime, unless we ask her to work overtime at an event."

"She could have left something here and come back for it." Melanie was grasping at straws and, judging from her grandmother's face, not doing a very good job of it.

"Well, we'll ask her when she gets here tomorrow," Liza said, picking up her mug. "And if she says she wasn't here, then we need to find out who was and why someone found it necessary to open the cellar door. Are you okay, by the way? I thought I saw you limping just now."

"I twisted my ankle when I fell. It's a little sore, that's all." She frowned. "I stepped on something on the stairs. I don't know what it was. I didn't see it when I fell."

"We'll go down and look in the morning. We have to change that lightbulb if we're going to see anything down there. Drink your tea, and let's go to bed. I think we've done enough worrying for one day."

Melanie sipped her tea, trying not to think about whatever it was she tripped on. It kept nudging at her, however, until finally she put down her mug. "I have to go and see what it is," she said, "or I'll be awake all night thinking about it."

Liza sighed. "I'll get the flashlight again."

"I'll get a new lightbulb."

Moments later they stood with Max at the foot of the cellar stairs. Using the step stool she'd carried down with her, Melanie reached for the bulb. To her surprise, it flickered on and then off again. "It's loose," she said, giving a twist. Immediately light flooded the room.

As she stepped down from the stool, Liza uttered a soft exclamation and stooped to pick something up from the floor.

Max barked, his tail wagging furiously.

"Shush!" Liza told him and held out her hand to Melanie. "It's one of his toys. We must have missed it with the flashlight just now. It's a wonder Max didn't pick it up."

Melanie took it from her while Max watched her with anxious eyes. It was a long, thick rope with a brightly colored tennis ball threaded on each end.

"No wonder you tripped on that thing," Liza said, nodding at the toy. "Max must have dropped it on the way down."

Melanie stared at the rope in her hand. The bad feeling that had been creeping up on her ever since she'd seen the dog attached to the wall was now a full-blown anxiety. "Or," she said slowly, "someone put it on the stairs."

Liza's eyes widened. "Are you saying Orville put it there?"

"And opened and shut the door, loosened the lightbulb, and hooked Max to the wall? I don't think so." The dog whined, and she handed him the toy. He took it in his mouth and bounded up the stairs.

Liza's voice shook. "What are you saying?"

"I'm saying I think someone wanted me to fall down the stairs."

"Oh, Mel." Liza shook her head. "Not again."

Remembering the last time a killer threatened her, Melanie felt a flash of fear. "I think someone went to a lot of trouble to send us a warning."

"I need some more tea. Preferably with a shot of brandy in it. Come on." Liza climbed the steps once more with Melanie following close behind her.

Minutes later, they sat in the nook, sipping the laced tea. "Who do you think it was?" Liza asked as she put down her mug. "You could have had a serious injury or even . . ." Her voice trailed off, as if she couldn't bring herself to finish the sentence.

"It could have been anyone in the house."

"It would have to be someone who could reach the lightbulb."

"We keep the stool right there in the corner. Anyone could reach it using that."

"It was well thought out, I will say that."

Melanie let out a sigh. "That's what scares me. If we're right about this, we're dealing with a clever mind."

"And a dangerous one. Maybe we should tell Grumpy what happened and let him deal with it." Liza's forehead was creased with worry.

Melanie met her gaze. "Is that what you want to do?"

Her grandmother raised her chin. "Hell, no. I want to find out who the bugger is and hand him over to the police so we can get on with our business. After all, we don't know for sure that someone planned all that. If we tell Grumpy, there'll be more questioning, more investigating, and this case will never be over with in time for our next guests."

"I know. Can you imagine what would happen to our reputation if we have to cancel all those reservations?"

"Exactly. So I vote we keep on asking questions until we get at the truth."

Melanie struggled for a moment longer with her doubts. "It could have been you on those stairs tonight."

"But it wasn't. And from now on, we'll be on our guard." Liza lifted her tea and held it out to tap her granddaughter's mug. "Here's to solving another murder."

"Amen to that." Reluctantly accepting the inevitable, Melanie put down her mug. "Now let's get to bed."

*   *   *

The following morning, she awoke with a start, the memory of last night's close call still fresh in her mind. For several minutes she tried to recall everything she and her grandmother had learned so far, but thinking about it made her head ache, and she made an effort to put the whole thing out of her mind for the time being. It was her birthday, and she was going to do her best to enjoy it.

To her surprise, when she sat up, she saw a card and a small package sitting on her bedside table. Smiling at her grandmother's thoughtfulness, she opened the card.

Here's hoping the next year brings you love and happiness so that you can put the past behind you, Liza had written. The front of the card showed a comical caricature of a woman dancing with obvious joy while flowers and lovebirds fluttered all around her.

Shaking her head, Melanie opened the package. Inside the small box, she found a beautiful opal pendant, its gorgeous colors flashing in the light from her bedside lamp. She held it in her hand, thrilled with the gift, and wondered when Liza had found the time to buy it.

When her grandmother wandered into the kitchen a short while later, Melanie hugged her. "Thank you for the lovely gift," she said, fighting tears. "The pendant is magnificent and such a wonderful surprise."

"Happy birthday." Liza hugged her back. "I'm so glad you like it."

"I do." Melanie took the box out of her pocket and opened it again. "It's my favorite stone. I didn't know you went shopping on your own."

"I didn't." Liza walked over to the counter and poured herself a mug of coffee. "It belonged to your mother. Your grandfather and I gave it to her when she got married. It's her birthstone. And yours."

Melanie blinked hard. "She left it behind when she went to England?"

"She left a lot of things behind," Liza said dryly. "Anyway, I was going to give the pendant to you when you got married. You know, something old, something new? But you wore your mother's veil at your wedding for the something old, so I decided to hang onto it for a more suitable occasion."

"So why now?"

"You've had a tough three years. Opals are supposed to be lucky for Scorpios. I'm hoping it will bring you luck and happiness."

"It's already made me happy." Melanie dropped the pendant back in its box. "It's so beautiful—I'm going to wear it tonight."

Liza smiled. "I was hoping you would."

Melanie couldn't suppress the anxious jolt to her stomach. "You have to promise me you won't say anything outrageous at dinner tonight."

Liza turned wide, innocent eyes on her. "What? Me? Outrageous? Never!"

Melanie rolled her eyes. "Please, Granny. I know how badly you want me to get together with Ben, but right now all I want is his friendship. I don't want anything to spoil that, okay?"

Liza sighed. "Don't worry. I'll be on my best behavior. Let's just go and have a good time. And quit calling me Granny. I thought we had an agreement about that."

"Sorry. Old habit." Melanie sat down in the nook with her coffee. "Now I think we need to talk to Cindi. Ben asked me if she'd said anything about Nick's reaction to Walter's insults. I'd like to get her take on it."

Melanie waited until breakfast had been served in the dining room and they were all ready to enjoy the eggs Benedict before she brought it up.

"I was talking to Beatrice yesterday," she said, handing Cindi her plate. "She was pretty upset about the mean things Walter said to Nick about his magic act."

Cindi shrugged. "Walter had been chugging wine. He was just making noise."

"But it must have been upsetting for Nick. He's so passionate about his performance."

Cindi gave her a hard look. "It didn't bother him. He just laughed it off and forgot it. The rest of them enjoyed the show, and that was all he cared about."

Afraid that she was approaching forbidden territory, Melanie changed the subject.

Later, however, as Cindi got up to clear the dining room tables, she said quietly, "You should talk to Nick about what happened at the party. He'll tell you he didn't kill Walter, and then maybe you'll believe him."

"I'm sorry, Cindi." Melanie stood up, feeling awkward. "I know this is hard on you, too. I'm not accusing Nick of anything. I'm just trying to get at the truth."

"Then talk to him." Cindi left the kitchen, her chin in the air and her back stiff with resentment.

"She's right, you know," Liza said as Melanie sat down and buried her face in her hands. "We should talk to Nick."

"I know." Melanie lowered her hands. "I hope I haven't lost us an assistant."

"She'll get over it. She's in love. She's going to defend her man to the death."

"What if he is the killer? It will destroy her."

"It's better she finds out now, before she gets in too deep with him." Liza looked down at her hands. "Of course, there's always the possibility that she actually helped him kill Walter."

Melanie groaned. "This whole thing is a nightmare."

Max growled, and a second later, Melanie heard a light tap on the door. Before she could say anything, the door opened, and Joe wandered in.

"Sorry to bother you," he said, his gaze sweeping around the kitchen, "but I was wondering if you had an extra pillow. I get a sore neck if I sleep too flat."

"Of course." Liza got up. "I'll fetch you one. Would you like a cup of coffee?"

"No thanks. I already drank two cups." Joe nodded at the window. "Nice view you have from up here."

"We like it." Melanie watched Liza leave the room, then added, "I'm sorry you're not sleeping well. I heard that some of you have been woken up by hearing laughter in the hallway."

Joe's eyes narrowed. "I heard it. The night Walter died."

"Someone saw you going downstairs that night."

She hadn't meant to blurt it out like that. Joe's expression darkened, and she wished she'd waited for Liza to come back before bringing up the subject.

He stared out the window for a few seconds, then looked back at her. "Like I said, I heard the laughing. I knew it wasn't

Walter. That old grouch couldn't crack a smile. Since I'm the only other man in the house, I got up to see what was going on. When I looked in the hallway, there was no one there. But I could still hear the laughing."

He gestured at a chair. "Mind if I sit down?"

"No, that's fine." She stood up. "Are you sure you don't want any coffee? I'm going to have some."

Joe shook his head and sat. "I'd heard all the stories about the ghost," he said as Melanie poured coffee into her mug. "We all knew about it. I figured it was him. It gave me the shakes, so I went downstairs to have a smoke and settle the nerves. That's when I saw him."

Melanie's hand jerked, spilling coffee onto the counter. "You saw the ghost?"

"No, I saw Walter. Look, I've been stewing over this ever since it happened. I didn't want to tell that detective anything, but I need to tell someone. It's keeping me awake at night."

Melanie's pulse quickened as she carried the coffee back to the table. "You saw Walter? Where?"

"Lying in the driveway. I went up to him. I thought he'd had a heart attack or something, but then I noticed the railings were broken."

Sitting down, Melanie carefully placed the mug on the table. "Why in the world didn't you wake one of us?"

Joe lifted his hands and let them drop. "I don't know. I should have. I guess I panicked. I could tell he was dead. I thought maybe he'd fallen through the railings, but then I wondered, what if someone had pushed him? There I was, standing over his body in the middle of the night. I'd be a prime suspect, considering how everyone knew there was bad blood between us. I figured there'd be no harm in waiting until the morning, since Walter was already dead."

He flicked a glance at her and then shifted his gaze to the window. "I know I should have said something to the cop, but like I said, I panicked. I was afraid I'd be blamed for it."

Melanie thought back to the moment when she'd announced to the guests in the dining room that Walter had died. Joe had seemed just as shocked as everyone else. She frowned. Something about his story didn't quite ring true. "You need to tell the detective what you told me," she said firmly. "It could help in their investigation."

"Yeah, you're right." Joe looked as if he would say something else, but just then the door opened, and Liza walked in, a pillow tucked under her arm.

Joe stood up, and she handed it to him. "There you go. That should help."

Clutching it, Joe looked back at Melanie. "There's one more thing. I thought I saw someone moving on the balcony that night. A guy. Tall, skinny, needed a haircut." He looked back at Liza. "Thanks for the pillow."

Liza stared after him as he went out the door. "What was all that about?"

Melanie repeated Joe's story. "I can't believe he actually went back to bed, leaving Walter lying out there." She sat down at the table again. "He said he could tell Walter was dead, but how could he be sure?"

"He probably felt for a pulse." Liza sat down with her.

"I guess so." Melanie shook her head. "It just seems so callous—so inhuman."

"Well, like he said, he panicked. He was afraid he'd be blamed for killing Walter."

"I think he still is." Melanie stared at her coffee. "I have a strong feeling he's hiding something."

"Why would he tell you all that if he was hiding something?"

"I don't know. He said it was keeping him up at night, worrying about it."

Liza shook her head. "What about the man he saw on the balcony?"

Melanie sighed. "It was dark, and Joe was in shock. He could have imagined it."

"But if he really did see someone . . ." Liza let her voice trail off. After a long pause, she added, "You know who it sounds like, don't you? The man Joe saw, I mean."

"Yes." Melanie lifted her mug. "We need to have a chat with Nick Hazelton. We need to tell the cops about all this too. Joe agreed with me when I said he should report this, but I'm not sure he'll go through with it."

Liza nodded. "We will. Right after we've talked to Nick."

*   *   *

A thick mist hung over the coast road as they drove to the campground, and the cold, damp air seemed to cling to Melanie's skin when she led her grandmother into the office.

A fireplace and armchairs welcomed them when they walked in. A revolving row of shelves offered DVDs, while another held postcards, brochures, and magazines informing the visitor of the various sights to see along the Oregon coast. Toward the back of the room, shelves were filled with supplies—everything from cereal and cookies to sunscreen and bandages.

Reaching the long counter, Melanie and her grandmother were greeted by the manager of the campground.

Rachel Wilson was a vibrant, friendly woman, eager to please. "You'll find Nick somewhere out in the campground," she told them. "He's evaluating the repairs and improvements we've got scheduled for the winter. We have to do them during the off-season, when we have more room. Of course, in Oregon, that means doing most of it in the rain."

"How long has Nick worked for you?" Liza asked as Melanie wandered over to look at the brochures.

"Just over a year now." Rachel smiled. "He's a good worker. We're lucky to have him."

"Cindi works for you too, doesn't she?"

"When she's not working at your inn." A note of wariness crept into her voice. "Is there something you're not telling me? I know you've had some trouble at the inn. I hope it doesn't involve Cindi."

Melanie swung around and walked back to the counter. "We just want to be sure she's not overworking herself, that's all. She works really hard for us."

"Oh, she doesn't have to do anything really physical here." Rachel waved a hand at the computers behind her. "It's all sitting-down stuff. She does a good job and really helps out."

"Well, thanks." Melanie nudged her grandmother's arm. "We'd better get going if we want to talk to Nick. I promise we won't keep him too long."

"Oh, take your time. We're not that busy right now."

Thanking her, Melanie walked back to the car with Liza, much to the delight of Max, who greeted them as if they'd been gone for hours.

After driving up and down two of the lanes, Melanie finally spotted Nick on the far side of the campground. He was talking to two other men, who were seated in what looked like a golf cart with a trailer on the back.

He looked surprised to see her and Liza when they stepped out of the car.

Melanie smiled at him, avoiding the curious glances from the other two men. "I'm sorry to interrupt, but we were wondering if we could have a word with you."

"Sure." Nick stuck his hand in his pocket. "What can I do for you?"

Melanie shifted her weight. "Is there somewhere we can talk in private?"

Nick's friendly smile vanished. "What's this about?"

One of the other men spoke up. "It's okay, Nick. We'll take a look at that fence and check out the damage."

Without taking his gaze off Melanie's face, Nick raised his hand. "I'll be there in a minute."

The men roared off in their cart while Nick folded his arms, a scowl darkening his face. "Okay, what do you want to know?"

Now that they were alone with him, Melanie was beginning to feel decidedly vulnerable. They were surrounded by trees, with no one else in sight. If Nick was the killer and wanted to silence them both, they were pretty much defenseless against the man.

It was a little late now to have second thoughts, however. They had started this, and they would have to finish it. She just hoped they hadn't taken on more than they could handle.

Chapter 8

Liza shuffled a little closer to her granddaughter and peered up at Nick's face. "We want to know what you were doing on the balcony of our inn in the middle of the night."

Melanie could feel the hair rising on the back of her neck as Nick turned his head to stare at her grandmother.

"What the hell are you talking about?" He jutted out his chin. "I have never set foot on your damn balcony."

With Ben's warning ringing in her head, Melanie took hold of Liza's arm and pinched it.

"Ow!" Liza glared at her, and Melanie briefly shook her head at her. "It's just that someone saw a man on the balcony the night Walter died," Liza said, turning back to Nick, "and we thought it might have been you."

"Well, it wasn't." Nick turned away, then paused and looked back at her. "Not that it's any of your business, but I'll tell you what I told the cops. I left the inn right after you paid me. I came back here and waited for Cindi in her trailer. We spent the night in there together. End of story."

Liza gasped, and he sent her another dark look before stomping off after his two workmates.

"Well," Liza said, looking shaken, "what an unpleasant man. What on earth does Cindi see in him?"

"You can't blame him for losing his temper," Melanie said as she opened the car door for her grandmother. "You practically accused him of murder."

"You know what they say about people who protest too much." Liza climbed back into the car. "I don't trust him."

"Cindi obviously trusts him." Melanie slid behind the wheel, trying to avoid Max's enthusiastic cold nose on her cheek. "Sit!" she told him, and he obeyed at once, squatting back on his seat as she started the engine.

"Cindi's young." Liza fastened her seat belt. "She's guided by her heart, not her head. We'll have to ask her if Nick really did spend the night with her."

"That's prying into her personal life."

"That's establishing an alibi."

"Right. But if it wasn't Nick who Joe saw on the balcony that night, then who was it, and how did he get in the house?"

"Like I said before, someone could have climbed up to the balcony."

Melanie tried to picture that as she pulled out of the campground. As far as she could remember, the only handhold on the outside walls was maybe a drainpipe.

"As long as we're out," Liza said as they turned onto the coast road, "how about lunch at the hardware store? We need to ask Doug Griffith if his brother knows anything about our murder. Maybe Grumpy Dutton knows something we don't."

Remembering how the cheerful pub owner loved to tease her grandmother, Melanie had to smile. "Even if he did, I doubt if he'd tell Doug's brother about it. Shaun's only a reserve police officer."

"Yet somehow, Shaun seems to know what's going on at the station. Someone must do a lot of talking."

Melanie slid a glance at her. "You don't have to make an excuse to see Doug. I know you like him."

"I like the pub."

"You know what they say about people who protest too much."

Liza laughed. "Touché. But it's true. I do like the pub. It reminds me of home. I met your grandfather in an English pub. Did I ever tell you that?"

"Many times." Melanie slowed down as they approached the main street of Sully's Landing. "But I love hearing about it."

"Remind me to tell you about it one more time when we get home. Right now I'm going to enjoy a plate of fish and chips."

Melanie parked in front of the hardware store and shut off the engine. The walls of the rustic building, like so many in the town, were covered with gray cedar shingles, and wide windows lined the lower floor.

The main door led directly into the pub, where voices were raised to be heard above the country music playing over the speakers. Posters and signs covered the wall of the large room, and off to the left, a fully stocked store supplied residents and visitors with everything they might need in the way of hardware.

A long bar took up one end of the room, displaying a vast array of wines and beers. Some of the small tables were occupied, but Liza headed toward one close by the bar, in the corner. It was her favorite table in the place and afforded her the opportunity to talk to the jovial owner of the pub.

Doug Griffith reminded Melanie of Santa Claus, with his twinkling brown eyes, white whiskers, and beer belly. Standing behind the bar, he called out to them as they sat down at the table.

"Hi there, English! How's my favorite limey?"

Liza pulled a face as heads turned her way. Doug had called her "English" ever since she'd forcefully corrected him when he'd mistaken her English accent for Australian the first day they met.

Melanie grinned. Doug was one of the few people who could get the better of her grandmother in a battle of words. She waved at the big man as she sat down.

"I don't know why I put up with him," Liza said as she picked up the menu. "He's so loud and uncouth."

"And you love it."

"I tolerate it. Doug is useful when we want to know what's going on at the police station."

"Or anywhere else in Sully's Landing." Melanie glanced at the man behind the bar. "He knows everyone and everything about this town."

"Which is why I put up with his nonsense." She visibly jumped when Doug appeared behind her and put a hand on her shoulder.

"What can I get for you, English?"

Liza gave him a fleeting glance. "I'll have my usual fish and chips."

"And a glass of wine, I'm sure." Doug winked at Melanie. "A cobb salad for you, right?"

She nodded. "Please."

"We're celebrating Mel's birthday," Liza told him.

"In that case, the wine is on the house." Doug grinned at Melanie. "Happy birthday."

"Thanks." Melanie smiled back at him.

Across the room, Fiona Donnegan, Doug's young server, watched him out of the corner of her eye. Melanie figured she was probably wondering why her boss was doing her job. Doug didn't usually wait on the tables. He spent most of his time behind the bar.

Liza, however, seemed not to notice anything unusual. "When you have a moment," she said, peering up at him, "we'd like a word with you."

Doug's expression was cautious, but he answered readily enough. "Sure. I can spare a minute or two. What's up?"

Melanie glanced at the rest of the tables. Apparently the rest of the patrons had lost interest in the limey, since no one was looking her way.

Liza lowered her voice. "We want to know what's going on at the police station concerning our situation at the inn."

Doug nodded. "I'll put your order in and be right back."

He disappeared behind the bar, and Liza leaned forward across the table. "I hope he has something he can tell us. We're halfway through the week, and we're still no closer to finding out who killed Walter."

"I know." Melanie sighed. "It seems the more we learn about what happened that night, the more confusing it becomes." She caught sight of Doug approaching, carrying two glasses of white wine. "Here he comes. Keep your fingers crossed."

Doug put the two glasses on the table in front of them and sat down. "Bottoms up."

Liza picked up her glass and raised it at Melanie. "Happy birthday and many more." She touched her glass to Melanie's and took a cautious sip. "Nice." She took a longer sip and put the glass down. "So what can you tell us?"

He tilted his head on one side. "What's it worth to you?"

Liza gave him a haughty look. "That depends if your information has any value."

"My information always has value."

"That's a matter of opinion."

"Who's opinion?"

"Mine, of course."

Melanie lifted her wineglass. She was used to the verbal sparring between them and enjoyed it at times, but right now she was eager to find out what Doug knew, if anything.

Doug finally relented and folded his arms. Leaning forward, he placed his elbows on the table. "I don't have much. They're keeping the case under wraps. Shaun did hear there were no fingerprints or DNA on the saw you found. Or on the victim. Guess the perp was wearing gloves."

Liza wrinkled her nose. "You sound like a bad cop movie."

Doug uttered a loud sigh. "Shoot. I was going for Sam Spade."

"Is that all you can tell us? Does Grumpy Dutton have any suspects?"

He leaned back. "From what I hear, everyone in your house is a suspect, including you two."

"What!"

"Huh?"

Melanie and Liza had both spoken at once and louder than either of them had intended. Once more, curious stares turned their way.

Doug held up his hand. "Simmer down. It's not official. They're just not ruling anything out right now. It's still early in the investigation."

"Too early," Liza said crisply. "We're running out of time. Our next guests are due on Sunday. We need to get rid of the ones we've got."

Raising his eyebrows, Doug murmured, "I'd be careful who you say that to if I were you."

"You know what I mean." Liza took a gulp of wine. "If they don't find out who killed Walter soon, we'll have five people looking for somewhere to sleep."

Deciding it was time to join in the conversation, Melanie said, "Ben said they'd make arrangements for them."

"He said he was sure that certain arrangements could be made, which tells me he wasn't sure of anything." Liza stared at her glass. "This whole thing is such a mess."

Doug reached out and patted her hand. "Don't worry, English. Something will turn up. I'll ask Shaun to keep his ears open, and if he finds out anything, I'll let you know." He got up and stretched. "I'd better get back to the bar before someone starts shouting for service. Enjoy your lunch."

He took off, leaving Liza still staring gloomily into her glass.

"Maybe we should ask some more questions," Melanie said, relieved to see that they were no longer the center of attention in the room.

"Like what? We've talked to everyone. No one seems to know anything, yet someone must know something." Liza frowned. "You said you thought Joe was hiding something."

"It was just a feeling. Nothing concrete."

"Well, let's talk to him again. See if we can trip him up or something."

"I guess it's worth a try."

Liza looked as if she was about to say something, then apparently changed her mind.

"What?" Melanie leaned forward. "What were you going to say?"

Liza shrugged. "Nothing. It's probably a ridiculous idea."

"What is?" Melanie felt like shaking her. "Tell me!"

Liza looked around and lowered her voice. "I just had this idea, and it probably won't work, but we don't seem to be getting anywhere, and time's running out, and—"

"Will you please tell me what you're talking about?"

"All right." Liza took a deep breath. "You remember when Sharon Sutton told us she holds séances for her friends?"

Melanie nodded. "She said she just did it for entertainment. I don't think she is a real medium."

"Probably not. But our guests don't know that."

Melanie stared at her. "Are you suggesting what I'm thinking?"

"Depends on what you're thinking."

"I'm thinking you've got the crazy idea to hold a séance for our guests."

"I told you it was ridiculous." Liza twiddled her glass in her fingers. "I was just thinking that if Sharon pretended to contact Walter and ask him who pushed him off the balcony, someone might give something away."

Melanie groaned. "You've been reading way too many mystery novels. That only works in books."

"I know." Liza lifted her glass and took a swig of her wine. "But it would be fun, though, right? And we might just pick up a clue. Maybe it will jog someone's memory or something."

Melanie gave it some thought. It probably wouldn't do any harm, and her grandmother was right. Maybe they could pick up a clue somehow. "You really want to do this?"

Liza's eyes lit up with excitement. "Yes, I do! We can tell the guests that it's to take their minds off the investigation. We can do it tomorrow night, if Sharon is free."

"But what about Sharon? Would she do it for us?"

"She'll do it for you. She adored having you work in her dress shop all summer, and the two of you have become good friends, right?"

"Yes, but this is a lot to ask."

"She can always say no if she doesn't want to do it. Let's go ask her. We can go right after we leave here."

Still not sure about the whole idea, Melanie slowly nodded. "Okay. We'll go ask her. But please, don't bully her into something she doesn't want to do. Okay?"

Liza opened her eyes wide. "Me? Bully someone? Never!"

Melanie looked up as Fiona arrived at the table with their lunch plates. She waited until the server had left before saying,

"Let's try to put all this out of our minds for a while and enjoy the food."

"Agreed." Liza lifted her glass. "Down the hatch!"

Melanie raised her own glass. "To success!" *And may it be soon*, she added inwardly.

"I've been wanting to stop by Felicity's Fashions," Liza said as they were leaving the pub later. "I keep meaning to stop in there to see if Sharon's got a fur cape. I saw one in a catalog, and I rather like it."

"As long as it's fake fur." Melanie reached the car and opened the passenger door for her grandmother.

Max uttered a couple of low woofs, his tail wagging frantically in greeting.

"Of course." Liza climbed stiffly into the car. "I wouldn't dream of wearing the real thing."

Melanie drove onto the street and headed into town, where Sharon's dress shop was located. She found a spot at the curb fairly close to the shop and parked the car. Max lay down on the seat again with a resigned sigh as she got out of the car and closed the door.

The middle-aged blonde woman behind the counter greeted them the moment they entered the small shop. "Liza! Melanie! How good to see you both!" She waved an arm at the empty room. "You picked a good time to visit. There's no one here. We'll have plenty of time to talk."

Melanie headed over to a rack of sequined sweaters. "These are pretty. Are they a new line?"

"Just came in last week." Sharon walked out from behind the counter. "I ordered them while you were working here this summer, but they've been on back order for months. Very popular, so I hear. Want to try one on?"

Melanie shook her head. "I'm not a big lover of sequins, but they are cute."

"Do you have a fur cape, by any chance?" Liza reached for a blue-and-purple silk scarf hanging on a stand on the counter. "This is nice. It would go with my blue sweater."

"A fur cape?" Sharon looked around the shop as if hoping a cape would materialize. "I don't think so. I might be able to order you one if you tell me what you want."

"I don't really know what I want until I see it." Liza pulled the scarf from the stand. "I will take this, though."

She handed it to Sharon, who carried it behind the counter. "I had some of your visitors in here this morning," she said as she folded the scarf. "I think two of the women were sisters, and they had another little woman with them."

"Oh, yes, I know who they were." Liza looked at Melanie as she joined her at the counter. "Are you going to look at clothes?"

"Maybe later." Melanie nodded at the scarf. "I like that."

"The sisters both bought scarfs like this one," Sharon said, wrapping the filmy fabric in pink tissue. "The other woman bought gloves and a beautiful white sweater with gold edging on the collar and sleeves. I was quite sad to see that one go. I'd been thinking of keeping it for myself."

Melanie tried to envision the mousy Beatrice in a fancy sweater and failed.

"I told them I was so sorry to hear about their friend's death." Sharon produced a small cream bag with black drawstrings from under the counter. "They didn't want to talk about it, though. I can't say I blame them. It must have been such a dreadful shock for them all." She slipped the scarf into the bag and handed it to Liza. "For you, too."

"It was indeed." Liza handed her credit card to Sharon.

"Did the police find out who killed him?"

"Not yet." Liza looked over her shoulder, as if to confirm the shop was still empty of customers. "In fact, we wanted to ask you a favor. We need your help."

"Me? What can I do?"

"We were wondering if you'd hold a séance for our guests tomorrow night."

Melanie held her breath as Sharon's eyes widened. "A séance? But I don't . . . I'm not . . . I only do it for fun."

"That's exactly what we want." Liza leaned over the counter. "We want you to pretend to contact the dead man and ask him who pushed him off the balcony. We're hoping someone will give us a clue."

"We'll pay you, of course," Melanie said as Sharon still looked doubtful.

"You don't have to pay me. I'd be happy to do it for you. It's just . . ."

Her voice trailed off, and Liza said anxiously, "It's just what?"

Sharon's hand strayed to her throat. "Will it be dangerous? I mean, being in the same room as a murderer?" She shuddered. "I don't know. It seems dangerous to me."

"Of course it's not dangerous. We've been living with a killer presumably in the house for days. Whoever killed Walter is not interested in killing anyone else. He just wants to get away with it. And it looks like he might do so if we don't find out who did it soon." Liza looked at Melanie for help.

"There'll be plenty of other people in the room," Melanie said. "I don't think for one minute that the killer will give himself away. We're just hoping that listening to you talking to Walter might trigger something from one of the group that could help us figure out who killed him."

"Besides," Liza added, "it will be fun. Our guests need something to take their minds off the investigation. They're supposed to be on vacation, and they've had to deal with the shock of Walter's death and all the questioning from a rather hostile detective. They don't know if and when they'll be able to go home, and they're very unhappy. A séance will be a nice distraction for them."

Sharon's skepticism still showed on her face, but after a moment's thought, she said quietly, "Well, if it will help, I'll be glad to do it."

"Great!" Liza straightened up. "Tomorrow night, then. Let's say . . . eight o'clock?"

"Okay." Sharon swiped Liza's card and handed it back to her.

Melanie could tell the woman still had serious reservations about the project, and she could hardly blame her. Being invited to entertain a group of strangers that almost certainly included a killer was not her idea of a fun evening, either. "I'm going to take a look at the racks," she said as Liza tucked her credit card back in her purse.

She left the women talking at the counter and wandered across the room to where a row of dresses beckoned to her. The holiday season was coming up, and just in case she was invited somewhere nice, she wanted something new and a little fancy herself.

Just for a second, she allowed a picture into her mind of a glittering ball of lights, soft music playing, and Ben's arms guiding her around the floor.

She quickly shut down on the vision. There was absolutely no point in getting ideas about Ben Carter. That ship could never be launched.

None of the dresses on the rack appealed to her, and she walked back to the counter, telling herself that a trip into Portland might be just what she needed.

Liza looked disappointed when Melanie told her she hadn't found anything she liked.

"I'll be getting a new batch in next week," Sharon told her. "The best ones go fast. Stop by on Saturday and take a look."

"I will," Melanie promised as Liza headed for the door. "And we'll see you tomorrow night."

"I'll be there."

Sharon waved at her, and Melanie joined her grandmother outside, feeling more than a little guilty for putting that kind of pressure on a friend.

"I didn't think she was going to do it," Liza said, stopping to look in the window of the candy store.

"She's scared, and I don't blame her." Melanie's mouth watered at the sight of a tray of decorated chocolates.

"She'll be fine. Nothing's going to happen with everyone in the room." Liza glanced at her. "We could invite Ben for protection."

"He'd put a stop to the whole thing if he knew about it."

"Probably." Liza moved on. "It's a shame you couldn't find anything you liked in Sharon's shop. We need to go to Portland. Sharon has some really nice things, but her shop is small, and she can't carry much of a selection."

Thankful for the change of subject, Melanie said, "I was just thinking the same thing. Though I don't know where we'd ever find the time."

"We could go one day right after breakfast is served. It only takes an hour and a half to get there. We could have lunch there. Max would love the ride."

"Sounds good."

They reached the car and got the usual boisterous welcome from Max. Arriving back at the inn later, Melanie parked the car in the garage and opened the rear door to allow the dog to leap out. While Liza hurried ahead of her to get into the house, Melanie followed more slowly, studying the wall beneath the balcony.

There didn't seem to be anywhere where someone could climb up. Not without a ladder or maybe a grappling hook and a rope. What about the saw? Why would the killer take the time and trouble to bury it if he could simply take it away with him? How could he saw through the railings late at night without someone hearing him? How could he be sure Walter would come out onto the balcony and not anyone else?

No, whoever was on that balcony that night was still inside the house. The railings could have been sawn through during the party, when everyone was downstairs and making too much noise for anyone to hear the killer at work.

She came to a halt, her mind furiously working. If that were so, then someone had to have been missing at some point.

Nick was at the party dressed as a skeleton, but then he left to change into his magician's outfit. But that was before Walter insulted him.

She thought back to his heated response to Liza's accusation. In any case, if he was with Cindi all night, as he so adamantly professed to be, then he couldn't have been on the balcony late at night. What if Joe had been mistaken? What if it wasn't a man he'd seen up there that night, but a woman?

Tall, skinny, needed a haircut. Only one woman fitted that description—Gloria Olsen.

The sound of a car's engine caught Melanie's attention. Turning her head, all thoughts about the murder vanished as she recognized the gray Honda pulling up at the curb.

Sick with dread, she watched the familiar figure of her ex-husband climb out of the car. The urge to run inside the house and slam the door was so strong, she had to force herself to stand still as he walked toward her.

His mouth was smiling, but his eyes were cold as he greeted her.

She didn't return the smile. "What are you doing here?"

His mouth hardened. "I was down here on business and heard about the unfortunate demise of one of your guests. I'm here to help."

Melanie felt like hitting him. Gary always talked like he was reading a textbook. "There's nothing you can do. The police are handling it."

"Yes, I know. But if there are charges, such as negligence, you'll need a lawyer."

There had been no mention of sawn-through railings in the news reports, and Melanie saw no reason to enlighten him.

"There will be no charges, and even if there were, I would not be hiring you as my lawyer. Now I have to get back to my guests."

She turned away, only to be halted by his sharp command. "Wait!"

Hating the fact that he could still manipulate her, she looked back at him.

"I'm taking you to lunch. It is your birthday, isn't it?" He looked at his watch. "I know it's late but—"

"I've already had lunch."

"Dinner, then. I can make it around seven."

"No, thank you. I have plans." She took another step toward the door.

"How long are you going to keep this up?"

She could feel her temper rising and made an effort to calm down. Slowly, she turned around to face him. "Forever," she said quietly.

"You have to forgive me sometime. What happened was an accident. I didn't crash the damn car on purpose."

"I know. But if you hadn't been so eager to see who was calling you on your cell phone, the accident wouldn't have happened. Your carelessness took away the most important thing in my life. Because of you, I can never have a baby. One day I might be able to forgive you. But I can never forget. How could I? It's over, Gary. I don't know how many times I have to tell you that."

His face was a stone mask, his eyes glittering with resentment. "Get over it, Mel. It's not the end of the world. Bad things happen. For pity's sake, grow up and deal with it."

It took all her willpower to keep from hitting him. "I did," she said shortly. "I got the hell out of your life. Go find someone else to boss around and leave me alone." She twisted away from him and headed for the porch.

"You'll come crawling back to me one day, you'll see," he called out after her, but she kept on walking, up the steps and inside the house. Closing the door, she leaned against it for a moment. The encounter had left her shaken, and she took a few deep breaths before heading for the kitchen.

Liza sat in the nook, reading the local newspaper, when Melanie walked in a moment later. "Oh, there you are," she said, turning a page. "I was wondering where you were. Max has been pacing up and down like an anxious parent."

Melanie glanced at the dog, who was now settling down in his bed. "I just had a fight with Gary."

Liza's chin shot up. "Gary? What in heaven's name is he doing here?"

Melanie walked over to the fridge and opened the door. "He's down here on business. He heard about Walter. It gave him an excuse to stop by." She grabbed a soda and flipped the lid. "He was his usual obnoxious self, demanding to know when we'd get back together. He remembered my birthday as an afterthought and actually wanted to take me to dinner."

Liza sniffed. "I hope you said no."

"Of course I said no. I told him to find someone else."

"I wish he would." Liza rattled the newspaper. "If Gloria was a bit younger, I'd have her go after him. Those two would hit it off like wildfire."

In spite of her churning stomach, Melanie snorted a giggle. "She'd keep him in line, that's for sure. Can I get you anything?"

"No thanks. I just had a cup of tea."

Melanie carried the soda over to the table and sat down. "Any news in there?"

"About us? No. At least I haven't seen any yet." She turned another page. "The problem with running a bed-and-breakfast is that we don't get time to read the paper in the morning. By the time we get to it, the news is already old." She flipped a page back and set the paper down in front of Melanie. "Look at this. They are building a fancy new hotel resort on the beach in Seaside. That town is growing. There's a lot of construction going on there lately."

"Not like Sully's Landing." Melanie took a draw from the can and set it down. "I don't think anything new has been built here in years."

"Which is the way I like it."

Melanie stared out the window. The mist had thinned out, leaving a slight haze over the ocean. She could see a ship close to the horizon, slowly making its way north. "Speaking of Gloria," she said, "do you think it's possible that Joe mistook her for a man that night on the balcony?"

Liza frowned. "Gloria? I guess so. It was dark, and the streetlight doesn't penetrate through the trees. You really think Gloria could have killed Walter?"

"I don't know what to think. I do think whoever sawed through those railings might have done so while we were all at the party. It's really the only time someone could do that without one of us hearing him. Or her."

"You may be right." Liza appeared to think about it for a moment or two. "We need to find out if anyone noticed someone was missing from the party for a while."

"Yes, we do." Melanie looked at the window. "I'm not sure how we do that without making it obvious that we're investigating the murder."

"We'll think of something." Liza glanced at the clock. "Maybe we can catch one or two of them alone."

"Well, it's cold out there and it's started to rain again. At least a couple of our guests will most likely be in the living room."

"Right." Liza pushed herself up from the table. "Let's go talk to them. We need to tell them about the séance, anyway. It will give us an excuse to ask some questions."

Walking into the living room with her grandmother a minute later, Melanie was surprised to see all of their guests in there. The sisters sat on the couch, quietly discussing something. Gloria sat next to them in the recliner, a tablet on her lap. Beatrice was dozing in an armchair in the corner, while Joe stood at the window, gazing at the tossing trees outside.

He turned to look at Melanie, his bored expression making him look disgruntled. "It rains a lot down here," he said as if it were her fault.

"It rains a lot everywhere in Oregon." She smiled at him, hoping to lighten his mood. "The forecast is good for tomorrow, though."

He shrugged and turned back to look out the window, obviously unimpressed by her prediction.

Gloria looked up. "Don't pay any attention to him. He's like a caged bear when he can't get outside."

"There's not much to do down here when it's raining," Amy said as if apologizing for Joe's bad attitude.

Eileen gave her a scathing glance. "There's lots to do. You just need to bundle up and wear a hat. You can walk on the beach or go window-shopping in town. There's a nice little museum I noticed when we were there yesterday. Getting out in the fresh air is good for all of us."

"Then why aren't you out in it?" Joe muttered.

Liza cleared her throat. "I know exactly what you need. A nice cup of tea. I'll go make one for you all." She nudged Melanie and headed for the door.

Melanie waited until they were back in the kitchen before asking, "What was that all about?"

Sitting down on a chair, Liza sighed. "We can't ask them who was missing from the party with everyone there. You know they're not going to rat on their friends. We have to get each one of them alone."

"And how do we do that?"

"I don't know. But I'll think of something."

"We didn't tell them about the séance."

"It didn't seem like a good time. They were all a little hostile."

The sharp ring of the front doorbell made them both jump. Melanie's fingers curled into her palms. "I hope that's not Gary."

Liza stood up, wincing as she took a step away from the chair. "Ouch. I keep forgetting I'm not thirty anymore."

"Wait here," Melanie said, starting for the door. "I'll go and see who it is."

"No, let me." Liza followed her out into the hallway. "If it's Gary, I want to give him a piece of my mind. I have some advice for that man, and I can't wait to deliver it."

"We'll both go." Melanie paused in front of her grandmother, preventing her from moving forward. "Just promise me that if it is Gary, you'll say nothing."

The doorbell rang three times, suggesting whoever was outside was getting impatient.

"Oh, all right." Liza hunched her shoulders. "But it won't be easy. There are things I'd like to do to that man that shouldn't be printed."

Hurrying to the door, Melanie prayed that it wasn't her ex-husband. She reached the door and braced herself. If it was Gary, she promised herself, she'd be polite but firm. She wouldn't let him speak. She'd just tell him to get the hell out of her life and leave her alone. Taking a deep breath, she opened the door.

It wasn't Gary.

She heard Liza groan behind her as the grim face of Detective Dutton stared back at her. Melanie let out her breath in a puff of exasperation. "What can we do for you?"

Dutton seemed unmoved by the cold welcome. "I'd like a word with one of your guests." He hunched his shoulders as a blast of wind blew the rain against his head. "Inside, if you don't mind."

Reluctantly, Melanie stood back to let him in. Liza hovered in the hallway, glowering at the detective.

Dutton gave her a cursory glance before saying to Melanie, "I need to talk to Joe McAllister."

Melanie could feel her grandmother's eyes burning into her head as she answered the detective. "I'll see if he's here."

"Alone." Dutton gave Liza a hard look.

Ignoring him, she kept her gaze on Melanie. "I'll be in the kitchen."

She stalked off, leaving Melanie to cope with the detective. "You can talk to him in the dining room," she said, gesturing down the hallway. "I'll send him in."

Dutton gave her a curt nod and strode off toward the dining room.

Reaching the living room door, Melanie noticed that she'd left it slightly open. The group had probably been listening to the conversation in the hallway.

The sisters looked up with innocent smiles when she walked into the room. Gloria kept her gaze firmly on her tablet as Joe turned to look at her, and she could tell by his set expression that he knew the detective was looking for him.

"Detective Dutton would like a word with you," Melanie told him. "He's in the dining room."

Amy uttered a soft gasp, while Eileen stared resolutely at her book. Gloria sent a brief glance Joe's way, then stared back at her tablet.

Beatrice seemed not to notice anything going on. She sat with her eyes closed and her hands folded in her lap.

Joe's lips were tightly compressed as he walked past Melanie and out the door.

The minute he'd left the room, Eileen put her book down. "What do the cops want with Joe? Do they think he killed Walter?"

Gloria's head shot up. "Joe would never kill anyone."

"You can't know that for sure." Eileen looked at Melanie for confirmation. "The detective must have a reason to talk to him."

Amy whimpered. "I can't believe Joe is a murderer."

"He's not a murderer!" Gloria shot up from her chair. "I can't believe you think he's capable of killing someone."

"Nobody's accusing anyone of anything," Melanie said as Beatrice mumbled something and sat up. "Detective Dutton just wanted a word with him and—"

She broke off as Liza rushed into the room. "Dutton is taking Joe to the police station for questioning," she said, nodding at the window. "He must be arresting him for Walter's murder."

Chapter 9

Gloria uttered a muffled yelp of protest and dashed to the window to look out. "He's putting him in his car." She turned back to look at them. "He's arrested Joe!"

Amy whimpered again. "I told you so."

Eileen shook her head. "Just goes to show, you never really know anyone."

Beatrice uttered a little sigh and closed her eyes again.

"Well, he's mistaken," Gloria declared, stomping back to her chair. "I just hope Joe has a good lawyer."

A vision of Gary popped into Melanie's mind. She immediately dismissed it. "Look, I know this is upsetting, but let's not jump to any conclusions, okay? Just because the detective is questioning Joe doesn't mean he suspects him. After all, he's questioned us all."

"Yes," Eileen said, "but none of us were taken to the police station."

Melanie had to agree with her. It did seem that Dutton had a strong reason to take Joe in for questioning. If he was charged with murder, that would solve all their problems. However, she still had a couple of days to contend with the rest of the group, and so far, no one had said anything about them being able to go home.

"Well, this is all very upsetting," Gloria said, picking up her tablet again. "What are we supposed to do now?"

"I want to go home," Amy said, sounding close to tears.

"We can't go home," Eileen told her. "Not until the police say we can."

Amy burst into tears.

Afraid things were getting out of hand, Melanie held up her hand. "Okay, let's all calm down. I suggest you all try to relax and enjoy the rest of your visit. The Arts Festival is on Saturday, and you've all been looking forward to that. By then, all this upheaval should be over, and you'll be able to go home on Sunday as planned."

"And leave Joe behind?" Gloria stood up again. "I can't deal with this. I need to get out of here. I'm going for a walk."

"It's raining," Liza said, not too helpfully.

"So I'll get wet."

Gloria left the room, and the sisters exchanged a long glance. "I think there's something going on between those two," Eileen said. "It wouldn't surprise me if they planned Walter's murder together."

Amy uttered a little moan of protest.

Remembering Beatrice's story about blackmail, Melanie watched Amy as she fumbled for a tissue. It was hard to imagine the timid woman having an affair and lying to her husband and daughter all these years. She wondered if Eileen knew the truth and was in on the secret.

"Well, I'm going to make that cup of tea," Liza announced. "Would anyone like one? I have some biscuits to go along with it."

Eileen gave her an odd look. "Like the ones we had for breakfast?"

"She means cookies," Melanie said. "Chocolate chip."

"I'll have some," Beatrice chirped, suddenly wide awake.

"I'll bring a plate of them in." Liza left, and Melanie followed her to the kitchen.

"I'm going to work on my computer for a while," she said as Liza filled the kettle with water. "I need to balance the bank account." What she needed, she added inwardly, was to focus on something else other than their dinner date with Ben tonight. Her stomach churned every time she thought about it.

"You don't want tea?" Liza carried the kettle to the stove and lit the gas under it.

"No thanks. I'd rather have a soda." Melanie walked over to the fridge. "So it looks as if Joe might have killed Walter after all."

"Maybe so. The cops must have found out he was in the driveway with Walter's body in the middle of the night." Liza opened a cabinet door and took down a large tin, decorated on the lid with a picture of Buckingham Palace. "He seemed like such a nice, refined gentleman. It's hard to imagine him actually killing someone."

"Much easier to imagine Nick Hazelton shoving Walter off the balcony."

"Exactly." Liza shook her head. "We misjudged that young man. At least now we can relax, knowing that the killer has been caught and our guests can go home on Sunday."

"And we won't have to hold the séance after all. I'll call Sharon and let her know."

"No, wait." Liza opened the lid of the tin. "As long as we have it all arranged, let's just go ahead and do it. It will be fun, and the guests deserve some entertainment after everything they've been through this week."

Melanie would much rather have cancelled the whole thing, but Liza seemed so excited. The last thing she wanted to do was take that away from her grandmother. It occurred to her that Liza might be hoping to contact her late husband, but then she remembered Sharon's confession that she wasn't a real medium. Liza had enough sense to know Sharon couldn't get in touch with dead spirits.

So what harm could it do? Besides, her grandmother was right. Their guests deserved a respite from all the gloom and doom. "Okay," she said, mentally crossing her fingers, "we'll go ahead with it."

"Good." Liza beamed. "We'll have Cindi make the announcement at breakfast tomorrow. Want a biscuit?"

"Thanks, but I'll pass." Melanie headed for the door. "I'll be in my room if you need me."

Liza waved a hand at her. "Take your time. I'm going to try to finish the new book I'm reading. We still have an hour or so before we need to get dressed for dinner."

Melanie looked at Max, who sat in his bed, watching her with expectant eyes. He thumped his tail as she beckoned to him, then jumped up and followed her to her room.

The moment she opened the door, he bounded inside and leapt for the bed. He landed on top of a newspaper that was spread out on the comforter. The rattling noise it made startled him, and he backed off, squatting up against the headboard.

"Oh, it's okay, Max. It's not your fault." Melanie patted his head to reassure him and got a lick on the hand in return. "Now what in the world is this doing here?" Picking up the newspaper, she noticed the picture of the new hotel being built in Seaside and realized it was the same paper Liza had been reading earlier.

Maybe Liza wanted her to read the whole article. Frowning, Melanie folded up the paper. It was odd that her grandmother hadn't simply given her the newspaper when she was in the kitchen. Then again, who knew how Liza's mind worked at times? She had long ago given up trying to second-guess her grandmother.

Max settled down now that the threat of the newspaper had been removed. Leaving him to sleep, Melanie switched on her computer. Once more she was disappointed to find no e-mail from Vivian. This latest lead on her missing mother had seemed so promising, though she had to admit, it was a long shot. The chance that her mother actually was a neighbor of Vivian's coworker just seemed too good to be true. The truth was, she was afraid to hope for too much. She'd been disappointed so many times.

Determined to put the matter out of her mind, she logged onto her bank account and began the tedious task of balancing it.

More than an hour later, she was still working on it when a tap on her door raised her head.

Liza poked her head around the door, and Max sat up, yawned, and stretched. "How are you doing?"

"I'm just about done."

"Good. It's time you were getting dressed." Liza walked into the room and sat on the edge of the bed. "Mel, I'm sorry, but I really don't feel good. My stomach is upset, and I feel a migraine coming on."

Immediately concerned, Mel jumped up from her chair. "Can I get you something? Do you need to lie down?"

"I've already taken some antacid, and yes, I think I have to lie down."

Liza's voice sounded weak, worrying Melanie even more. "Maybe I should give Dr. Winston a call?"

"Oh, no. That's not necessary." She gave Melanie a feeble smile. "A couple of hours in my room in the dark will soon get rid of my headache."

Still worried, Melanie laid the back of her hand on her grandmother's forehead. "You don't have a fever, so that's good."

"I told you, all I need is to lie down for a couple of hours and I'll be fine."

"I didn't know you suffered from migraines." Melanie sat on the bed next to her. "Do you have meds for it?"

"I have meds for just about everything." Liza patted her hand. "Now stop worrying about me and go get dressed for dinner."

"What?" Melanie jerked her head up. "I'm not going without you. I'll call Ben and let him know, and then I'll cancel the reservations."

"No, you won't. It's your birthday, and I'm not spoiling it for you. You can't do anything if you stay here. I'm just going to sleep for a couple of hours." Liza looked agitated. "I'll feel terrible if you cancel everything now. Plus, it will make my migraine much worse if I'm stewing about wrecking your birthday. Please, Mel. You have to go."

Alarmed by her grandmother's obvious anxiety, Melanie reluctantly gave in. "All right, if you insist. But I'm not going to enjoy it if I'm worrying about you."

"Then don't worry about me." Liza got up. "Now I'm going to bed. Just do me one favor."

"Anything."

"Tell me all about it when you get home. I'll probably be feeling a lot better by then."

Melanie studied her for a moment. Surely Liza wasn't putting on a pretense just so her granddaughter would have dinner alone with the man? In the next instance, she chided herself for being so suspicious. Her grandmother's skin was pale, and her eyes seemed dull and half-closed. "Of course I'll tell you about it. Though there probably won't be too much to tell."

"Well, from what you told me, you spent last night with Ben discussing our murder case. I hope the conversation tonight is a bit more exciting."

Melanie stood up. "Don't go getting any ideas."

Liza looked brighter as she headed for the door. "Who, me? Whatever do you mean?"

She was almost at the door when Melanie spotted the newspaper on the bed. "By the way, thanks for leaving the article for me."

Liza turned back to look at her. "What article?"

"This one." Melanie picked it up. "I haven't had time to read it yet, but I will get to it later."

Liza shook her head. "I have no idea what you're talking about."

Melanie held out the newspaper. "You left this on my bed."

Liza took it from her and peered at it for a long moment before lifting her head. "I didn't put this on your bed. I put it in the recycling bin while you were talking to the visitors in the living room."

Melanie was beginning to get the cold, itchy feeling she had whenever something odd was going on in the house. "Are you sure?"

"Of course I'm sure. It was only an hour or so ago." Her eyes opened wide. "Orville. He must have put it there." She stared at the paper. "Now why on earth would he do that?"

Grappling with confusion, Melanie wasn't sure what was more comforting to believe—that a ghost had put the newspaper on her bed or that her grandmother had some kind of brain seizure and had forgotten she'd put it there.

"Ah, well," Liza said as she walked back to the door, "I'll drop this in the bin again and hope it stays there this time." She paused and looked back. "By the way, did you ever try to find out Orville's real name?"

Still shaken, Melanie hesitated, unwilling to admit she believed the ghost had prevented her from researching him. This whole business was getting out of hand. If they weren't careful, she and her grandmother would end up the same way as that Sullivan daughter. "I tried," she said at last, "but I had no luck."

"Then we'll have to ask Josh. Maybe we should invite him to lunch. Enjoy your dinner. I'll look forward to hearing all about it when you get home." She left the room, leaving Melanie to deal with her twitching stomach.

It took her several minutes to decide what to wear. She much preferred casual clothes to dressy outfits, and she finally decided on a slim black skirt and royal-blue silk blouse. Her mother's opal pendant was the perfect finishing touch, and halfway satisfied with her appearance, she headed for the living room to wait for Ben.

Much to her relief, when she walked into the room, she was alone. The guests had to be out somewhere having dinner. She wasn't in the mood for small talk, especially if it was about Walter's murder. She needed to focus on the evening ahead.

It would have been a great deal more relaxing if Liza had been able to go with her. If only the invitation had come from Ben and he hadn't been coerced into it, she might have looked forward to it. Right now she was feeling decidedly uneasy about the whole thing. Would he think Liza's headache was an excuse for her to be alone with him?

She sat in the window to watch for the lights of his car, still stewing about what she would say to him, when the door opened and Gloria rushed in.

"Oh, hi," she said, flapping her hand at Melanie. "I think I left my glasses in here. Oh, there they are." She leaned over an armchair and snatched something up from the seat. "Thank goodness. I thought I'd lost them." She slipped the glasses in her pocket. "You look nice. Are you going out somewhere?"

"To dinner." Melanie hesitated a minute, then added, "To celebrate my birthday."

"Really? Happy birthday." Gloria tucked a wisp of blonde hair back in place. "I don't celebrate birthdays anymore. When you get to my age, they are a miserable reminder that you're getting old."

Melanie smiled. "I don't think you have to worry about getting old. You and my grandmother both look great. I hope I do as well when I get up there."

Gloria studied her for a moment. "You will. You have good bones. By the way, did you know that Joe is back? He walked in about half an hour ago. He hasn't been arrested after all. Though why the detective needed to question him again and why he couldn't do that here, I just don't understand."

Melanie caught her breath in dismay. She was happy for Joe, but this meant they were back to square one again. "Did he say what happened at the police station?"

"No, he won't talk about it." Gloria started for the door. "And when Joe doesn't want to talk, an atom bomb won't shake him. Have fun tonight. Hope he's a hot one."

Melanie could feel her cheeks warming as the door closed behind Gloria. She was still trying to recover when the lights of Ben's car swept into the driveway.

He seemed genuinely concerned when she told him that Liza wasn't well enough to join them. "Is she going to be okay?" he asked as Melanie slid onto the front seat of his car.

"She insists that it's just a migraine and she'll be fine in a couple of hours." Melanie sighed. "I do wish she'd been able to come, though. It doesn't feel right, celebrating my birthday without her."

"We'll bring some dessert back for her." Ben drove out of the driveway and headed down the coast road. "I'm glad you didn't cancel."

"Liza insisted. She said it would make her migraine worse if I didn't go."

"Your grandmother is a very thoughtful woman."

"I know. And a very devious one."

He sent her a quick glance. "What does that mean? You think she's putting on an act?"

"I don't want to sound unsympathetic, but I think it's a distinct possibility."

"Then in that case, we should do what she wants and enjoy the evening."

He'd sounded amused, and she leaned back with a sigh of relief. The awkward moment was over, and she could finally relax.

The hostess at the Seafarer showed them to a booth next to a window overlooking the beach. The sun had already set over an hour earlier, and only the faintest of light-blue streaks hovered far out above the ocean's horizon.

Inside the restaurant, candles flickered on the tables, casting warm glows across the customers' faces. Muted lamps from chandeliers above their heads provided enough light to read the menus, and Melanie studied hers before deciding on the salmon, while Ben ordered a steak.

Waiting for their drinks to arrive, Melanie decided this was a good time to ask Ben about Joe's visit to the police station. "I guess Joe was cleared of suspicion," she said, "since he's back at the inn."

Ben looked as if he didn't want to answer, but after a moment's hesitation, he said, "We didn't have enough evidence to hold him. It doesn't mean he's in the clear."

"Oh." Melanie felt a stab of apprehension. "So you still think he's the one who killed Walter?"

Ben smiled. "It's your birthday. Let it go for tonight and just enjoy a nice evening out, okay?"

It was a nice way of telling her he didn't want to discuss it. "Okay." She smiled back at him. "So tell me, what made you decide to become a cop? I know you told me a lot about what you do, but you never told me why you wanted to do it."

Ben laughed. "I wish I had a dollar for every time someone asked me that question." He looked up as the server arrived with the drinks—Chardonnay for Melanie and a Scotch and soda for Ben.

"So what's the answer?" Melanie asked after the server had left.

He shrugged. "It's simple. I come from a family of cops—my grandfather was police chief in Seattle, my father and two uncles are retired cops, my brother is a detective in the San Francisco PD, and two of my cousins work in law enforcement."

Remembering everything he'd told her about police work the last time they'd had dinner together, she shuddered. "It's such a dangerous job. I often wonder why anyone would want to do it."

"It has its rewards. And like I told you before, much of the time, it's pretty much routine. A lot of paperwork and sitting or standing around." He stared at his glass, twisting it around in his hands. "I guess there's something satisfying about knowing you're there to protect the community, to keep order and help people in a crisis and, maybe once in a while, turn a bad guy's life around and give him hope."

Impressed, she murmured, "When you look at it that way, it makes sense."

He smiled. "It does to me. So what about you? What made you want to run a B and B in a sleepy little town like Sully's Landing?"

"It was my grandmother's idea. My grandfather died a couple of years ago, and I think Liza missed him so much, she wanted to do something completely different. We had always had an interest in cooking. She taught me how to bake Christmas cookies when I was in third grade."

"I remember you telling me your grandparents raised you."

"Yes." She hadn't told him why, and she wasn't sure she wanted to tell him now. "My father died when I was four years old," she said, "and my mother . . ." She paused, wondering how to explain her mother's disappearance. "I lost my mother shortly after that."

He gave her a sharp look, and she knew he must be wondering why she didn't expand on that. "I'm sorry. That must have been hard."

"It would have been a lot worse if it hadn't been for Liza and my grandfather. They were wonderful parents, and I had a wonderful life with them. Then I got married. And divorced." She sighed. "I was in a pretty bad place when Liza bought the house, so when she suggested we partner up and turn it into an inn, I figured I had nothing to lose."

Ben started to say something, but just then the server arrived with the meals. He waited until she had left before saying, "Is it working out for you?"

Melanie picked up her fork. "I hope so. So far our first week isn't going too well."

"No, I meant getting you out of your bad place."

She tasted the salmon, wondering how much she should tell him. "This is very good."

He looked a little disappointed, and she said quietly, "I was working at a job I didn't enjoy and living in an apartment beneath a couple who fought long and loud just about every night. The prospect of living at the beach and cooking for people seemed like paradise."

"I'm sorry."

She looked at him, and he added, "About the divorce, I mean."

"I'm not."

"Oh."

"It was the best thing that happened to me." She'd sounded bitter, and she made an attempt to lighten her tone. "That marriage was a mistake from the beginning."

"Any kids?"

A stab of pain took her breath away. "No."

"Maybe it's just as well. It's hard on the kids when the parents split up."

She couldn't answer him. A dark memory had surfaced. She was sitting in the passenger's side of a car. Gary was driving, speeding down the freeway. She heard his cell phone ring and saw the pickup pulling in front of them. There was a moment when she knew they were going to hit it . . . then darkness.

"Are you okay?"

She pulled herself together with a start. "Sorry. I was just remembering something."

"Judging from the look on your face, it wasn't a pleasant memory."

To her surprise, she found herself telling him. "I was in a car wreck. My ex-husband was driving. He was distracted by his cell phone and hit a truck."

Ben winced. "You were injured?"

"Yes." She sighed. "Gary is a lawyer. He'd always put his work before anything else—including me and our marriage. I never felt I was important to him. That lousy phone ruled his life and almost killed us both. I spent weeks in the hospital. I tried to put it behind me, but after that, things between us just kept getting worse. It took me another two years to realize my marriage was over and I needed to leave."

"I'm so sorry."

"Thank you." She didn't know why she'd told him all that. Maybe it was the wine or the sympathy she saw in his eyes. Or maybe it was the way he always made her feel—protected, understood, and respected. She'd never felt any of those things with Gary.

Even so, there was one part of the story she hadn't told him. Only Gary and Liza knew that the accident had caused injuries that would forever prevent her from bearing a child. She didn't know if her ex-husband would ever have her forgiveness for that.

"I was married once too," Ben said, slicing into his steak.

Melanie swallowed a mouthful of rice. It was the last thing she'd expected him to say. Remembering that he'd once told Liza he had no wife, she wondered if the woman had died. Afraid to ask in case it brought back bad memories, she murmured, "I'm sorry."

Ben shrugged. "She was young and couldn't handle the uncertainties of my job. She was convinced she'd end up a widow. I was on the Seattle PD when one night I had a close call while trying to arrest an escaped convict. It was too much for her to take. When I got home that night, she was gone, taking my baby son with her."

Melanie put down her fork. "Oh, Ben. I'm so sorry. Is your son still in Seattle?"

His jaw tightened. "Laura got married again and got full custody. I fought like hell to get joint, but Laura painted me as an unfit father. It's amazing how lawyers can pick on the smallest thing, bend the truth, and make you look guilty."

"Yes, I know." Looking at the pain in his eyes, she wanted so badly to reach out and take his hand.

"I did get visitation rights," he said, "but because of my job, I missed so many. My son didn't know me and would cry when I tried to hold him. It broke my heart. Laura told me that my visits were upsetting him too much and that if I really loved him, I'd let him go. I put in for a transfer after that."

"That must have been so hard."

"It was. It still is. I send him gifts for his birthday and Christmas, but I never know if he gets them. I'm not giving up on him. I'm hoping when he gets older, he'll want to meet his real father."

"One day you'll marry again and have another son to love."

"I can't see that happening. Cops don't make good marriage material. It takes a tough woman to put up with the odd hours and never knowing if your husband is coming home in one piece or in a body bag. It's hard on the kids too. Cops shouldn't have kids, I guess, but then it's the kids that make a marriage. I can't imagine anything more rewarding than watching your own flesh and blood growing up." He drained the last of his Scotch and scanned the room, apparently look-ing for the server.

Now Melanie felt uncomfortable. The conversation had taken a personal turn she hadn't expected or wanted, and she needed to steer it back to safer topics.

To her relief, Ben did just that by asking how Liza had come to the country to live.

"She met my grandfather when he was stationed with the USAF in England back in the early sixties," Melanie told him. "According to Liza, it was love at first sight. She married him six months later, and when he was sent home, she left every-thing she knew and loved to come back with him."

"That must have been hard."

"It was, and she was homesick for a long time, but I don't think she ever regretted marrying him. They had a wonderful, happy marriage."

"That's nice. Does she mind that you call her Liza and not Grandmother?"

Melanie laughed. "She insists I call her Liza. She says that calling her Granny makes her feel old."

"There's nothing old about that lady."

"I couldn't agree more."

By the time they were ready to leave, Melanie was totally relaxed and enjoying Ben's company. He'd kept her entertained with stories about his job that actually made her laugh. There were always two sides to a story, she thought, as she led the way out of the restaurant and into the parking lot. She really liked this comfortable, humorous side of Ben and was impressed that he could appreciate the lighter moments in what must be a demanding job.

He'd insisted on paying the bill—as his birthday gift to her, he'd told her—and had ordered an extra dessert to go for Liza. In all, it had been a thoroughly enjoyable evening, and she was sad to see it end.

"This was nice," Ben said as he drove her home. "We'll have to do it again sometime."

"I'd like that."

"Great." He was silent for a moment, then added, "If something turns up at the inn, like you hear something or see something you think we should know, I hope you'll call me."

"Of course I will."

"That doesn't mean I want you to go asking questions."

"I know."

"Just promise me you'll both be careful, okay?"

"I promise." His concern for their safety warmed her heart.

He parked in her driveway, and now her heart started thumping. If this had been a real date, he might have kissed her good night, and she would have welcomed that with open arms. This wasn't a real date, though, and she needed to get out of the car before she did something stupid.

She opened the door and swung her legs outside. "Thank you so much for dinner, and for Liza's dessert. She will love this. Chocolate mousse is one of her favorites."

"You're welcome." He sounded a little subdued, but in the next breath, he added, "I hope Liza's recovered from her imaginary headache. Tell her the strategy worked. I had a great time."

She turned to grin at him. "So did I. Thanks again."

"My pleasure. See you soon."

She nodded and scrambled out of the car, her purse in one hand and Liza's mousse in the other.

Reaching the door, she looked back at him as he pulled out of the driveway but couldn't tell if he saw her raise her purse at him.

Max gave her a tumultuous welcome when she walked into the kitchen, wagging his tail so hard his entire back half wiggled with it. Liza sat in the nook, a book propped up in front of her and a mug of steaming cocoa sitting next to it. She wore her pink robe and looked a little tired, but the color was back in her cheeks.

Melanie put the mousse in front of her. "Ben sent that for you. He was sorry you missed the dinner and hopes you're feeling better."

"That was sweet of him, and I am." Liza gave her a searching look. "How did the evening go?"

"Good." Melanie walked over to the counter and opened the flatware drawer to take out a spoon. She brought it over to the table and handed it to Liza before sitting down. Max immediately deposited himself at her feet, his furry body pressed against her legs.

"Thank you." Liza opened the carton and dug into the mousse. "This looks so good."

"It is. I had some at the restaurant. Have you heard about Joe?"

Liza frowned. "Joe? Is he in jail?"

"Nope. Gloria told me he's back here at the inn. He wouldn't tell her what happened at the police station, but Ben said Dutton released him because he didn't have enough evidence to hold him."

"What does that mean?"

"It means we're back to not really knowing who killed Walter."

"Bugger." Liza popped a spoonful of mousse into her mouth and swallowed. "Delicious. So maybe we can get Joe to talk to us and find out what went on at the police station."

"If he won't talk to Gloria, there's not much hope of him telling us anything."

"Well, then, we will have do what we always do when we want to know what's happening with the cops."

Melanie eyed her warily. "What's that?"

Liza raised her spoon in the air. "Lunch at the hardware store again!"

"Of course. I should have known."

"So tell me about the evening. What did you have for dinner?"

Melanie described the meal and then told her grandmother about Ben's failed marriage and the loss of his son.

"That's so sad," Liza said when she was finished. "He's seems like such a good man. He must miss his son terribly."

Melanie didn't want to dwell on that. "He talked a lot about his job, though this time it was mostly the funny side of it. He has a quirky sense of humor."

"And you like him." Liza's gaze was intent on her face. "So when are you seeing him again?"

Melanie sighed. "He's a nice man, but if you've got wedding bells ringing in your head, you can throw them out right now." She yawned and stood up, bringing Max to his feet. "I like him, yes. But as a good friend. That's all. And now I'm going to bed." She bent over and kissed her grandmother's cheek. "Good night and sleep well."

She escaped before the disappointment on her grandmother's face could make her feel guilty. Liza's words tormented her, however, as she got ready for bed. *And you like him.*

Yes, she did. But even if he returned those feelings, there was no chance of them getting together. If Ben got married again, he'd want kids. He'd made that very clear. *I can't imagine anything more rewarding than watching your own flesh and blood growing up.*

And that was the one thing she couldn't give him.

Chapter 10

The following morning, Cindi arrived in the kitchen wearing a black-and-white-striped sweater that hung off one of her shoulders and reached down to her knees, black tights, and a scowl on her face that didn't bode well for the morning breakfast rush.

"That mouthy detective came to the park to question Nick last night," she said when Liza asked her if she was okay. "He acted like Nick was guilty or something."

"Did he take him to the station?" Liza picked up a frying pan and tossed the pancakes in it.

"What? No!" Cindi tied an apron around her waist. "He just asked him a few questions and left. It was his lousy attitude that upset Nick. He was like, 'What the heck is wrong with me that everyone thinks I'm a murderer?' And I go, 'Nobody thinks you're a murderer,' and he goes, 'Well, your bosses think I am.'" She glared at Liza. "You accused him of killing Walter?"

Melanie's stomach started fluttering again.

"I didn't mean it to sound like that," Liza said, putting a soothing hand on Cindi's arm. "I was just trying to eliminate suspects, that's all."

Cindi seemed unimpressed. "He said he told you he was with me all night."

"Yes, he did." Liza waited, spatula in hand, for Cindi to continue.

"Well, he was." Cindi gave a defiant toss of her head. "I didn't tell you that before because I didn't think you'd approve."

Liza sighed. "It's none of my business what you do in your own time. I only care what you do while you're working here. And time's moving on, by the way. The guests are already in the dining room, waiting for their breakfast."

Cindi shot a look at the clock. "Okay. I'm on it."

"Wait, we need you to make an announcement. We're holding a séance tonight for the guests, and we'd like them all to be there."

Cindi stared at her. "A séance? What for?"

"To entertain the guests, of course. We thought it would be fun. We could use your help with refreshments, if you don't mind doing a little paid overtime."

"Okay." Cindi seemed to like that, but then she frowned. "They'll all think you're doing it to catch the killer. It wouldn't work, though."

Liza studied her for a moment before asking, "Why not?"

"Because everyone knows you can't talk to the dead."

As if in answer to her, a ghostly chuckle filled the room. Melanie jumped, and Max lifted his head and barked.

Liza grinned. "That Orville has perfect timing."

Cindi rolled her eyes. Grabbing a tray of glasses filled with orange juice, she headed for the door.

"Tell them eight o'clock in the dining room," Liza called out after her.

Cindi paused in the doorway and looked back at her. "You know what I hope? I hope the cops catch this lousy killer soon and leave us all alone."

"Amen to that," Liza murmured as the door closed behind her assistant.

"Do you think she's telling the truth? About Nick spending the night with her, I mean." Melanie pricked at the scrambled eggs with a fork and tasted them. "This needs more pepper."

Liza reached up to the shelf for the pepper shaker and handed it to her. "It's hard to say. These young people speak a different language than when I was growing up. Then again, when I first came to this country fifty years ago, everyone was speaking a different language, except for the few English people I met."

Melanie sprinkled pepper onto the eggs. "You lived with foreigners? I don't remember you telling me that before."

"I lived with Americans. It took me months to get used to their fractured English. Now I talk like an American."

Melanie laughed. "Which is why everyone knows you're English the moment you open your mouth."

"You know what I mean. I call a 'bonnet' a 'hood' now, a 'dustbin' is a 'garbage can,' and a 'waistcoat' is a 'vest.' I could go on and on." She slipped two pancakes onto a plate and handed it to Melanie. "I still can't call biscuits cookies, though. They will always be biscuits to me. 'Tea and cookies' just doesn't sound right."

Cindi burst into the kitchen just then, announcing, "They're ready for their eggs!"

Melanie spooned scrambled eggs next to the pancakes and handed it back to her grandmother.

Liza dropped two fresh orange slices onto the plate and handed it to Cindi. "Did you tell them about the séance?"

"I did. They didn't look too thrilled."

"But they're coming?"

"I guess so. They didn't say they wouldn't."

"If Cindi's right and they all think that we're doing it to catch the killer, then they'd have to come." Melanie spooned more eggs onto a plate. "If they didn't, it would make them look guilty."

Liza let out a triumphant laugh. "You're right! I hadn't thought of that."

"We should ask Nick to be there," Cindi said, balancing a third plate on her arm.

Melanie swung around to look at her. Liza was staring at her as if her assistant had confessed to the murder herself.

Apparently realizing the stir she'd caused, Cindi said hurriedly, "I just meant he could hide somewhere and move stuff around. Make it look more real. He's done it before for his aunt. She's a medium too."

Liza's face cleared. "Oh, good idea! Ask him. It will add to the fun."

"I will."

Carrying the plates, she left the room again, and Liza shook her head. "He moves things around to make it look real? How many fake mediums are out there?"

Melanie grinned. "I thought for a minute she was suggesting having Nick come to the séance to find out if he was guilty."

"I think she got that."

Melanie turned back to the stove. "I just hope this whole thing doesn't backfire on us."

Liza reached for more plates. "Now what can possibly go wrong? The guests will have a little fun, and just maybe we might pick up a clue. After all, what better place is there to hold a séance than a haunted house?"

The next half hour passed quickly as Cindi sailed back and forth between the kitchen and the dining room. Finally the breakfasts had been served, and there was time to relax.

Cindi joined Melanie and Liza in the nook, and everyone was very careful not to mention the murder or the police. Cindi talked about her life in foster homes, and by the time they had finished with breakfast, Melanie was feeling more than a little depressed.

After setting out with Max for his daily walk, however, she began to feel better. The skies were clear, and the sun actually felt warm as she walked down the lane to the beach, with Max impatiently tugging at his leash.

Liza was waiting for her when she got back to the inn. "I tried talking to Joe," she said as Melanie joined her in the living room. "He won't tell me what happened at the police station last night. He said they just asked him a few questions and sent him home." She sat down on the couch, looking worried. "He seemed upset, though. I know something's going on. We have to talk to Doug today."

"We'll go there for lunch," Melanie promised. "Just give me an hour to do some work in my room."

"Of course." Liza glanced at the clock. "I think Eileen took Amy and Beatrice into town. I don't know where Joe went, but he left soon after they did. I have to do some laundry, so I'll get that done before we leave."

As usual, Max followed Melanie to her room and settled himself on the bed while she sat down in front of the computer. The second she logged onto her e-mail, she saw a note from Vivian. It had an attachment with it, and her heart leapt with anticipation. Was it possible she was finally going to find her mother?

Her hands shook as she opened the e-mail. The text was brief. *Here's the pic Brian took of his neighbor. Let me know if she's your mother.*

Melanie sat staring at the computer for so long that Max sat up and whined. She looked at him and found him gazing at her with anxious eyes. "It's okay, buddy. I'm just nervous, that's all."

He kept his gaze on her as he laid his jaw on his paws.

Bracing herself, Melanie made her hand guide the mouse to the attachment. One click and it would open, either making her dream come true or dashing her hopes once again. *Just one click.*

Her finger hovered over the button, but she couldn't bring herself to press down.

Then from behind her came the familiar sound of a deep-throated chuckle.

Her hand jerked, accidentally pressing the button, and the attachment opened to reveal a fuzzy picture of a woman.

It wasn't her mother.

Even given the twenty-eight years Janice had been gone, and with the different hair color and style, Melanie could tell right away it wasn't the woman pictured in the precious, faded photos she had tucked away in a box.

Max sat up on his haunches, uttering a warning growl. The room had grown cold, and Melanie started up from her chair, turning to see what was behind her.

There was nothing, of course. The room was warm again, though Max still sat staring at the wall as if he could see something she couldn't. Convinced that the ghost had triggered her hand, she turned back to the computer, muttering, "Thanks, Orville."

Struggling with her disappointment, she stared at the photo for several more seconds. It was so hard to accept the fact that once more, her hopes had been dashed. Finally she had to acknowledge that the woman was, indeed, a stranger. She tapped out a message to Vivian, thanking her for sending the pic and telling her the woman was not her long-lost mother. Then she leaned back, feeling drained.

It didn't seem possible that someone could vanish so completely without a trace. She wouldn't let herself believe that her mother had deliberately abandoned her young daughter when she'd needed her the most. Then again, why hadn't she taken her child to England with her?

Liza had told her that Janice was too distraught and unstable to take care of her when she'd left, but all Melanie knew was that she could never have left a four-year-old daughter behind, no matter how desperate and shattered she felt.

Reaching for the keyboard, she opened up the accounts file. Those kind of thoughts were depressing, and she was not about to wallow in grief. She'd shed enough tears already. Someday she'd find out what had happened to her mother—hopefully finding her alive. Until then, she would concentrate on the business at hand, which was to pay some bills and update the website.

Liza was ready and eager to get to the hardware store when Melanie found her in the kitchen an hour later. "I got the laundry done," she said as she pulled on a white wool coat over her black sweater and pants, "and did some ironing as well." She picked up a red scarf and wound it around her neck, tucking the ends inside her coat. "Now I'm ready to eat."

"You're always ready to eat." Melanie stopped by the hall closet and took out her blue jacket. "You live to eat, while most of us eat to live."

"It's the British in me. We're a nation of guzzlers. None of that greens and grains stuff for us. Give us a plate of roast beef and Yorkshire pudding, followed by a slice of sticky pudding and custard, and we're happy."

Rolling her eyes, Melanie led her grandmother outside to the car. As usual, Max beat them there and waited impatiently for Melanie to open the back door for him.

They arrived at the hardware store as large gray clouds began to roll in from the ocean. Doug greeted them with his usual exuberance, once more generating glances from the handful of customers at the tables.

Melanie recognized a couple of them as regulars at the pub and returned their greetings with a smile while Liza settled herself at her usual table. "I think Doug keeps this table open for us," she said as Melanie sat down. "It's hardly ever taken when we come in."

"That's because it's tucked away in a dark corner." Melanie took off her jacket and hung it over the back of her chair. "Nobody wants to sit here."

"Well, I like it." Liza unbuttoned her coat and pulled off her scarf. "It's private." She looked up as Doug loomed over her.

"Two days in a row, English? My considerable charm must be getting to you."

"You're insufferable ego is getting to me." Liza struggled to get out of her coat, and Doug took hold of it to help her. "Thank you." She allowed him to pull the second sleeve off her arm and leaned forward so he could hang the coat over the back of her chair.

"My pleasure. Now what do you two ladies want from me?" Doug sat down at the table. "Somehow I don't think it's a passion for my fish and chips."

"We came to ask you something." Liza softened her voice. "The police took one of our guests in for questioning last night."

Doug nodded, looking grave. "I heard."

Melanie's pulse quickened. "Do you know what he told them?"

Doug looked around the room to make sure no one was listening. "I don't know much. Like I told you, Shaun only hears a word here and there from the other officers. He told me that the main suspects in your case are either the maintenance guy at the RV park or your visitor who was at the police station last night. They just don't have enough evidence to arrest anyone yet."

Liza sighed. "We've had our doubts about Nick Hazelton too." Doug raised an eyebrow, and she added, "He's the maintenance man."

Doug nodded. "Shaun also said your visitor found a note at the crime scene and gave it to the police."

Melanie caught her breath. "Joe found a note? He didn't say anything to us about it. Do you know what's on it?"

Doug shook his head. "Sorry. Shaun didn't say. He probably doesn't know. Like I said, he only gets bits and pieces of what's going on. Why don't you ask your guy about it?"

"He probably wouldn't tell us. Joe's being very tight-lipped about this whole thing." Liza picked up the menu.

"I had a feeling he was hiding something," Melanie said, looking up as Fiona arrived at their table.

The server slid a sideways glance at her boss before asking, "What can I get for you ladies?"

Liza was still studying the menu, and Doug poked her in the arm. "Why are you reading that, English? You must know it by heart by now."

"I do. I keep hoping to find a lobster tail or scampi listed on it."

Doug sighed. "We're a pub, not a five-star restaurant. What do you want from me?"

Liza grinned. "Don't get your knickers in a twist. The Caesar salad will do nicely." She looked up at the server, who had been hovering behind Doug with an anxious frown. "Thank you, Fiona."

"I'll have the Caesar too," Melanie said, giving the server an apologetic smile.

Fiona nodded and rushed off, and Doug shook his head. "Knickers in a what?"

"Twist. English expression." Liza turned her head to look at the bar. "Oh, bugger. I forgot to order a glass of wine."

"There's that word again." Doug got up from his chair. "I'll have to remember it. I can swear at my ornery customers without them knowing it."

Liza peered up at him through her lashes. "I'm sure you have a few choice words of your own to use."

"Enough to make your hair curl." He looked at Melanie. "Both of you want wine?"

Melanie smiled up at him. "Yes, please."

"Coming right up." He took off toward the bar, where a couple of customers were waiting to be served.

"You do enjoy pulling his chain." Melanie glanced over at the bar, where Doug was now talking to a customer.

"I don't often get the better of him." Liza propped the menu behind the salt and pepper shakers. "So what do you think about Joe finding that note? I'd give my right arm to know what was on it."

"Well, Joe's probably not going to tell us."

"No, I guess not." Liza sighed. "I don't suppose Ben would tell you?"

"Nope. He told me he can't discuss the details of the case while it's under investigation."

"Then we'll just have to try to worm it out of Joe." Liza smiled as Fiona arrived with the wine. "Meanwhile, let's enjoy our lunch."

They were deep in conversation about breakfast recipes when the food arrived, and Liza spent the rest of the time recalling memories of her adventures with Melanie's grandfather. Doug arrived at their table just as they were standing up to leave.

"Hope we see you two ladies again soon," he said as Liza wrapped her scarf around her neck.

"Oh, we'll stop by the next time we have nothing better to do." She picked up her coat, and he took it from her and held it up for her. Slipping her arms into the sleeves, she looked up at him. "You're a gentleman after all. Who would have thought?"

He grinned. "There's a lot you don't know about me, English. We'll have to get together sometime and swap stories."

For once it seemed Liza had no smart answer. Instead she picked up her purse and murmured, "See you later."

Having thoroughly enjoyed watching the exchange, Melanie smiled as she followed her grandmother out of the pub.

"Was that big baboon actually hinting at a date?" Liza marched over to the car as large drops of rain began to fall.

Reaching the car, Melanie opened the passenger door. "Would that be so terrible? He seems like a great guy."

"I know." Liza shook her head. "It's been fifty years since I last dated. I'm not sure I know how anymore."

Melanie laughed. "It's not that hard. You just meet somewhere, talk a lot, and see what happens after that."

Liza wrinkled her nose. "That's the part I'm most worried about. I'm not a young woman anymore."

"All Doug was asking for was a conversation. It never needs to go beyond that."

"I guess you're right."

She still looked doubtful, and Melanie gave her a little push. "You don't have to do anything you don't want to do. Remember that. Now hop in before the downpour gets here."

"It's been quite a while since I hopped in anywhere," Liza said as she struggled onto the seat.

"You do more than okay for an old fogey."

Liza grunted. "Thanks for nothing."

Smiling, Melanie joined her in the car. Max poked his nose into her back, and she turned to give him a pat. "Yes, I know. You're ready to get out of here. We're going home."

The rain started pouring down in earnest as they drove onto the coast road. The first thing Melanie saw as she rounded the curve was the black police car sitting at the curb outside the inn. Her pulse raced as she thought it could be Ben stopping by, but in the next instant, she reminded herself that it could also be Detective Dutton.

Liza confirmed her thoughts as she gazed through the windshield at the car. "Oh, bugger. It looks like Grumpy Dutton is back. Has he come to arrest Joe after all?"

Melanie could feel the tension in her shoulders as she parked the car in the garage. Max leapt to the ground the moment she opened the door and dashed past her, heading for the house. Liza followed more slowly, her face creased in a worried frown.

Beatrice met them at the door, apparently on her way out. "That horrible detective is here," she hissed at Melanie as she pulled the hood of her jacket over her head. "He was asking me all kinds of questions, and now he's talking to Gloria. I'm going for a walk. I don't want to run into him again."

She stepped out into the rain, hunched her shoulders, and set off down the street.

"Will she be okay?" Liza watched the woman for a moment trudging down the road before closing the front door. "It's raining quite hard out there."

"She probably won't go far." Melanie took off her jacket and hung it in the closet. She waited for Liza to shed her coat and scarf before heading down the hallway to the kitchen. "I wonder why Dutton is talking to Gloria," she said as she opened the fridge door. "Do you think he's asking her about Joe? Eileen said she thought the two of them were close. Maybe Dutton thinks Gloria knows what happened that night."

"Who knows what that man thinks?" Liza picked up the kettle and took it over to the sink. "He even suspects us of killing Walter, for heaven's sake. That tells you what a total idiot he is." She stuck the kettle under the faucet and turned it on. "I have to admit, I find it rather intriguing to be a murder suspect."

"You wouldn't think it was so exciting if Dutton took you away in handcuffs and threw you in jail."

Apprehension spread over Liza's face. "You don't really think that would happen, do you? I mean, you hear all the time of innocent people being arrested for a crime they didn't commit."

Melanie smiled. "Don't worry. I wouldn't let that happen to you. I'd have a lawyer at your side before you ever got close to jail."

"Well, as long as it isn't Gary." Liza stood the kettle on the stove. "I'd rather go to jail than deal with that skunk."

"It won't be Gary," Melanie promised her. She took a soda out of the fridge and closed the door. "Besides, I would think that our guests would be stronger suspects than either of us. The only reason we were included was because we were in the house the night Walter died. I guess Dutton can't rule anyone out until the investigation turns up the killer."

"Which had better be in the next two days, or we'll have a huge problem on our hands."

Melanie carried her soda to the nook and sat down. "I know. I guess we should contact someone and find out what arrangements can be made for our guests if they can't leave town on Sunday."

"That someone should be Ben." Liza sat down at the table. "He was the one who told you they'd make arrangements."

"I guess I could call him." Melanie pulled her cell phone from her pants pocket. "He probably won't be there." She dialed the number and waited.

Nadine, one of the police station's administrative assistants, answered right away and told her that Ben was not at the station and wasn't expected back that day. "I can give you his cell number," the assistant added, "if it's important."

Melanie wasn't sure how she felt about that. She'd always called him at the station. Calling his personal cell phone with police business seemed like an invasion of privacy. "Thank you," she said at last, "but I'll just leave a message for him, if that's okay."

"Sure. I'll tell him you called." The line clicked, cutting her off.

Melanie slipped the phone back in her pocket and found Liza watching her. Answering her grandmother's unspoken question, she said, "Nadine wanted to give me Ben's cell phone number."

Liza's eyebrows twitched. "You didn't want it?"

"I didn't want to invade his privacy with police business."

"You could have taken his number down, just in case you need it sometime."

"Then Nadine wouldn't have given him the message."

Liza sighed. "Why is romance so complicated these days? When I met your grandfather, there was none of this ducking and bobbing around, trying to figure out our next step. We met and felt a spark. Then he asked me out and boom, fireworks. That simple."

Melanie rolled her eyes. "And what I keep telling you is that there is no romance as far as Ben is concerned. There never will be. No spark. No boom. No fireworks."

"I don't believe that for one second. The spark is there. I can see it in the way you look at each other. It just needs a little flame to set off the fireworks."

For long seconds Melanie struggled between the desire to keep her feelings private and the need to set her grandmother straight once and for all. The need won. "Ben wants children. I can't give them to him. End of story."

The kettle started whistling, but Liza ignored it, her stricken eyes staring at her granddaughter. "Oh, Mel. I'm so sorry. I didn't even think . . ."

"I'm fine with things the way they are." Melanie softened her next words with a smile. "Just let it go, okay?"

Liza wiped two fingers across her mouth. "Not one word." She lowered her hand. "Well, maybe just one more. Ben is a good man—and they are hard to find. I'm sure if he knew what happened and why, he wouldn't let that dictate his feelings." She got up and walked over to the stove. "You could always adopt children, you know."

Melanie winced. How she hated that phrase. Why couldn't anyone understand that she desperately wanted her own children? Her own flesh and blood? Yes, she could adopt. And she could love her adopted children. But there would always be that underlying ache, that constant longing. Always wondering what kind of person a child of her own would have grown up to be. She was certain that Ben would also feel that way, and she just couldn't deny him that chance to hold in his arms another baby of his own.

The whistling stopped as Liza filled the teapot with boiling water. She opened the cabinet door and took down a mug. "Want a cup?"

"No thanks. I have my soda." Melanie reached for the can but paused with her hand in midair when Gloria barged into the room.

The woman's eyes were red rimmed and smudged with mascara. Her usual immaculate hair hung in wisps around her face, and she seemed to have trouble getting her breath. She stared wildly at Melanie, her hand hovering at her throat.

Melanie could hardly breathe herself. Something bad must have happened to get Gloria so upset. She prayed this wasn't another deadly blow to the Merry Ghost Inn.

"Sit down here," Liza told the stricken woman, guiding her onto a chair.

Gloria slumped down and buried her face in her hands.

"Whatever is the matter?" Liza asked. "Are you in pain? Do you need a doctor?"

Gloria shook her head, mumbling, "What I need is a drink."

"We just have wine . . . wait." Liza rushed back to the cabinets and opened a door. "We have a bottle of brandy in here we sometimes use in cooking. Ah, here it is." She pulled out a bottle and closed the cabinet door. "It will have to be in a wineglass."

She uncapped the bottle and poured a generous amount in a glass as Gloria sat shuddering with her elbows on the table and her hands covering her face.

"Here." Liza placed the drink in front of her. "Take a good swig of that. You'll feel better in no time."

Gloria slowly lowered her hands, stared at the glass for a long moment, then lifted it with a shaking hand to her mouth. She gulped, flinched, and screwed up her face in a grimace of pain.

"There!" Liza beamed. "Doesn't that feel better?"

It seemed to Melanie that Gloria was feeling anything but better. Then, to her surprise, the woman nodded, lifted the glass again, and took another gulp.

Liza sat down at the table, and Melanie took a seat next to her.

They waited while Gloria drained the glass and let out a long sigh. "Oh, God. What am I going to do?"

Liza leaned forward and covered the woman's shaking hand. "Why don't you tell us what happened?"

Gloria stared at her with anxious blue eyes. "I've been accused of murder. That's what's happened. Me. Gloria Olsen, who's never had a traffic ticket or missed a mortgage payment in my life." Her voice started rising. "That disgusting man accused me of killing Walter!"

Liza struggled back to her feet. "Hold on." She grabbed the glass and carried it over to the counter, where she poured another few fingers of brandy.

The second she put it in front of Gloria, the woman snatched it up and took another long gulp. Apparently the liquor no longer burned, as she hardly flinched this time. "Joe found a note," she said, her head nodding up and down as if to confirm her words. "It was lying close to Walter's hand. He must have been holding it when he fell."

She leaned forward, her eyes now shining and watery. "Did you know Joe found Walter's body in the middle of the night?"

She shook her head. "He never told us about that, did he? Why didn't he tell us about that? He should have told us about that."

Her words were beginning to slur, and Melanie watched in alarm as Gloria took another swig of the brandy. Much more of that and the woman would be flat on her back.

Liza apparently realized the same thing, as she moved the glass out of Gloria's reach while saying gently, "Maybe we should go a little slower on the booze."

Maybe her grandmother shouldn't have given Gloria a second glass, Melanie thought, but she wisely kept her mouth shut.

"Did the detective tell you what was on the note?" Liza asked as Gloria's eyes began to flutter.

"Of course he did." Gloria leaned forward, then jerked back, as if afraid of toppling over. "He thought I wrote it."

Melanie caught her breath. "Why would he think that?"

"Because it was signed with my name." Gloria raised her hand and pointed an unsteady finger at Melanie. "You know I wouldn't write a note to Walter and invite him to meet me on the balcony in the middle of the night, don't you?"

Melanie gave her a solemn nod. "Of course I do."

"Well, then, tell that to that miserable cop. I didn't write the note. I gave him a sample of my handwriting to prove it, but he didn't seem too convinced." Gloria pounded the table with her fist, making Melanie jump. "I didn't meet Walter on the balcony that night, and I sure as hell didn't shove him off it." She closed her eyes and swayed backward. "I think I need to lie down."

Melanie exchanged an anxious glance with Liza.

"I'll put her in my room to sleep it off." Liza stood up again. "She'll never make it up the stairs." She took hold of Gloria's arm. "Come on, dearie, let's go have a nice snooze. You need to be wide awake for the séance tonight."

Melanie jumped up to help, and between them they got a wobbly Gloria to Liza's room and on the bed.

"She's going to have one heck of a headache when she wakes up," Liza said, closing the door.

"Well, you did get a little lavish with the brandy." Melanie followed her grandmother back to the kitchen. "Why did you give her so much?"

"Well, in the first place, she said she needed a drink, and in the second place, I thought it might loosen her tongue. It's worked before when we needed someone to tell us something. It's surprising what you can learn from a person under the influence. I didn't think she'd drink the whole of that second glass, though."

"You are devious."

"Maybe, but I get results. Do you think she wrote that note? I was wondering how someone managed to get Walter out onto the balcony alone that late at night. Simple, when you think about it. A note from the woman he had the hots for, inviting him to meet her after everyone had gone to bed."

"I don't think Gloria wrote that note." Melanie sat down once more at the table and picked up her soda.

"You don't?" Liza sat down too. "Why?"

"I don't know why. Just a gut feeling. I just can't see her pushing Walter to his death just because he made a pass or two at her. Gloria's a strong woman. She could squash him like a bug any time she felt like it."

"Well, then, if Gloria didn't write the note, who did?" Liza frowned. "Do you think Joe could have written it himself?" She shook her head and answered her own question. "No, of course he didn't. If he had, he wouldn't have taken it to the cops. He would have simply destroyed it."

"I guess that leaves Nick." Melanie stared at her empty can of soda. "Then again, I can't imagine Nick killing Walter just because he made fun of him."

"I think we're forgetting something here." Liza leaned back. "We're forgetting about Amy being blackmailed. She had a strong motive to get rid of Walter. I'm surprised Grumpy didn't question her too."

Melanie stared at her grandmother. "You think Amy might have killed Walter?"

"I think the sisters could have planned it together. Eileen is very protective of Amy. I can imagine her going after someone threatening her sister. Can't you?"

Reluctantly, Melanie nodded. "I guess so. We should have another chat with them. Not that they're likely to admit anything."

"No, but as I've said before, they might let something slip that we can use against them." Liza stood, and wincing a little, she stepped away from the table. "But first, I want to talk to Joe and ask him about that note."

"He didn't want to talk to us last night."

"That was before Gloria was accused of murder. He might be more eager to talk now."

"I guess we can try." Melanie looked out the window. "It's still raining. He's probably in the living room watching TV."

"Then let's go and find him." Liza trotted to the door. "We can offer him a cup of tea."

"He'll probably prefer a beer."

"We don't have any beer, do we?"

"No. We still have a little brandy left. Not much after you plastered Gloria with it."

"Yes, I don't think we have enough to loosen Joe's tongue. We'll just have to hope he feels like talking." With that, she opened the door and charged into the hallway.

Chapter 11

Following her grandmother to the living room, Melanie hoped they would find Joe alone.

He was sitting on the couch, watching a soccer game. "I'd rather be watching football," he said as he reached for the remote and turned off the TV, "but this is okay. I have to grab the chance to watch while the ladies are out. They don't like sports programs, and I'm a little outnumbered here."

Melanie smiled. "Where are the ladies?"

"The sisters and Beatrice are out on the porch, watching the rain."

Liza raised her eyebrows. "Really? It's a little chilly out there."

Joe shrugged. "They said they needed some fresh air."

"We were wondering if you'd like a cup of tea," Liza said, sitting down on the couch next to him.

Joe looked at her as if she'd sprouted horns. "Tea? I don't think so. But thanks."

Liza smiled. "I'd offer you a beer, except we don't have any."

"We have wine," Melanie told him, feeling uneasy as Joe's dark gaze rested on her face.

"I'm good. Thanks." Joe looked back at Liza. "Is there something else you wanted?"

"Yes." Liza looked him straight in the eye. "We want to know about the note you found by Walter's body."

Joe's features hardened. "What about it?"

"You didn't mention it when we talked about it before."

"I didn't think it was any of your business."

"What happens at this inn is my business." Liza raised her chin. "We have a business to run here, and it's suffering because of what happened to Walter. We need to get this case solved so that you can all go home. Now is there anything else you haven't told us or the cops?"

For a long, tense moment they stared at each other, and Melanie held her breath.

Finally, Joe's shoulders relaxed. "Look, I didn't tell you or the cops about the note because I was trying to protect Gloria. I thought she'd killed Walter, and I didn't want to be the one who turned her in."

Liza leaned back. "Of course you didn't. But what about the person you saw on the balcony that night? Did you tell the cops about that?"

Joe looked sheepish. "I didn't see anyone. I just told you that to take the focus off Gloria."

Melanie sat down on an armchair. "The note asked Walter to meet Gloria on the balcony?"

"Yes." Joe stretched out his legs and stared at his shoes. "I was so sure she'd killed him. It nearly did me in to think that, but I wasn't going to be responsible for her getting caught."

"And now?"

"And now what?" Joe lifted a hand and let it drop. "Do I still think she killed him? I don't know. I don't know what to think."

"Well," Liza said briskly, "it's obvious the police don't think she did it, or she would be behind bars right now."

"Or maybe they just don't have enough evidence." Joe looked up at her. "I wouldn't blame her if she did kill him. He was a miserable bastard who wouldn't leave her alone."

There was so much venom in his voice that Melanie's blood ran cold. If she had to choose between Joe, Nick, and Gloria for a major suspect in the murder, Joe would win hands down.

"He ruined her life, you know," Joe added, leaning his back against the cushions. "She was in love with a rich dude, and it looked like he was going to propose, until Walter stepped in and told him some lies about her. The guy dumped her. Just about broke her heart." He sat up again. "There were times I felt like murdering him myself."

Liza's thoughts had to be running along the same lines. "So why did the police take you to the station for questioning? They must have had a reason."

It seemed as if Joe wasn't going to answer, but then he muttered, "Someone told the detective I was out in the driveway that night. He wouldn't tell me who it was that told him."

Maybe it was just as well, Melanie thought, or judging by Joe's tone, whoever had tattled on him would be in a lot of trouble by now.

"I finally figured I had to tell him about the note," Joe went on, "or I was going to end up in jail. Much as I like Gloria, I wasn't about to take the rap for her."

Apparently Liza was satisfied with his answers, as she stood up. "Thank you, Joe, for talking to us. We're doing our best to find out who was responsible for Walter's death. You've been very helpful, and we appreciate it."

Joe actually looked surprised. "Sure. If there's anything else I can do to help, just let me know."

"We certainly will. I hope we'll see you at the séance tonight?"

"I'll be there." He picked up the remote again. "But I have to tell you, I don't believe in all that crap. Like your ghost. That laughing sound you hear? It's air bubbles in the pipes somewhere."

Liza smiled. "If you say so." She looked at Melanie. "You know, I could use a little fresh air myself. Want to join me?"

Melanie jumped up. "Sure." She waited until they were out in the hallway before asking her grandmother, "Do you think he was telling the truth? About the note, I mean. He could be lying about trying to protect Gloria. He could have killed Walter and given the note to the police to put the blame on her."

"He could have," Liza agreed as she paused to take her jacket out of the hall closet. "But then, if that were so, why didn't he give the note to Grumpy right away?"

Melanie grabbed her own jacket off its hanger. "There is that, I guess."

"Besides, I've seen the way he looks at Gloria. There's definitely something there. Remember Eileen saying she thought there was something going on between them?"

"So if Joe didn't write the note, and Gloria didn't, that leaves the sisters and Beatrice."

"And Nick," Liza reminded her. "Or even Cindi. We haven't ruled either of them out yet." She opened the front door. "I'd like to know who told Grumpy that Joe was in the driveway that night. As far as we know, nobody knew that except you and me. Until now, at least." She stepped outside, squinting at the sky, then turned back to look at Melanie. "I think that whoever told the detective that Joe was standing over Walter's dead body could have been the person who killed him."

Melanie stared at her. "But wouldn't Dutton figure that out?"

"Not necessarily. Our killer is obviously an accomplished liar. He or she would have made up a story of how he or she happened to see Joe in the driveway. Without hard evidence, as the cops are so fond of saying, Dutton's hands are tied."

"Well, if Dutton wouldn't tell Joe who told him that, he's definitely not going to tell us."

"You're probably right." Liza looked along the porch. "The sisters are over there. Let's go talk to them."

She took off to where the sisters sat together on the swing. Beatrice sat in a rocking chair, hunched up against the cool wind in spite of her hat, gloves, and thick scarf. Eileen and Amy seemed not to notice the cold as they greeted Liza.

Melanie reached them as Liza was saying, "I see the rain has stopped. We might even get a spot of sunshine before the day is out."

"That would be nice." Eileen smiled at Melanie. "That was a good breakfast this morning. We enjoyed it, didn't we, Amy?"

Amy nodded. "Yes, we did."

Liza looked pleased. "Thank you. We do our best. You will be coming to the séance tonight, I hope?"

Eileen's eyes brightened. "We'll be there. We wouldn't miss it, would we, Amy?"

"Wouldn't miss it," Amy echoed.

Liza turned to Beatrice. "What about you? Will you be joining us tonight?"

Beatrice appeared to be thinking it over as it took her a moment or two to respond. "I've never been to a séance. I don't really believe in them."

"You didn't believe in ghosts, either, until you heard this one laughing," Eileen said, her voice a little sharp.

"Everyone is coming," Liza said, smiling at the solemn woman. "We'd love to have you join us."

Beatrice finally gave in. "All right. As long as everyone else is going."

"Good." Liza sounded relieved. "Then we'll see you all tonight."

"We were wondering if you've heard anything from the police about when we can go home." Eileen nudged her sister's arm. "Weren't we, Amy?"

"Yes," Amy said, her voice trembling just a bit. "We were wondering."

"All this is nonsense." Beatrice turned up the collar of her coat. "I don't think anyone killed Walter. If you ask me, he was the one who sawed through those railings and fell through them while doing it."

Melanie stared at her. It was an interesting theory, and one they hadn't thought of yet. "What makes you think that?" She moved over to Beatrice's chair and took the one next to her.

"Walter was upset the night of the party. He was belligerent and threatening. Who knows what was in his mind? He could have planned to get rid of someone. Like that magician. He really didn't like him."

"That's crazy," Eileen said sharply. "It's more likely the magician killed Walter."

Amy whimpered. "I wish we didn't keep talking about Walter. It gives me nightmares."

"She's right." Eileen gave Melanie a murderous glare, as if it was all her fault. "We'd just like to know if we can go home on Sunday. This hasn't been exactly a relaxing vacation, by any means."

"I've left a message at the police station to talk to someone about what arrangements can be made." Melanie looked at Amy. "I'm sorry. I wish this hadn't happened, of course, but there's not a lot my grandmother and I can do about it. It's up to the police now."

"Unless," Liza said as she sat down next to Eileen, "someone can tell us something helpful about the night Walter died." She looked at Eileen. "Like who told the police that Joe was in the driveway that night, standing over Walter's body."

Eileen stared up at her. "Joe found Walter's body? That night? Why didn't he tell someone?"

"I guess he was afraid he'd be blamed for the murder," Melanie said.

Amy whimpered again.

"Someone must have seen him and told the detective," Liza added.

"Well, it wasn't me," Eileen declared. She put an arm around Amy's shoulders. "And it wasn't her. Was it, Amy?"

Amy shook her head.

"Maybe you should ask the magician," Beatrice said. "He could have told the police. After all, he wasn't inside the house that night, like the rest of us were."

Eileen looked relieved. "Of course, that must be it. He could have seen Joe in the driveway. He probably was there to make sure that Walter was dead after he pushed him off the balcony."

Liza threw a look at Melanie. "Well, none of you will be going home until the murder is solved. So if anyone thinks of something that might help, I hope you will come and tell us." She stood up.

"It was a nice party, though," Eileen said. "It was a shame someone had to go and spoil it. Everyone was having such a good time."

Liza smiled. "Thank you. Though I do wish we'd hired a piano player. I always think there's nothing like a rousing sing-along to liven up a party."

Beatrice looked up at her. "I thought you played the piano."

Liza's face registered astonishment. "How did you know that?"

Beatrice pointed to Liza's hands. "You have piano hands. My mother had long, slender fingers like yours, and she was a wonderful pianist."

"Well, thank you," Liza said again, looking somewhat confused.

"It's getting too cold to sit here." Beatrice struggled up from her chair. "I'm going inside where it's warm." Hunching her shoulders, she shuffled along the porch and disappeared into the house.

Watching her leave, Eileen shook her head. "Don't mind her," she said. "Beatrice is a good woman, but she's missing a few stitches in her sweater, if you know what I mean. I think it was the shock of losing her husband that way."

Liza, obviously sensing a story, sat down again. "She lost her husband?"

Eileen nodded and sent a searching look at the door, as if afraid that Beatrice was still hovering there. "Beatrice told us all about it when she first joined the book club. It happened about five years ago. Beatrice's husband, Steven, owned a construction company in Portland. His project manager was on the take. He was using cheap products, then charging the customers for the most expensive stuff and keeping the difference. Of course, eventually people complained about the shoddy work and started suing Steve's company. The media got hold of it, and it was all over the news. The business went downhill, and things got so bad, Steve couldn't take it anymore. He ended up hanging himself. Beatrice was the one who found him."

Liza seemed to take a long time digesting the news, and Melanie felt like crying. Poor Beatrice. No wonder she was always looking so miserable and defeated. She wanted to go back in the house and give the woman a big hug.

"That's so sad," Liza said, getting up again. "I lost my husband too not so long ago. But he died from a heart attack. I can only imagine how Beatrice must have felt, knowing her husband had taken his own life."

Eileen sighed. "I think it did something to her mind. She gets confused a lot. She means well, though, and she can hold her own in our book discussions. She loves to read."

"So do I." Liza shivered as a gust of wind ruffled her hair. "And on that note, I'm going inside to finish my book."

Melanie jumped up. "Me too. It's getting cold out here."

Eileen looked at Amy, who seemed unaffected by anything that was said. "We'd better go in too. Right, Amy?"

Amy nodded and waited for her sister to stand before getting up.

"I guess we'll see you at the séance tonight, then." Eileen took hold of her sister's arm.

"Will there be refreshments?" Amy asked.

Eileen looked at her. "You're always thinking about your stomach."

"Of course there'll be refreshments," Melanie hurried to assure them.

"I was just asking so I wouldn't eat too much for dinner," Amy said, giving her sister a resentful scowl.

"You can always find room for more. You eat twice as much as I do." Eileen started down the porch, propelling her sister along with her. They could still be heard arguing as they disappeared into the house.

"I hope they settle that before the séance," Liza said as she headed for the front door. "We don't need any tension there tonight."

"I would imagine there'll be plenty of tension if Sharon starts talking to Walter's spirit." Melanie followed her grandmother inside and closed the door. "They'll all be watching each other like hawks."

"Well, let's hope somebody gives us something we can work with." Liza headed for the kitchen. "We'd better get started on those refreshments. We don't want to disappoint Amy."

Melanie laughed. "We haven't yet. What are we making for tonight?"

"Not much. They'll all probably have eaten dinner, so they won't be that hungry." She opened a cabinet door and peered at the shelves. "Crackers and cheese, some fruit. I can whip up some miniature mince pies." She reached up to a shelf. "We can open these tins of mixed nuts." She took two cans of the nuts and dropped them on the counter. "We have chips and dip we can put out." She looked at Melanie. "How about making some of your scrumptious brandy balls? Amy would love those."

"Eileen would probably ration her." Melanie opened another cabinet. "I think I have a couple of boxes of wafers in here somewhere. Ah, here they are." She took down two boxes and checked the pull date on them. "Yep. We're in business."

"Great!" Liza beamed. "Then let's get to work."

*   *   *

Cindi arrived shortly before eight, frazzled and out of breath. "Sorry I'm late. Nick had an emergency, and I was waiting for him, but it looks like he'll be stuck in the park for a while longer. Someone backed into a power box, and he has to fix it." She stared at the island counter, where Liza had laid out the refreshments. "Wow. You two have been busy. This looks awesome."

Liza smiled. "We did what we could, considering it was an unplanned event."

Cindi reached out to the pyramid of brandy balls and plucked one off the top.

Melanie watched her intently as the assistant took a bite.

Cindi chewed for a second or two, and then her wary expression changed to one of sheer ecstasy. "This is totally lush. What is it?"

"A brandy ball," Liza told her, "and you're only allowed one."

"How come? I'm over twenty-one."

"We need our assistant sober for the evening."

Cindi grinned. "Better lock them up, then. Did you make them?"

"Melanie made them."

Looking at Melanie, Cindi nodded. "Good stuff. They won't last long." She reached her hand toward the plate, but Liza gave it a soft slap. "They're for the guests. If there's any left over at the end of the evening, you can have another one then."

"Yes, ma'am."

"We'd better get these dishes into the dining room," Melanie said, glancing at the clock. "Sharon should be here any minute."

"I'll take care of it." Cindi grabbed up the plate of brandy balls and a plate of tiny pastries. "What are these?"

"They're mince pies," Liza told her. "You can have one when you finish taking all this into the dining room. I saved some for us to eat later."

Cindi hoisted the brandy balls higher. "I hope you kept some of these too."

"I did," Melanie assured her. "Here, I'll help." She picked up the tray of cheese and fruit in one hand and the plate of crackers in the other.

Just as Cindi reached the door, the bell rang in the hallway. "I hope that's Nick," she said, pausing to look back at Liza.

"I'll get the door. You two get this stuff into the dining room." Liza hurried out into the hallway.

Melanie followed Cindi to the dining room, where expectant faces turned in their direction as they walked in. Beatrice and the sisters sat at one end of the long table, which was actually the smaller tables pushed together and covered with a black sheet. Two tall silver candlesticks sat on the table, with a bowl of yellow chrysanthemums nestled between them.

Joe stood with his back to the window, talking to Gloria, who sat on a chair next to him.

Melanie placed her tray on the buffet table, greeting everyone with a smile. "We should be able to get started soon," she told them. "Meanwhile, help yourself to the refreshments."

Amy shot up from her chair and scurried over to the table. "Are those brandy balls? Oh, my. Can I have one?"

Eileen loomed up behind her. "You'd better go easy on those. They can be potent."

Ignoring her, Amy plucked two of the balls from the pyramid. She had to open her mouth wide to stuff one of them in and then almost choked as she tried to chew on it.

Eileen clicked her tongue in annoyance but said nothing as she hooked a square of cheddar cheese from the tray.

"I'll get the rest of it," Cindi said and left the room.

Seconds later, the door opened again, and Liza walked in, followed by Sharon. "This is our medium," she announced. "Sharon Sutton. She's going to entertain us tonight by communicating with the spirits."

Sharon waved and smiled, looking almost unrecognizable with a purple-and-gold silk scarf wound around her head like a turban and her eyelids heavy with false eyelashes and purple shadow. She wore a black skirt and a silk purple blouse with long lace-edged sleeves, reminding Melanie of a fortune-teller she'd consulted one year at the Portland Rose Festival.

The woman had predicted a happy and successful life with a handsome, loving husband and three children. She couldn't have been more wrong.

Liza went around the room introducing Sharon to everyone. Joe seemed ill at ease and barely nodded at the shop owner when Liza announced his name. Gloria looked nervous and kept fiddling with the tassels on her gold-fringed top.

Beatrice greeted Sharon like an old friend. "We've met," she said as Liza introduced her. "I bought this sweater in your shop."

"Of course you did." Sharon smiled at her. "It looks very nice on you." She turned her head to look at the sisters. "I've also met these two."

Amy was still trying to digest the brandy ball and flapped her hand at Sharon, and Eileen gave her a curt nod. "Nice to see you again," she said, her expression suggesting the opposite. Apparently she had taken a dislike to the shop owner for some reason.

Cindi arrived back in the room with more refreshments and set them down on the buffet table.

"We'll be holding the séance in a few minutes," Liza announced as a hush fell over the room. "So go ahead and enjoy the food. Cindi will pour wine for anyone who wants a drink." She glanced at Joe. "Sorry we don't have any beer."

"I'm okay with wine," he told her.

"More than okay," Gloria murmured, earning a resentful frown from him.

Amy giggled and nudged her sister's arm. "We like wine too, don't we?"

Eileen's answer was a scathing look that made her sister visibly cringe.

Melanie felt sorry for the younger woman. Obviously the sisters were at odds over something, and it hadn't yet been resolved.

"This all looks very appetizing," Sharon said as she walked over to the buffet.

Melanie watched her stack her plate with cheese and fruit and balance a couple of mince pies alongside. "We're putting you at the head of the table," she said, gesturing at the empty chair at the farthest end of the table. "You can eat there."

Sharon smiled her thanks, then walked over to the chair and sat down.

Amy seemed fascinated by the woman and kept glancing over at her as she loaded her own plate with a sampling of everything on the table.

Joe appeared to be having an earnest conversation with Gloria, who kept tossing her head as if disbelieving whatever he was saying.

Eileen had filled a plate for Beatrice and, carrying her own plate in the other hand, took her friend's food over to her as Amy trailed behind her back to the table.

Melanie could almost feel the tension in the room. Nobody seemed relaxed, except perhaps for Beatrice, who sat nodding, her eyelids drooping as if she were ready to fall asleep at any minute, despite Sharon chattering in her ear.

Liza wandered over to Melanie, chewing on a handful of nuts. "Look at this lot," she muttered, sending a glance around the room. "They look like they're at a funeral service."

Melanie smiled. "They're probably apprehensive about the séance."

"Yes, well, someone in this room should be seriously worrying about now." She sent another searching look around the room. "The problem is, they all look worried. I was hoping we'd pick up some vibes of guilt from someone, but it's hard to tell with this gloomy bunch."

Melanie looked at her watch. "Speaking of the séance, shouldn't we be getting started?"

Liza sighed. "I was hoping Nick would be here by now. I warned Sharon he would be here, moving things around. She loved the idea. It looks like she'll be disappointed, though." She nodded at Cindi, who stood by the window with a glass of wine in one hand and a mince pie in the other.

The assistant quickly drained her glass, then sauntered over to them. "What's up?"

"We need to start the séance now." Liza took the empty glass from her and set it down on the table. "We'll have to go without Nick."

Cindi looked frustrated. "I'll give him a call. You guys go ahead. I'll wait for him to get here, and if the séance is still going, we'll sneak into the room somehow so he can do his thing." She pulled a cell phone from her pocket. "Just make sure it's good and dark in here."

"We'll just have candles burning," Melanie assured her. "In fact, you can go ahead and light them now." She reached for the gas lighter in the buffet drawer and handed it to Cindi.

"Sounds good." The assistant took the lighter and walked over to the table, where she leaned across to light the candles. "Hope everyone has a good time," she said as Gloria sat down at the table.

Melanie watched Joe walk over to the table and take a seat next to Gloria. Neither of them had come near the buffet table. Apparently they weren't hungry.

Cindi brought the lighter back and handed it to Melanie, then snatched a brandy ball from the table, grinning as Liza uttered a sound of protest. "Just in case they're all gone by the time I get back." She took a bite out of it and sailed out the room.

"All right, everyone!" Liza looked at Sharon. "Are you ready, medium?"

"I am." Sharon folded her hands in front of her and looked serious.

Melanie waited until everyone was settled before turning off the lights. The room was plunged into darkness, with just a faint glow from the flickering candles.

Someone uttered a nervous gasp, and Melanie guessed it was Amy. She made her way to the table, where Liza was already seated. She could barely make out faces in the dim light and wondered how Liza's plan could possibly work if they couldn't read the expressions on the faces of their guests.

"Don't you have a crystal ball?" Gloria demanded, temporarily breaking the eerie atmosphere.

"I don't need a crystal ball." Sharon had dropped her voice to a low, husky drawl, bringing a chill to the room again. "I talk directly to the spirits. But I need complete and utter silence or you will scare them all away."

Amy uttered a soft giggle and was immediately shushed by her sister.

For several long, tense-filled moments, the only sound in the room was the heavy breathing of someone at the table. Then Sharon moaned, making Melanie jump.

"I see a young woman." Sharon swayed on her chair. "She is trying to reach someone here. Her name begins with the letter . . . *C*."

Gloria uttered a gasp. "My niece! She died many years ago in a skiing accident. What does she want?"

Sharon did some more back and forth swaying before answering, "She wants you to know she's well and happy."

Melanie almost choked. The woman was dead. How the heck did well and happy work for her?

Gloria, however, sounded emotional when she said, "I'm so glad. Tell her we all miss her."

Melanie squinted at her through the haze of flickering light. Surely Gloria wasn't swallowing all this? How in the world did Sharon hit on a real dead person connected to someone in the group? Had she and Gloria cooked this up beforehand? But then they had acted as if they'd just met for the first time that evening.

Liza leaned closer to her and whispered, "She's good."

Good enough to make Melanie uncomfortable. She nodded at her grandmother, then jumped again as Sharon let out a louder moan. "Who at this table has recently lost a husband?"

Melanie looked at her grandmother. This, she knew, had to be rehearsed beforehand. Presumably Sharon knew that Liza's husband had died two years ago.

It was Beatrice, however, who answered the medium. "I did," she said quietly.

Sharon nodded. "He wants you to know he's sorry and he loves you."

There was a long pause before Beatrice muttered, "Thank you."

"Oh!"

Sharon's loud exclamation made everyone sit up. She sat swaying back and forth for several seconds before uttering a long, chilling moan. "Oh, the poor man. I can see him now, falling, falling . . ." Her voice trailed off, and she clutched her throat.

Melanie strained to see the faces staring at Sharon, but they were mostly pale blobs in the shadows.

Just then a soft laugh echoing above her head made Melanie go cold, until she remembered Nick. Cindi must have smuggled him into the room while everyone's attention was on Sharon. She peered around the room but could see nothing but the dark walls and curtained windows.

"What was that?" Eileen's sharp voice cut through the silence.

"Hush," Sharon murmured. "You will disturb the spirits." She swayed some more. "He died quite recently. His spirit is very much alive in this room."

As if in answer to her, a tiny pinpoint of blue light danced across the ceiling.

A laser beam, Melanie told herself. Nick was inventive.

Sharon looked up at the light. "He is trying to communicate with us."

The blue light traveled down the wall and rested on an empty chair by the window. All heads turned to watch it. Then very slowly, the chair started rocking—slowly at first, then faster and faster until it almost tipped over.

Amy uttered a little scream, and several gasps echoed around the table.

Melanie stared hard at the chair. She could see no one standing there. Nick must be dressed all in black with his face covered. Or there was some other trick to it. She let out her breath. Of course. He was a magician. He'd know how to pull off a trick like that. She'd have to congratulate him later.

The rest of the guests at the table were clearly unsettled. "This is ridiculous," Gloria said, her voice harsh with fear. "How did you do that?"

Sharon answered her in what was probably meant as a soothing tone but came off as creepy. "I didn't do anything. It was the spirit of the dead man."

"Dead men can't move chairs," Joe said, sounding a little strained.

"The spirits can do far more than you think." Sharon leaned back in her chair. "This man is telling me something. He is walking down the upstairs hallway. He has something in his hand. It's . . . it's . . ." Sharon paused for effect, then finished in a hushed voice, "It's an invitation."

Someone uttered a soft gasp, but Melanie couldn't be sure who it was.

Sharon leaned forward. "The man is excited. He's opening the door to the balcony." She lowered her voice again. "It's dark when he steps outside. He takes one step, then two, looking for the one who lured him there. He sees a shadow, moving toward him. Closer, closer, and then . . ."

Melanie's shoulders ached with apprehension. The silence was terrifying, as everyone seemed to be staring at Sharon, waiting for her to reveal the killer. Was this the moment they would finally find out who murdered Walter Dexter?

Chapter 12

"And then justice was served," Gloria said, in a low, throaty voice.

From the end of the table where the sisters sat came a hoarse "Amen."

An unmistakable nervous giggle from Amy broke the eerie tension. Eileen said something to her sister while Gloria declared, "I'm getting another glass of wine."

She stood up, and Joe stood up with her. "Give me your glass. I'll get it for you."

"I'd like one too," Beatrice piped up.

"I'll get the lights," Melanie said, pushing back her chair. "I think this séance is over."

"But I was just getting started," Sharon said as Melanie edged over to the wall and flipped the switch up, turning on the lights in the chandelier above the table.

"Thank you, Sharon," Liza said, getting slowly to her feet. "That was very entertaining. I'm sure we all enjoyed it, didn't we?"

Murmurs of agreement answered her.

Melanie studied the faces at the table. Gloria looked bored. Amy, as usual, was chewing on her lip, and Eileen's face was set in stone. Beatrice seemed ready to fall asleep, and Joe stood at the buffet table, concentrating on the wine he was pouring into Gloria's glass.

The chair by the window sat still now, and Melanie walked over to take a look at it. As far as she could see, there were no strings or straps attached to it. She'd have to ask Nick how he did it, she told herself.

Thinking of Nick reminded her that he was probably still somewhere in the house with Cindi, since there was no sign of him in the room. He must have slipped out again.

She looked for Liza and saw her sitting next to Sharon, where they appeared to be deep in conversation. She should find Nick and thank him, she decided. That trick with the chair had been the highlight of the whole séance.

She left the room and headed for the living room, fully expecting to see Cindi and Nick on the couch. The room was empty when she walked in, however, and she walked over to the window to look outside.

There was only one car in the driveway, and it wasn't Cindi's. She had to assume that the car belonged to Sharon. Cindi and Nick must have left already.

The door opened behind her, and Liza walked into the room. "Have you seen Cindi? I was hoping she'd stay and help us clean up."

"I can't see her car. I think she might have left." Melanie moved away from the window and sank on the couch. "Where's Sharon? Isn't that her car outside?"

"She's talking to Beatrice. They seemed to be enjoying the conversation, and I didn't want to interrupt them." Liza sat down next to her. "So what did you think of the séance?"

"It didn't tell us much." Melanie pulled her cell phone from her pocket and turned it on. There was one voice mail waiting for her; it was Ben telling her he was returning her call and would try to get hold of her tomorrow.

As always when she heard his deep voice, everything seemed a little warmer.

She was still enjoying the sensation when Liza asked, "Was that Ben?"

"Yes." She slipped the phone back in her pocket. "He called while I had the phone turned off. He said he'll call again tomorrow. We'll need to talk to him about relocating our guests. I wonder how long the police can hold them in town. There must be a limit if they're not under arrest."

"That's something else you'll have to ask Ben." Liza sighed. "I was so hoping we'd pick up something concrete tonight and solve the case before the weekend."

"Yeah. Like I said, this kind of thing only works in books."

"I imagine you're right." Liza chuckled. "The rocking chair caused quite a sensation, though. It even gave me goose bumps. Nick did a really good job. I didn't see him at all. Did you?"

"No, I didn't." Melanie sat up. "I wanted to thank him, but I guess he left with Cindi." The phone in her pocket buzzed against her hip, and she reached for it.

"Maybe that's Ben," Liza said, her face lighting up.

Melanie tried to ignore the little skip of her heart and spoke into the phone.

Cindi's voice answered her. "Sorry I had to bail on you. You were still doing the séance, so I couldn't tell you I was leaving. It's over now, though, right?"

"Yes," Melanie assured her. "They're finishing up the refreshments right now."

"Yeah, I figured it was over when you answered your phone. I was going to leave you a message. Tell Liza I'm sorry I couldn't help with the cleanup."

"That's okay. There's not much to do." Melanie frowned. Cindi had sounded upset. "Is everything okay?"

"Yeah, I guess. Nick was on his way over there and got a flat. He wasn't carrying a spare so I had to go take him mine. Now he can't get the car to start. I keep telling him that old junker is on its last legs, but he never listens to me. Anyway, he says to tell you he's sorry he didn't make it to the séance."

Melanie felt as if she'd been punched in the stomach. It took her a moment to get her breath back. "That's okay," she said at last. "We'll see you tomorrow. Thanks for letting us know."

Liza was watching her, curiosity playing across her face. "I take it that was Cindi?"

"Yes." Melanie slowly slid her phone into her pocket.

"Is she okay?"

"She's fine. Nick had a flat and she went to help him." She met Liza's anxious stare. "Nick says he's sorry he didn't make it to the séance."

Liza's face mirrored Melanie's confusion. "But the blue light? The rocking chair?"

They stared at each other for a few more seconds, then whispered in unison, "Orville."

For several long seconds, they sat mesmerized, until Liza stirred and stretched her feet out in front of her. "We'd better get this mess cleaned up or it will be midnight before we get to bed."

Melanie was still having trouble collecting her thoughts. Part of her still balked at accepting the fact that a ghost could make noises and move things around, yet she had witnessed just that with her own ears and eyes. Only the knowledge that everyone else had seen and heard the phenomena reassured her that she wasn't going crazy. Still, getting used to sharing the house with a ghost was going to take some time. Lots of time.

"Orville outdid himself tonight," Liza said as she helped Melanie carry what was left of the refreshments back to the kitchen. "That was spectacular but so ill-timed. If it hadn't been for him, we might have discovered our killer tonight."

"I doubt that. We're no closer to solving this murder than we were the day I found Walter's body." Melanie piled empty dishes in the sink and turned on the faucet. "It could still be any one of the guests sitting at that table."

"I know." Liza opened a tin and started fitting the leftover brandy balls into it. "Frustrating, isn't it? I do think, however, that we're a little closer. We just have to put all the pieces together."

"What pieces?" Melanie began rinsing plates and stacking them in the dishwasher.

"Little things we've learned about the guests. I think the clues are there. We just haven't connected them yet."

Melanie tried to remember their recent conversations with everyone, but her head hurt with the effort. "I'm tired," she said, "and you must be exhausted. Let's just go to bed and we'll worry about all this tomorrow."

Liza dropped mince pies into a plastic container and snapped on the lid. "Sounds good to me. At least Sharon had a good time tonight. Though I think she was disappointed it didn't last longer. She was really impressed with the rocking chair. I can't wait to see her face when I tell her our merry ghost did the rocking."

"She probably won't believe you." Melanie frowned. "I wonder how she knew about Gloria's dead niece."

"I think that was just a lucky shot in the dark. She just threw something out there and Gloria jumped on it."

"And Beatrice's late husband?"

"She knows your grandfather died not too long ago. I think she was expecting me to answer, but Beatrice got in there first."

Melanie closed the door of the dishwasher. "Well, you were right. She's good. And she proved my theory tonight."

"What theory?"

"That most mediums are fake."

"Oh, ye of little faith." Liza looked up at the ceiling. "Don't mind my granddaughter, Orville. She knows you're not a fake."

Melanie wasn't about to admit it, but she was a little disappointed that Orville didn't answer with one of his ghostly cackles.

She slept well that night and woke up to Max's loud snoring close to her ear. The dog lay spread eagle on his back, his ears twitching as he chased after some prey in his dreams.

It was Friday, she reminded herself. On Sunday four more guests would arrive, with no room to put them in, unless she found somewhere else for her current visitors to stay. All she could hope was that Ben would call her with arrangements for them.

It was still dark outside as she showered and dressed. When she opened the kitchen door to let Max out, however, thin streaks of light had begun to reach out toward the dark horizon of the ocean. She could barely see the outline of the massive rocks rising out of the water, but she could hear the wind rustling the branches of the hemlocks and the cries of the sea gulls welcoming the dawn.

It had to be cold out there in the yard, as Max barked to come back in shortly after she'd closed the door.

It was warm in the kitchen, though, and Max soon settled down in his bed. She had the coffee percolating when Liza walked in a few minutes later.

"For someone who has always been used to drinking tea first thing in the morning," Liza said, "I just adore the smell of coffee. There's nothing better to get the juices flowing."

Melanie laughed. "Spoken like a true American."

"I suppose I am." Liza poured coffee into a mug and joined Melanie in the nook. "I've been here twice as long as I lived in England."

"Do you ever miss it?"

"No, not anymore. When your grandfather died, I played with the idea of going back there for a long visit, but I just couldn't get up the enthusiasm to go." She gazed into her mug. "I thought I might try to find out what happened to your mother, but I decided to leave well enough alone." She looked up, and her eyes were bleak. "I'm sorry, Mel, but I honestly believe if your mother had wanted to come home, she would have. If she'd died, there would have been some record of it somewhere. I think she was so heartbroken about losing your father, she just cut her ties away from the memories and started a new life."

"And abandoned us." Melanie had a hard time swallowing past the lump in her throat. "How ironic is that. I can't have the child I want, and she had a child she didn't want."

Liza's hand shot out to cover hers. "Don't be bitter, Mel. We don't know that for sure. I'm sorry. I shouldn't have said all that. Don't give up your search for her. We both need closure on this, even if it's to learn she died."

"I don't know which would be the less painful." Melanie sighed and lifted her mug. "Anyway, we'd better get started on breakfast. What's on the menu today?"

Liza brightened. "It's specials day, so I thought we'd go with one of my Buckingham Palace recipes."

Melanie swallowed a shot of coffee and put down her mug. "Great! Which one?"

"How about pancakes royale? They're richer than American pancakes and so delicious. We can serve them with sausage, fried eggs, and mushrooms."

"They serve pancakes at Buckingham Palace?"

"Special pancakes. Trust me. The guests will love them. They're literally fit for a queen."

Melanie smiled. "Now I can't wait to try them."

"You'll love them." She glanced up at the clock. "Cindi should be here soon to set the tables. I wonder if they ever got Nick's car started."

"He probably stayed with her again last night. At least he won't have far to go to work."

Liza shook her head. "I still can't see those two together. He seems so standoffish and self-centered. Not at all who I would imagine Cindi would be interested in. She's just the opposite."

"Well, you know what they say"—Melanie got up from the table—"opposites attract. Though I do know what you mean. I think Josh would be a better fit for her. He's lively and outgoing, like she is."

"You're right! Why didn't I think of that?" Liza stood up, her empty mug in her hand. "Josh would be perfect for Cindi! Let's get them together."

Melanie sighed. "Isn't it enough that you keep matchmaking me? Now you have to start on Cindi?"

Liza grinned. "Love's what makes the world go around. I just like giving it a little helping hand now and again."

"Well, I don't think either Josh or Cindi would appreciate your efforts, so you might want to rethink that little scheme. Besides, I think Josh is interested in one of the assistants at the police station. He told me—"

A voice from the doorway interrupted her. "What wouldn't Cindi appreciate?"

Startled, they turned to stare at their assistant.

"Er . . . we were wondering if you'd met Josh Phillips. He's a local newspaper reporter." Melanie covered her embarrassment with a warm smile. "He stops in here now and again."

"He's a very nice young man," Liza began earnestly, "and we—" She broke off as Melanie gave her a sharp nudge with her elbow.

Cindi looked at Melanie. "What's going on?"

Melanie smiled back at her. "Nothing. We were just going to start breakfast. Did Nick get his car fixed?"

To her relief, after a probing look at both of them, Cindi shook her head. "Not yet. He's staying with me while it's in the shop." She slipped her purse off her shoulder and stashed it in the broom closet, then sauntered to the sink and washed her hands, drying them on a kitchen towel before pulling open the tableware drawer. "What are we going to do if the police haven't solved this murder by Sunday?" After taking down a small tray from the cabinet above, she started piling knives and forks on it.

"We were wondering the same thing," Liza said, heading for the fridge. "We're hoping the police can find somewhere for our guests to stay. That's if they still can't go home by then."

"I'm talking to Ben today." Melanie took a clean apron out of a drawer and tied it around her waist. "I'll find out as much as I can from him."

"Good." Cindi carried the tray over to the door. "They're all getting antsy about it. They keep asking me if I know when they can go home."

"I know. They ask us too." Melanie sighed. "I hope I can tell them something today."

"Let me know if you find out anything." Cindi balanced the tray on one arm and opened the door. "I can't wait for this whole thing to be over."

"She's not the only one," Liza murmured as the door closed behind their assistant. She opened the fridge door. "Okay, let's get started on these pancakes."

When Melanie sampled one of the pancakes later, she had to agree they were different from regular pancakes. They were lighter and fluffier, and the addition of lemon juice and sugar sprinkled on them gave them a tangy taste that went surprisingly well with the sausage, eggs, and mushrooms.

When Cindi reported that the guests were raving about them, Liza declared them a success and added them to their permanent menus.

"I've invited Josh to lunch," she announced when Cindi left the kitchen to clear off the tables in the dining room.

Melanie frowned. "I hope you're not figuring on getting him together with Cindi. I told you he was interested in someone else. Besides, Cindi already has a boyfriend. One who's living with her right now, I might add. Or did you forget that?"

Liza put on a hurt look. "Of course I didn't forget. And no, I'm not trying to get them together. There's something I want to ask Josh, and I thought it would be better to do it over lunch. Besides, Cindi isn't the only single young woman in this house, you know."

Melanie rolled her eyes. "Seriously? You just can't leave this alone, can you?"

Liza laughed. "I'm just kidding. I know you only have eyes for Ben. Anyway, what do we have in the fridge we can give Josh for lunch?"

Melanie pulled open the fridge door and inspected the contents. "Some ham, bacon, eggs, cheese, sausage . . . that's about it."

"Looks like my specialty grilled cheese sandwiches then." Liza looked up at the clock on the wall. "If it's not raining, I'd like to come with you on your walk with Max."

"I think that's an excellent idea. Just as soon as we get the dishes in the dishwasher, we'll go."

Upon hearing the word "go," Max leapt from his bed and padded over to the door, his tail stirring up a breeze behind him.

"Look at him," Liza said, giving him an admiring glance. "He understands every word we say."

"He's like a kid," Melanie said, opening up the dishwasher. "He understands what he wants to and ignores the rest."

Liza chuckled. "Ain't that the truth."

Cindi arrived in the kitchen just then and piled the used dishes onto the island counter. "I'm going up to clean the rooms," she said, heading back to the door. "Everyone should be outside by now. The sun's shining."

Melanie looked out the window. Cindi was right. The sun was shining through a hazy mist. Max was going to enjoy his walk.

As soon as the dishes were in the dishwasher and the kitchen was sparkling clean again, Liza went back to her room to get ready for the walk.

Melanie waited in the hallway for her, with an impatient Max straining on his leash. He turned his head as Eileen appeared at the foot of the stairs and walked toward them.

"Amy is lying down for a while," she said. "She has a migraine."

"Oh, I'm sorry." Melanie put her hand on Max's head to stop him bouncing around. "My grandmother had one of those a couple of nights ago. They can be brutal. Can I get some ibuprofen for her?"

"I've already given her some medication, thank you." Eileen looked at Max as if he were about to attack her. "That's a big dog. I don't like big dogs. You can't trust them."

"I promise you, you can trust this one." Melanie patted Max's head to take away the sting of the criticism.

Eileen looked unconvinced. "Yes, well, I was wondering if I might borrow one of your books in the living room to read. I've read the two I brought with me."

"Of course! Help yourself."

"Thank you. Oh, and I asked Cindi if she'd clean Amy's room later. I hope that's all right with you."

"Absolutely. Cindi won't mind at all. She's a very easygoing person."

"Yes, she is. I like her."

Melanie got the impression that Eileen didn't like too many people.

"I was a bit wary of her when I first saw her," Eileen went on. "All those weird clothes and that dreadful makeup. Underneath it all, though, I think she's a very kind and sensitive young woman."

"She is, which is surprising, considering her unfortunate upbringing."

Eileen's sharp eyes probed Melanie's face. "Oh? She's had some trouble in her life?"

Uncomfortable now that she was caught gossiping about her assistant, Melanie tried to brush it off. "She grew up in foster homes. That's never an ideal situation for a child."

"Oh, I know." Eileen looked over her shoulder, then turned back and said in a soft voice, "Amy fostered a child. She was told she couldn't have children, so she decided to foster a little girl. Crystal was a beautiful child, with blonde hair and the most gorgeous big blue eyes you ever saw. Amy fell in love with her right away. She and Phil, Amy's husband, ended up adopting her, and now Crystal has beautiful children of her own."

Melanie stared at her, Beatrice's words running through her head. *Her husband doesn't know it, but he isn't the father of their daughter.* "That's a lovely story," she said slowly. "Does Amy have any other children besides Crystal?"

Eileen nodded. "Right after she adopted Crystal, she got pregnant with Tyler. Just goes to show, the doctors don't know everything."

"Tyler? That's a boy, right?"

Eileen looked confused. "Well, he's grown up now. He's a pilot for the airlines."

"And Amy doesn't have another daughter?"

"No, just the one." She stared at Melanie. "Why do you ask?"

"Oh, nothing, really. I was just interested in the fostering, since Cindi talks about it quite a bit." To Melanie's relief, Liza walked around the corner and up the hallway toward them. "Oh, here's my grandmother. We're going to take Max for a walk now. Go ahead and pick out whatever you want from the bookshelves. I'm sure you'll find something you like."

She'd been opening the door as she spoke, which resulted in Max lunging outside and dragging her with him. She caught a glimpse of Eileen's puzzled face for a second before she turned and hauled Max to a stop.

Liza stepped through the doorway, said something to Eileen, and closed the door. "What the heck was all that about?" she demanded when she caught up with Melanie. "Eileen looked as if she'd bitten into an apple and found it was a lemon."

"She was telling me about Amy having adopted her daughter." Melanie tugged on Max's leash, slowing him down.

"Oh. I'm sorry, Mel. That must have been painful for you."

"What?" Melanie turned to look at her. "No, it's not that. It's what Beatrice said about Walter blackmailing Amy. I guess she got it wrong about Amy's daughter after all. But why would she think Walter was blackmailing her?"

"I think there are quite a few questions about Beatrice that need answering." Liza turned up the collar of her coat. "Like how she knew I played the piano."

Melanie frowned. "I thought she said you had piano fingers or something."

"And you thought that sounded feasible?"

"I guess I didn't think too much about it." They had reached the lane leading down to the beach, and Max had already turned the corner, his nose in the air, busily sniffing the inviting smells.

"Well, I did." Liza took off her scarf and wound it around her head, tucking the ends inside her coat. "I started wondering how she really could have known that I played the piano. Then I remembered last week, when I was in the garage sorting out my sheet music. I left it lying on the shelf until I had time to deal with it. The song sheets have my name written on them."

"You think Beatrice saw them? But what would she be doing in the garage?"

"Exactly. I asked myself the same question. I think she might have been looking for something to dig a hole for the saw."

Melanie stopped dead in her tracks. "You think Beatrice killed Walter? But why would she do that? I thought she was the only one in the group who actually liked him. She cried when she heard he was dead."

"I think that whole crying over Walter thing was an act. Remember when Gloria said last night at the séance that justice had been served? I think it was Beatrice who said, 'Amen.' It came from her end of the table."

Urged on by an impatient Max, Melanie started walking again. "And then there's the gloves."

Now it was Liza's turn to frown. "Gloves?"

"Yes. Doug told us that whoever used that saw wore gloves. You know how bundled up from the cold Beatrice always is, with a hat, scarf, and gloves. Well, when I saw her out in the yard, she wasn't wearing any gloves. I noticed her ring. It was flashing in the sunlight. Anyway, Sharon told us that Beatrice bought new gloves. So I wondered at the time what had happened to the old ones."

"Ah." Liza nodded. "You thought she might have messed them up while burying the saw and got rid of them."

"I do now." They had reached the sand, and Melanie bent down to unhook Max's leash. Watching him race to the ocean's edge to join another dog already frisking in the water, she struggled to capture something else teasing her mind. After a moment or two, she remembered what it was. "She didn't hear Orville," she said.

Liza stared at her. "What?"

"The night Walter died, when they were all out in the hallway. Everyone heard Orville laughing, but when I asked Beatrice about it, she said she didn't hear anything or see anyone.

I wonder now if it was because she was out on the balcony, pushing Walter to his death."

"Which is probably why Orville laughed." Liza gave a triumphant fist pump in the air. "I do believe we have our killer!"

"We don't know that for sure," Melanie warned her. "All this is just speculation. We have no proof and no motive. Remember what you're always saying? That every murder has means, motive, and opportunity? We only have two of them."

Liza sobered. "You're right. We have no proof. If we take this to Grumpy, he'll just tell us to mind our own business and stay out of his. It's circumstantial evidence. We have to rule out the alternatives."

"What does that mean?"

"It means that if we can find no alternative to the evidence, then it becomes less circumstantial."

Melanie took her time to digest that. "All right. What's the alternative for Beatrice being in the garage and seeing your song sheets?"

"In the first place, we don't know for sure that's what happened. She could have been in there for another reason. Or she might not have gone in there at all."

"Then how did she know you played piano?"

Liza shrugged. "I'm just saying that you're right. We can't rule out the possibility that we're wrong about all this. We need to find out if she had a motive, which is the reason I invited Josh to lunch. I have some questions for him."

Her pulse quickening, Melanie asked eagerly, "What questions?"

"For one thing, since you're having so much trouble finding out Orville's real name, I'm going to ask Josh to find out what it is." Liza pointed at the ocean, where Max was rolling on his back in the wet sand. "That dog will need a bath when we get back home."

Feeling frustrated, Melanie called out to the dog. Her grandmother had something else in mind, obviously. Since Liza seemed unwilling to discuss it, however, she would just have to wait until Josh joined them for lunch to find out what questions her grandmother had for him.

At the sound of her voice, Max had rolled over, scrambled up, and shaken himself, sending grains of wet sand from his coat in all directions.

Melanie marched down to him, picked up a pebble, and threw it in the ocean. Max plunged in after it, then just as quickly leapt back out of the frigid water and shook himself once more.

"That's got rid of some of it," Melanie said when she walked back to join Liza.

Her grandmother laughed. "That water must be freezing cold."

"Yeah, we'd better get him home." She grabbed hold of Max's collar before he could run off again and fastened his leash.

Liza looked at her watch. "Good idea. Josh should be here in about half an hour."

As they walked across the sand to the lane, Melanie turned over in her mind their conversation about Beatrice and the possibility that she had killed Walter. Envisioning the frail little woman who had cried at the news of his death, it just didn't seem possible. She could much more easily imagine the sisters, Joe, or Gloria planning the murder.

"I actually feel sorry for Beatrice," Liza said as they walked up the lane. "She seems so vulnerable."

"I know." Max was taking too long to sniff at something in the grass verge, and Melanie gently tugged on his leash. "In a way I hope we're wrong about her."

"But you don't think we are."

"No. It all seems to add up. She was very quick to blame someone else for killing Walter. She was the one who told us about the skeleton, then she said Nick could have killed him for making fun of him, and then she said Walter was blackmailing Amy when he couldn't have been. I wonder now if she misunderstood about Amy's daughter or if she made it up to throw suspicion on Amy."

"I think she was probably the one who told Grumpy that Joe was standing over Walter's body. She must have seen him from her window. Her room is the only one directly over the driveway."

"If we're right about this, she engineered my plunge down the stairs. She's a lot more devious than we realized."

"Yes, which means it will be difficult to prove anything."

"We have to try. We only have two days left."

Liza hunched her shoulders. "Well, let's find out if she had a motive first, then we'll worry about the rest later."

"How are we going to do that? Find out the motive, I mean."

"That's where I'm hoping Josh will be able to help us."

They turned the corner of the lane and started up the highway toward the inn. Melanie knew better than to bug her grandmother, but she was dying to know what it was Liza wanted to ask Josh.

Liza seemed determined to keep it to herself for the time being, however, and Melanie decided she would just have to be patient and wait until they talked to Josh.

Chapter 13

Josh arrived shortly after they got back from their walk. He'd brought a bottle of wine with him and offered to open it while Liza was grilling the sandwiches.

"We don't usually drink wine in the middle of the day," she told him, "but we'll be happy to make an exception for you."

Melanie wisely refrained from reminding her grandmother about their lunches at the hardware store.

"I hope you like this one," Josh said as Melanie handed him three wineglasses. "It's a new winery. I went to a wine tasting the other day and found this one. I know you both like Chardonnay, so let's enjoy it together."

"I knew there was a good reason I liked you." Liza put a sandwich in front of him. "Help yourself to the salad."

"I will. You guys make the best salads." Josh poured the wine, then heaped tossed salad onto his plate. "Once word gets around about your fabulous cooking, you'll be booked solid all year round."

Liza beamed. "You'll have to come to breakfast some morning. Then you can meet our assistant, Cindi. You two should have a lot in common."

Melanie hastily cut in before Liza could expand on her matchmaking. "I guess you don't have any fresh news about our murder case?"

"No, I don't. In fact, I was going to ask you guys if you have anything new to tell me." Josh took a bite out of his sandwich and chewed with a look of bliss on his face.

He must not eat well on his own, Melanie thought, watching him devour his lunch. It was just a grilled cheese with ham, but it might as well have been filet mignon by the way he was relishing every bite.

Liza waited until she had served the frozen yogurt before asking Josh her first question. "Remember the story you told us about the artist who committed suicide and came back as our ghost?"

Josh nodded. "Have you heard him lately?"

"All the time," Melanie said dryly.

Josh raised his eyebrows. "What do your guests think of that?"

"They're intrigued," Liza said, giving Melanie a sharp look, which her granddaughter interpreted as a warning to be careful what she said.

Melanie got it. Josh was a reporter, after all. It probably wouldn't be a good idea to say too much about their capricious resident. She wondered what he'd say if they told him about the blue light and the rocking chair. No doubt that news would cause a sensation. Either they'd be swamped with requests for reservations or they'd be the laughingstock of the town and everyone would think they were totally insane.

"Anyway," Liza said, "we call our ghost Orville, but we're both curious about his real name. Could you find out for us?"

"Sure." He finished the last spoonful of his yogurt. "I'll do some more research on it."

"Thanks." Liza reached for his empty bowl. "Would you like some more yogurt?"

"Thanks, but I think I'll pass." He looked at his watch. "I have an appointment this afternoon, so I have to run. That was a great lunch, you guys. Thanks."

"You're welcome," Melanie murmured.

"Next time, breakfast," Liza reminded him as he stood up.

"You're on."

"And thanks for the wine. It was delicious."

"Yes, it was," Melanie echoed, wondering when Liza was going to get to the question she was supposedly going to ask.

As if reading her mind, Liza added, "Oh, by the way, I wonder if you'd mind doing a little research on something else for us. When you get a spare moment, of course."

Josh smiled. "I figured there was a reason behind the invite."

"Nonsense. You're welcome any time," Liza said, looking a little abashed.

"It's okay. I'll gladly do anything you ask if it means a chance to enjoy your cooking." He flicked a glance at Melanie. "As long as it's legal, that is."

Melanie smiled back at him, hoping that whatever her grandmother was going to ask wasn't breaking any laws. Liza wasn't known for her appreciation of rules and regulations.

"It's about a suicide case." Liza got up from her chair. "It happened about five years ago. His name was Steven Carr, and he owned a construction company. We'd like to know anything you can tell us about it."

Josh took out his phone and starting thumbing text. "Steven Carr, five years ago, construction company. Got it." He closed his phone. "I'll get to it after my appointment, and I'll let you know what I find out. You okay, Melanie?"

Melanie realized she was staring at her grandmother and quickly switched her gaze back to Josh. "Yes, of course. It was good to see you, Josh."

"You too. I'll get back to you soon." With a quick wave, he disappeared through the door.

Melanie reached for her wineglass and drained the last drop. "So what was all that about?"

Liza sat down again. "It's a shot in the dark but worth a look, don't you think?"

"You think Walter had something to do with Beatrice's husband's suicide?"

"Remember the newspaper you found on your bed? The one that I didn't put there?"

Melanie frowned. "Of course. What about it?"

"What page was it opened to?"

Melanie had to think about that one. "It was an article you'd been talking about earlier. Oh, I remember. Something about a new hotel being built in Seaside."

"Right." Liza's smug expression made Melanie smile. "I think Orville was trying to tell us something. New hotel? Construction? Steven Carr's company that went bankrupt? Somehow there's a connection."

Melanie groaned. "Not Orville again."

"Don't forget, he helped us the last time when we were trying to solve the mystery of the skeleton we found behind the wall. I think he's helping us again now. Remember Gloria saying she found her gloves at the end of the hallway? I think Orville put them there to tell us about Beatrice's missing gloves."

"So why didn't he put Beatrice's gloves in the hallway?"

"Because they were missing, silly."

"Okay, so what do you think Walter's connection is to Beatrice's husband?"

"I don't know. But I'm hoping Josh will be able to tell us." Liza got up again. "Now I'm going to clear away these dishes. My head is aching with all this speculation."

Melanie got up to help her grandmother, her mind spinning with possibilities. Had Walter been responsible for Steven Carr's suicide? It would certainly give Beatrice a motive to hate the man. Was it enough for her to plot his murder? So many unanswered questions, and they would have to wait until Josh called back for the answers.

Liza decided to take a nap, leaving Melanie to work on the computer that afternoon. After working on the accounts for an hour or so, she gave in to the itch nagging in the back of her mind.

She tried putting Steven Carr's name into the search engine. She came up with a chef, a Swedish tennis player, a doctor, a writer, and one obituary that didn't seem to be about Beatrice's husband.

After playing around with it for a while, she finally gave up. Although she didn't expect any results, she put her mother's name in the search engine, and as usual, came up with nothing new.

She was playing with the idea of publishing a photo of her mother in the English newspapers when Liza opened the door.

"Am I disturbing you?" Her grandmother walked into the room, satisfaction glowing in her face.

"You heard from Josh," Melanie said, her pulse quickening.

"I did." Liza sat on the edge of the bed. "He called my cell phone."

"So? What did he say?"

"He found an article about Steven Carr's suicide." Liza folded her arms. "It gave the name of the manager who swindled all those customers and cost Beatrice's husband his company."

Melanie caught her breath. "Walter Dexter."

Liza smiled. "Right on."

*   *   *

Sitting in the kitchen nook a few minutes later, Melanie watched her grandmother pour steaming hot tea into two mugs and carry them over to the table.

"I should have twigged the connection," Liza said, "the night you found that newspaper on your bed." After handing a mug to Melanie, she sat down. "It's surprising what you miss when you're not looking for something."

"I still have trouble visualizing Beatrice planning a murder like that. It's so cold-blooded."

"She's a very good actor." Liza sipped her tea. "Remember how she cried when you announced Walter was dead?"

"And the séance, where she seemed to sleep through the whole thing."

"Except when Sharon mentioned her dead husband."

Melanie thought back to the night before, reliving the moment the chair had started rocking. Had she known at that moment that it wasn't Nick rocking the chair, she would have totally freaked out.

"So now we have means, motive, and opportunity," Liza said, bringing Melanie back to the present.

"So we can take it to Detective Dutton now and let him handle it," she said, feeling a sense of relief that it was finally over.

When Liza didn't answer right away, she gave her grandmother a sharp look. "What are you thinking?"

"I'm thinking that since we've come this far, wouldn't it be great if we could hand Grumpy Dutton a confession and wrap this up once and for all?"

"And how are we supposed to do that?"

Liza looked smug again. "Just leave it to me."

"I don't know." Melanie picked up her mug. "I don't think Dutton is going to be too happy with us if we mess this up. I think we should just tell him what we know and let him handle it."

"And let him poke around here for another two or three days? Meanwhile, we're stuck with five guests overstaying their welcome."

Melanie sipped her tea. Her grandmother was right. Until this case was solved, they were at the mercy of the surly detective. On the other hand, what if they were wrong about Beatrice? The real killer would know they were on the hunt, and they would lose any chance of finding the truth. Or what if they were right about Beatrice but she refused to admit to the crime? They would just put her on her guard and make it all the more difficult to prove she killed Walter.

"Well?" Liza sounded impatient. "Do we do this or not?"

Melanie put down her mug. "Either way is a risk, so we might as well go for it."

Liza punched the air. "I knew you would make the right decision. Now listen. Here's what we'll do."

*   *   *

Melanie had heard Liza's plan and had to admit that it might work. She was still wary about it all, however, when she followed her grandmother out to the garage later that night. If Beatrice was guilty, as they believed, they were dealing with a devious and dangerous killer.

After climbing into the back seat, Liza made herself comfortable, and Melanie took her place in the front seat of the car.

"It's a good job Max isn't in here with us," Liza murmured as she covered herself with the blanket she'd brought out from the house. "He'd have taken up all the room."

"He'd have given one of us something warm to cuddle up to," Melanie said, thankful that she'd also brought a blanket with her. "It's darn cold in here."

"Well, we shouldn't have to wait too long. Just remember to lie down when you see the door open."

Melanie peered in the direction of the door that led to the kitchen. "I can't see a thing."

"I know, but when the door opens, we should be able to see from the light behind it."

"I just hope this works." Shivering, Melanie drew the blanket closer around her shoulders. "What happened when you told Eileen the story?"

"She seemed shocked. I caught her coming down the stairs and told her that we'd found evidence in the garage that would implicate Walter's killer and that we'd left it there so that Grumpy Dutton could come by in the morning to collect it. I said that he would probably make an arrest at that time, which meant the rest of them would be able to go home on Sunday as planned."

"I hope she tells Beatrice all of that, or we'll be sitting out here all night."

"Are you kidding? You know Eileen. She was practically foaming at the mouth. She couldn't wait to get back into the living room and tell everyone the news. Which is exactly what we want her to do."

"Well, I—" Melanie broke off as the door to the kitchen opened without warning. She ducked down on the seat and made herself as invisible as possible beneath the blanket.

Light flooded the garage, and Melanie had to fight the impulse to raise her head to see who had turned on the switch.

She heard a soft grunt behind her as Liza moved her position and held her breath in case the intruder had heard her.

It seemed, however, that whoever had entered the garage was more interested in what was on the shelves. Melanie could hear objects being moved around and the clinking of glass.

She realized she was holding her breath and let it out just as Liza gave her a sharp poke in her shoulder.

"It's time," Liza hissed and opened her door.

Melanie threw off the blanket, sat up, and opened her door. She put one foot out, then had to untangle the other from the blanket before she could step out of the car.

By that time, Liza was on her feet, her voice sounding hoarse as she demanded, "What are you doing in here?"

Beatrice's voice answered her, faint with shock. "I was looking for my gloves."

Melanie finally got her foot free and scrambled out of the car. She saw Beatrice facing Liza with a look of frustration on her face. She wore a white terry cloth robe and pink slippers and looked so vulnerable in that moment that Melanie had a strong urge to go hug her—until she remembered that Beatrice had shoved a defenseless old man to his death.

"The gloves you wore when you buried the saw?" Liza asked, moving toward her.

For a long moment, it seemed that Beatrice would keep up the pretense of an innocent, helpless old woman, but then her eyes narrowed, and all traces of weakness left her face. "He killed my husband," she said between her teeth. "He deserved to die."

The change in her sent chills down Melanie's back. She wondered if Beatrice would try to fight them off, but when Liza took hold of the woman's arm, she offered no resistance.

Instead, she allowed herself to be led through the kitchen door and over to the nook. "Sit there," Liza ordered. "I'm going to make some tea."

She signaled to Melanie with her eyes for her to join Beatrice at the table.

Sitting down opposite the woman, Melanie felt sick to her stomach. Cold-blooded killers weren't supposed to look like somebody's beloved grandmother. She was relieved when Liza sat down next to her to wait for the kettle to boil.

"We know that Walter was responsible for the failure of your husband's company," Liza said quietly. "I want you to know we're both sorry about that, but that doesn't give you the right to take his life."

Beatrice's chin shot up. Her eyes were bright with unshed tears, and red patches burned in her cheeks. "He took my husband's life. An eye for an eye."

"No, your husband took his own life. Walter had no hand in that."

"He caused Steven's depression. He would never have killed himself if it hadn't been for Walter's betrayal." Beatrice slumped back on her chair as if her show of bravado had sapped the last of her energy. "My husband couldn't live with the fact that he'd put all his trust in a common thief," she said, her voice now dull with resignation. "Walter not only stole money, he stole my husband's good name and reputation, and Steven lost everything—his business, valued customers, and friends. Walter had to pay for that."

"But surely Walter had to answer to the law for embezzlement?" Melanie leaned forward. "Your husband did sue him, right?"

"Oh, he took him to court." Beatrice hunted in her pocket, pulled out a tissue, and blew her nose. "Because it was a first offense, Walter got three years' probation. He was ordered to pay back the money he stole, but we never saw a penny of it." She gritted her teeth for a moment. "It wasn't the money, though. It was the betrayal that killed Steven."

Max sat up in his bed and whined. Melanie glanced over at him. He was probably wondering why he wasn't asleep on her bed; it was way after his bedtime. Turning back to Beatrice, she asked, "So you tracked Walter down and found him here in Oregon?"

"Yes. I found out he was living in the Springlake retirement community, and I moved up here. When I discovered he belonged to the reading group, I joined it too." She met Melanie's gaze. "I just wanted to make his life miserable, the way he made mine."

"But he must have known it was you," Liza said. "Didn't he wonder why you'd tracked him down?"

"Not until the day he died. We'd never met in person before that. I made it a rule never to associate with my husband's business associates. Steven didn't believe in combining professional and personal relationships. He said it was bad for business. He kept a photo of us on his desk, but it was taken fifty years ago. I looked a little different back then."

"So you did everything you could to make Walter's life miserable?" Liza got up as the kettle's sharp whistle pricked Max's ears.

"That's what I intended to do." Beatrice stared at her wrinkled hands. "But every idea I came up with seemed like nothing more than a childish prank. I just couldn't think of anything that would satisfy the burning need to punish him for what he did. He was already miserable, always complaining about something. I found out his wife had divorced him after the trial, but even that didn't help. He did seem to enjoy the reading group, though none of us liked him much. I thought about getting him thrown out of the club, but I was afraid if I complained too much about him, they'd turn on me instead. They are the only friends I have here, and I didn't want to lose them."

"I can understand that," Liza murmured. "There's not much else that's worse than loneliness when you get old."

Beatrice nodded. "Anyway, as time went by, I got more and more frustrated. It infuriated me to know Walter was living a comfortable life while my husband was rotting away in his coffin." She let out a long sigh.

Liza had poured the boiling water into the teapot and was taking down the mugs from the cabinet.

Max lifted his head again.

For a moment or two, the silence in the room was so thick, Melanie could hear her heartbeat thudding in her ears. She half expected Orville to break the charged silence with one of his chuckles, but the seconds ticked by in silence until Beatrice spoke again.

"When Eileen announced the planned trip, I remembered seeing a picture of the inn in the newspaper. It was earlier this year when you found that skeleton hidden behind the wall. I looked it up on the Internet and saw the balcony on the upstairs floor." She looked over at Liza, who seemed transfixed, the teapot poised in her hand over one of the mugs. "I knew Walter had signed up to go, and I kept fantasizing about him falling from that balcony."

She fell silent, and after a moment, Liza said quietly, "And that's when you planned to give him a little help."

Beatrice briefly closed her eyes. "I bought the saw and wrote the note before we left Portland. I had a birthday card that Gloria had given me, and I copied her handwriting from that. As close as I could, anyway. I knew Walter wouldn't be able to resist a rendezvous with Gloria."

Liza carried two of the steaming mugs over to the table and went back to get the third.

Melanie still had a hard time imagining how the woman who sat opposite her could have planned to kill another human being. "When did you saw through the railings?"

"During the party that night. I made sure everyone was in the living room, then slipped out onto the balcony. No one noticed that I was late to the party, or if they did, they paid no attention."

Liza brought her mug of tea over to the table and sat down. "So how did you give Walter the note that night?"

"I waited for everyone to get settled down in their rooms, then I slipped the note under his door and knocked to make sure he found it. My room is next to his, so it was easy for me to run back inside before he opened his door. I peeked through the crack, though, just to make sure."

Melanie was beginning to feel sick again. "Then you waited for him to go out on the balcony."

"Yes. I needed to tell him who I was and how utterly despicable he was, and how much I hated him for what he'd done. I wanted to see fear in his eyes. The kind of terror I felt when I found my husband's body swinging from a hook in the garage."

Melanie shuddered. "I'm sorry. That must have been a terrible shock."

Beatrice's eyes were filled with pain. "I hope and pray you never have to go through what I went through that day."

"Amen to that," Liza murmured.

"Walter was out there," Beatrice said, "standing with his back to the railings. I could see his face in the glow from the moonlight. He was shocked to see me and even more shocked when I told him who I was. All the anger that had been building up in me came out as I told him how much I hated him."

She paused, and when she spoke again, the bitterness had crept back into her voice. "I raised my fist, and he backed away from me. When he reached the damaged railings, I jumped forward and shoved him, hard, with both hands on his chest."

The look of vindication on her face destroyed the last of any compassion Melanie might have felt. This woman had taken a man's life, with no apparent regret for what she'd done. She deserved to be punished.

Max whined and trotted over to her, nudging her with his nose. Her hand strayed out to pat his head while she reached for her cell phone with the other.

"You realize we have to call the police," Liza said as Melanie dialed 9-1-1.

"Yes." Beatrice closed her eyes. "In a way, it's a relief. I feel like I've been living with a time bomb ever since it happened." *It should be a relief to everyone*, Melanie thought as she waited for the dispatcher to answer the call. But somehow, looking at the elderly woman slumped on her chair, it was hard to feel anything but regret that she and Liza had been the ones to seal Beatrice's fate.

"Yes," she said into the phone in answer to the dispatcher's voice. "I need someone to come to the Merry Ghost Inn immediately. We have a murderer sitting in our kitchen."

Detective Dutton arrived a short while later, wearing his usual inscrutable expression. Melanie met him at the door, feeling a little uneasy about leaving Liza alone in the kitchen with a killer and even more uncomfortable having to tell Dutton how they trapped Beatrice.

To her disappointment, Ben wasn't with him. The two officers he'd brought along quickly headed for the kitchen while Melanie repeated everything that the woman had told her.

Dutton seemed shocked by her revelation, but her satisfaction was short-lived when he growled at her. "You both took an enormous risk, and once again you disobeyed my orders to stay out of police business. I hope you realize that this could have ended badly for you, not to mention the possibility of you totally ruining my case. I thought you had learned your lesson from the last time this happened. I said it then and I'll say it again"—he leaned forward, his eyes glittering with anger—"stay out of my way and mind your own damn business!"

To Melanie's relief, the two officers appeared in the hallway again, one of them holding Beatrice by the arm. Liza hovered behind them, her eyes wide and anxious.

Dutton barked at the officers, and they led Beatrice out the front door. Her gaze briefly met Melanie's as she passed, but her face was devoid of expression. To the last, apparently, Beatrice would feel justified in what she had done.

* * *

The following morning, Melanie made the announcement of Beatrice's arrest to a shocked group of guests. She left them speculating with each other in the dining room and went back to the kitchen where Cindi and Liza were dishing up breakfast.

"I can't believe it," Cindi said as she balanced plates on her arm. "She seemed like such a feeble old woman. I can't believe she killed a man."

"Just goes to show you can't trust anyone by their looks," Liza said, giving her assistant a meaningful look.

Cindi appeared to ignore that as she headed for the door. "Well, at least this lot can go home now," she said as she disappeared into the hallway.

"I'll drink to that," Liza said, raising a glass of orange juice.

Ben stopped by soon after they had cleared away the breakfast dishes. Liza was in her room and Cindi was cleaning bedrooms when he rang the bell.

Melanie let him in, unable to hide her delight at seeing him.

"I heard about what happened last night," he said as she led him down the hallway. "How'd you get Mrs. Carr to confess all that?"

Sitting him down in the nook, Melanie told him how they'd come to suspect Beatrice and Liza's plan to confront her in the garage.

"Well, it was very ingenious of you both," he said when she was finished. "And totally irresponsible, given you were both warned to stay out of the investigation."

Melanie avoided looking at him. "I know. But it worked, and I can't say I'm sorry about that."

"I don't expect you to."

Risking a look at him, she was relieved to see his smile. "Thanks."

"You can thank me by having dinner with me."

For a moment, she hesitated, torn between protecting her vulnerable heart and going for it. "You're not going to lecture me again about getting involved in police business, I hope?"

He gazed at her for so long, she was finding it hard to breathe. "I promise," he said softly, "we'll keep the evening strictly personal and pleasurable."

She was on dangerous ground again, but right then she was willing to take the risk. "It's a date. Just let me know when."

His grin made her forget the trauma of the past few days. "I'll get back to you soon." He stood up. "Now I have to get back to the station."

She followed him to the front door and watched him stride down the driveway without looking back, then closed the door and leaned against it. Something told her she was fighting a losing battle with her feelings for him. It was the last thing she needed right now, but she couldn't deny it felt good to be interested in a man again. Even if there was no future to it.

*   *   *

"All out on time," Liza said as she closed the door behind the departing book club members. "We have a couple of hours break before our next guests arrive. Let's hope this next lot is a little more predictable."

Melanie silently agreed as she followed her grandmother to the kitchen. She couldn't stop thinking about Beatrice and how easy it was to make the biggest mistake of your life. Walter had paid deeply for his mistakes, and now Beatrice had to pay for hers. She could only hope that the widow would survive her prison term and eventually find peace.

"By the way," Liza said as she put the kettle on for tea, "I forgot to tell you—Josh gave me the name of the artist presumably haunting the inn."

"He did?" Melanie opened the fridge and took out a soda. "What was it?"

"It was Arthur Mansfield." Liza shook her head.

"Arthur. Somehow that doesn't seem like a good name for a ghost."

"I prefer Orville. How about you?"

Before Melanie could answer, a familiar sound filled the kitchen. It started as a snicker, then a giggle, then a full throttle belly laugh.

Max barked, and Melanie put her hands over her ears while Liza stood staring at her with wide eyes.

The laughing cut off abruptly, leaving an eerie silence behind. Max whined and pressed his furry body against Melanie's leg.

"That was so weird," Liza said, her voice shaking. "He's never sounded that loud before."

Melanie's heart was thumping so hard, she could hear its echo in her ears. She no longer had any doubts. The Merry Ghost Inn was undeniably haunted.

It made her wonder what Orville—and fate—had in store for them.

Melanie's Tasty Lemon Poppy Seed Muffins

1¾ cups all-purpose flour
½ cup granulated sugar
1 tablespoon poppy seeds
1 tablespoon finely shredded lemon peel
2 teaspoons baking powder
½ teaspoon salt
¾ cup fat-free milk
1 beaten egg
¼ cup cooking oil
2 tablespoons coarse sugar

Grease twelve 2½-inch muffin cups or line with paper baking cups. Set muffin cups aside.

In a medium mixing bowl, stir together flour, granulated sugar, poppy seeds, lemon peel, baking powder, and salt. Make a well in the center of flour mixture.

In another medium bowl, combine milk, egg product, and oil. Add egg mixture all at once to flour mixture. Stir just until moistened (batter will be lumpy). Spoon batter into the prepared muffin cups, filling each full. Sprinkle tops with coarse sugar.

Bake in a 375 degree oven for 20 to 25 minutes or until golden. Cool in muffin cups on a wire rack for 5 minutes. Remove from pans. Serve warm.

Read an excerpt from

BE OUR GHOST

the next

MERRY GHOST INN MYSTERY

by KATE KINGSBURY

available soon in hardcover from
Crooked Lane Books

**CROOKED
LANE**

NEW YORK

Chapter 1

"What I love most about springtime," Liza Harris said as she pulled her white woolen scarf from her head, "is the smell."

Seated across from her in the dark corner of the hardware store, Melanie West studied her grandmother. It never ceased to amaze her that Liza could look so vibrant, especially after mornings like this when they'd cooked and served breakfast to eight guests. With her stylishly short, white hair tinted a pale blonde and a discreet touch of makeup, Liza looked closer to her fifties than her seventy-three years.

Realizing that her grandmother was waiting for an answer, Melanie sniffed the air. "All I can smell right now is beer and hamburgers."

Liza smiled. "I didn't mean in here. This place smells like an English pub. Only someone with an offbeat imagination would put a bar and a restaurant inside a hardware store. Though I have to admit, it is rather unique." She looked around at the scattering of small tables bordering the curved bar. A large poster of a bulldog holding a glass of beer leered at the customers from the wall. Liza studied it for a moment, then turned back to Melanie.

"Anyway," she said, "I was talking about the smell outside." She waved a hand at the window on the other side of the room. "The blossoms, the new leaves on the trees, the ocean, the wet sand, the seaweed, the sea breezes, it all carries the promise of warmer weather and fun in the sun."

Melanie reached for the menu. "Very poetic. It also brings the promise of crowded rooms at the inn, more time slaving over a hot stove, and the end of our peace and quiet."

Liza raised her eyebrows. "I thought you loved all that work."

"I do." Sensing that she'd upset her grandmother, Melanie stretched out a hand and patted Liza's arm. "I was just kidding. Owning a bed-and-breakfast at the beach has to be the absolute best way to make a living. Even if it does mean putting up with a ghost."

To her relief, Liza grinned. "We haven't heard from our merry ghost lately. Maybe he's found somewhere else to haunt."

"One can only hope."

"Oh, go on with you. You love Orville as much as I do, and he does bring in the guests. He's the first thing most of them ask about when they arrive at the inn."

Melanie was about to answer when she caught sight of the burly owner of the hardware pub striding toward them. Doug Griffith was a big man with a hearty laugh and a quick wit—one of the few people who could match words with her grandmother. His white whiskers and beer belly reminded Melanie of Santa Claus, and she always looked forward to his bantering with Liza.

Doug was one of the first friends they'd made in Sully's Landing. He and Liza had established a rapport the moment they'd met. The two of them acted at times as though they were siblings, engaged in petty teenage rivalry. Melanie, however, could tell that Liza loved the attention, more than she was willing to admit.

Her grandmother never missed an opportunity to have lunch at the pub, and there'd been more than a few. Doug's brother, Shaun, was a reserve police officer, and when Liza and Melanie had become involved in a murder investigation, Doug had provided useful information with the help of his brother. The access to otherwise classified material had given Liza the excuse she needed to visit the pub, and she'd taken full advantage of it.

"Hi, English!" Arriving at the table, Doug paused next to Liza's chair and laid a hand on her shoulder. "Slumming again, I see."

Liza rolled her eyes. Doug had called her "English" since the day they'd met. Much to Liza's disgust, he'd mistaken her English accent for Australian. She had forcefully set him straight and he'd never let her forget it.

She looked up at him now, her smile deceptively sweet. "One has to eat, and the food is passable here."

"Passable." Doug nodded and pulled a chair over from a nearby table. "Well, your majesty, I suppose I should feel privileged that you honor us with your presence."

"I said the food is passable. That doesn't include the company."

"Ouch." Doug looked at Melanie. "Is she including you, or am I the only derelict here?"

Melanie dropped the menu on the table. "Take no notice of her. She's spaced out on the smell of spring."

Liza frowned at her. "I thought you were on my side."

"I am. So behave."

Lowering himself onto the chair, Doug laughed. "Nothing I enjoy more than two females fighting over me."

Liza gave him a look that would have stopped a charging rhinoceros. "Don't flatter yourself. No man is worth fighting over."

Deciding it was time to change the subject, Melanie turned to Doug. "We didn't see you at the town hall last night. Were you there?"

"I would hope so," Liza put in. "After all, most of the towns-folk were there to hear what the mayor had to say about the new arcade. It got pretty contentious, too, with so many for and against the whole thing."

"I know. I got there late." Doug's grin faded. "I still can't believe the committee is actually going to vote on that damn arcade. They should have thrown it out the moment Northwood presented the idea."

Liza nodded. "I have to admit, building a games arcade in the middle of town would change the face of Sully's Landing forever. I read somewhere that Jason Northwood plans to put in over a hundred video games and pinball machines."

"That's not all," Doug said in a voice gruff with disgust. "He's planning a full-service bar, trivia nights, host DJs, game tournaments, and, believe it or not, a rock band karaoke."

Melanie stared at him in dismay. "That sounds terrible."

Doug shrugged. "If it was in Seaside, I'm sure it would be welcomed with open arms. It's that kind of town. The visitors who go there would love it. But like so many of the residents said last night at the hearing, this isn't Seaside. This is Sully's Landing and people come here for the peace and quiet."

Liza nodded. "It's a unique town with a character all its own, that's for sure. It's on such a beautiful part of the Oregon coast, and you won't find lovelier natural scenery anywhere."

"It's the small-town atmosphere that sells it—no fast-food or drive-in restaurants or noisy music blaring down the streets." Obviously warming to his subject, Doug picked up a fork and started tapping it on the table. "It says right there in the Comprehensive Plan for the town that commercial amusement activities are prohibited, which is why the Planning Commission and the city councillors are voting at the end of the week. If they agree to change the clause, then the arcade project will go ahead."

"Well," Liza said, "you're on the Planning Commission, and I know you'll vote no, and surely the rest of the committee will, too? They all love this town as much as you do."

Doug sighed. "Maybe they do, but Jason Northwood is a hard-nosed businessman and usually gets what he wants. Paul Sullivan will most likely vote yes, since Northwood will be leasing from him and paying a good deal more than the tenants there now. His wife will probably vote for it, too."

Liza nodded. "Brooke Sullivan would vote for anything that means more money for her."

"Even if it means destroying part of Main Street." Doug shook his head. "Foster's bakery and the two stores next to him will have to be torn down to make room for the arcade."

Melanie's cry of dismay mingled with Liza's shocked "Bugger!"

"I can't believe Paul would get rid of the bakery." Melanie shook her head. "It's one of the main attractions here."

"Well, since Sullivan owns the town, I guess he can do what he likes." Doug dropped the fork on the table with a clatter. "Northwood has called a meeting tonight in his room at the

Windshore Inn for all the members who will be casting a vote. We'll all be there—the mayor and the council members as well as the Planning Commission. I guess he's going to try and persuade us to approve his damn project." He shoved his chair back, his face darkening with anger. "Here's one person he won't be able to sucker into his precious plan. Jason Northwood is the scum of the earth and belongs in the depths of hell. Now, if you'll excuse me, ladies, I have to get back to the bar."

Liza waited until he was out of earshot before muttering, "Well, he's sure got his knickers in a twist. I've never seen him so steamed. It sounds like he has a personal grudge against the man. I wouldn't want to be in Jason Northwood's shoes at that meeting tonight."

Melanie reached for the menu again. "I just hope Doug can convince the others not to vote for that miserable arcade. I'm getting tired of reading about it in the paper. I'd like to see an end to the whole thing."

"I'm sure there are plenty of people who agree with you. Me included." Liza picked up her own menu. "On the other hand, Jason Northwood does have points in his favor. As he's been constantly telling us in all those noisy ads on TV, the arcade would bring more jobs to the town, and more money coming in from tourists, which would benefit the local businesses. It could lead to more construction, helping the housing shortage here."

"And Sully's Landing would turn into another Seaside."

"Exactly, and that makes it hard to imagine how the committee will vote at the end of the week. In any case, we'd better order our food before we outstay our welcome here."

In spite of her concern over the future of the town, Melanie had to laugh. "You could never do that in Doug's eyes."

Liza shrugged. "Right now I don't think Doug is in any mood for our company." She sent a worried look at the bar, where the owner stood talking to a customer. "I just hope the meeting tonight goes better than he's anticipating."

Liza's words seemed to echo in Melanie's head for the rest of the day. Although she and Liza watched the news on TV that evening, the anchor made no mention of the meeting. Obviously, the problems of Sully's Landing were too insignificant for Portland's newscasts unless there was a murder or something equally drastic.

Her thoughts came back to haunt her the following morning, when Josh Phillips, the local news reporter, paid them a visit.

He had planned it well, as usual, arriving after the breakfast meals had been served and in time to enjoy the leftovers.

Liza had made a sausage-and-egg casserole, while Melanie had created the perfect accompaniment with her blueberry French toast—a delicious mixture of bread, eggs, cream cheese, and blueberries.

Cindi Metzger, their eager young assistant, had brought back plates from the dining room that were scraped clean of every crumb, much to Melanie's delight. Nothing made her happier than seeing their guests enjoy an appetizing start to their day.

Unless it was doing exactly what she was doing right then— sitting in the nook in the corner window of the roomy, warm kitchen watching frothy waves race to the sandy shore below her. She never tired of the view from that window. The shoreline stretched into the distance, sometimes visible in all its glory, sometimes shrouded by the sea mist rolling off the mighty Pacific Ocean.

This morning the sky was clear, allowing the sunlight to sparkle on the roofs of the houses and condos that bordered the cliffs. Seagulls swooped hungrily over the sand, while below them dogs bounded and chased in the joy of freedom from fences and leashes.

"It looks like it's going to be another nice day," Cindi said as she plopped down on a chair opposite Melanie with a loaded plate of casserole and French toast. As usual, her unconventional outfit must have raised eyebrows in the dining room. Her bright-yellow top completely bared one shoulder, and its long sleeves were full of holes, allowing her tattoos to peek through. She wore her black hair shaved on one side and chin length on the other, with pink streaks for the final touch. Gold studs gleamed in her nose and one eyebrow, reminding Melanie of a female pirate.

Liza had been dead against hiring such an unconventional assistant to wait on their guests. Having listened to Cindi's story of her past, Melanie had been equally determined to hire her, and it had taken some persuading for her to change her grandmother's mind. Once she had told Liza about Cindi's unfortunate upbringing, her grandmother had reluctantly agreed to a trial period.

Much to the surprise of both of them, the guests had nothing but praise for the young woman, and Cindi had firmly cemented her position in the household. Even Max, the mostly sheepdog they'd rescued from the shelter, adored her and followed her everywhere. Although Liza still occasionally fretted about the unsuitability of their new assistant's outfits, as long as no one complained she managed to refrain from commenting too strongly on the subject in front of Cindi.

"That was a busy breakfast," Liza said, sinking down at the

table with a sigh. "So many people asking for seconds. It's a good job I made an extra casserole, though I was hoping to freeze it and use it later."

"You say that every time," Cindi said, wiping her chin with the back of her hand, causing Liza to wince. "You know they're going to ask for more. Why don't you just, like, make more?"

"Because the day we do will be the day no one wants another helping, and then we'll be stuck with all that extra food. We've only got so much room in the freezer." Liza plucked a napkin from the holder and handed it to Cindi, who promptly dropped it in her lap.

"Maybe we should get another freezer," Melanie said, reaching for her coffee. "We could put it in the garage and—" She broke off as the front doorbell echoed down the hallway. Max raised his shaggy head and uttered a soft bark in protest at being disturbed from his morning snooze.

"I'll get it," Cindi said, pushing back her chair.

Melanie held out a detaining hand. "Finish your breakfast. I'll go." She got up and headed for the door. Max jumped out of his bed to follow her.

"If it's someone looking for a room, we're full until tomorrow," Liza called out.

Melanie flapped a hand in the air and hurried out of the room with the dog right behind her. Someday, she promised herself as she walked briskly toward the front door, they would get rid of the ancient wallpaper in the hallway and that monstrous chandelier and replace them with something a little more inviting.

They were the first things people saw when they entered the house, and although so far no one had commented on either one, first impressions were important. The wallpaper, with its faded pink roses on an ugly beige background, and the tarnished metal chandelier didn't exactly shout comfort, convenience, and civility—Liza's three Cs of hospitality.

The hallway had escaped the fire that had damaged the living room, dining room, and two bedrooms a year earlier. Therefore, it hadn't been included in the redecorating. An omission Melanie hoped to take care of in the near future. Thinking about the cost involved in such a project, she pulled open the door.

The young man standing on the porch was gazing above the dense stand of trees across the road at the ridge of mountains beyond. Unlike at the beach, here the morning mist still lingered over peaks, waiting for the sun to banish it until nightfall. It shrouded the pines, making them look like wispy ghosts.

The collar of the visitor's New York Yankees jacket was turned up, and his dark hair sprung from his head in spikes.

Melanie smiled. "Good morning, Josh. You're just in time for breakfast."

He looked back at her, his grin spreading over his face. "That's what I was hoping." He held out his hand to the dog. "Hi, Max."

Max sniffed his hand, then, looking bored, padded back down the hallway.

"Come in." Melanie stood back to let him enter and closed the door. "We're all in the kitchen. Liza will be happy to see you. We're dying to know what happened at the arcade meeting last night."

"That's why I'm here. I figured you'd want to hear the news."

She had turned away from him to lead him down the hallway,

but something in his voice made her twist back sharply to look at him. "What happened?"

The kitchen door opened just then, and Liza popped her head out. "Is that Josh? I thought I recognized your voice. Come in and sit down while the casserole is still warm."

"Casserole!" The reporter rudely brushed past Melanie and charged into the kitchen. "I hope it's sausage." He waved a hand at Cindi. "Hi, gorgeous."

Shaking her head, Melanie followed him into the room.

Cindi stuck out her tongue and went back to checking her phone, while Max loped over to his bed next to the refrigerator and settled down again.

Josh took the empty place at the table, sniffing the air with a look of pure contentment on his face. "That smells like heaven."

Behind him, the light from the windows reflected on the copper pots Liza had brought back from a visit to England. They hung over the island counter and sent a glow like a halo behind Josh's head.

"If we ever knew what heaven smells like," Liza said as she ladled piles of the casserole onto a plate.

"Are they blueberries?" Josh plucked a blueberry from Cindi's plate, and she swiftly slapped his hand. "Ow! That hurt." He popped the berry into his mouth.

"It was meant to." She glared at him, but her mouth twitched in a reluctant grin.

Melanie waited until Liza had finished waiting on Josh and sat down before saying, "I think Josh has something important he wants to tell us."

The reporter's face sobered at once. "I do, but you may want to finish your breakfast before I tell you."

Cindi looked up from her phone. "What's happened? Is it something bad?"

Melanie felt a tug of apprehension. Judging from the look on Josh's face, it was very bad.

Josh shoved a mouthful of sausage and egg into his mouth and chewed for a few maddening seconds while all three women sat staring at him, waiting for the bomb to drop.

Finally he swallowed. "That's good. That's really good."

Unable to bear the suspense any longer, Melanie said sharply, "Josh, for pity's sake, tell us what's going on."

Josh drew a deep breath, obviously savoring the moment when he would deliver the startling news. "A busboy went to fetch the room-service trolley from Jason Northwood's room late last night. He found Northwood lying dead on the floor. He'd been stabbed in the heart."

Liza and Melanie both uttered a shocked gasp, while Cindi muttered, "Bummer."

Liza was the first to ask the obvious question. "Do the police know who did it?"

Josh shook his head. "The cops aren't saying much about it, but from what I hear, everyone who was at that meeting last night is a suspect."

"Oh, wow." Cindi leaned back and folded her arms. "That should make things interesting."

Melanie had to agree with her. All those attending the meeting were prominent members of the community. That kind of notoriety was bound to be embarrassing.

"Everyone who was at that meeting?" Liza echoed, her face shadowed with worry. "That includes Doug."

Melanie exchanged a sympathetic look with her. "As well as our bank manager, the city planner, and our esteemed mayor," she reminded her grandmother.

"Paul Sullivan and his wife were there as well," Josh put in, "and Foster Holmberg, who owns the bakery, and . . ." he frowned. "What's the name of the woman who owns the Seabreeze Hair Salon?"

"That's Amanda Richards," Cindi said. "I can't believe she's a murder suspect. She's so, like, gutless."

Liza scowled at her. "If you can't say something nice about someone, don't say anything at all."

Cindi rolled her eyes but mercifully chose not to answer.

Melanie went over the list in her mind. "What makes them think it was one of the committee members?" She stared at Josh. "Anyone could have gone to that hotel room after they left."

"Word is that there were so many fingerprints in the room, the forensics department had trouble sorting them out. So far, they haven't found any that don't belong to the members of that meeting." Josh leaned forward. "Think about it. They were all there because some arrogant, self-serving billionaire wanted to turn our town into a screaming, decadent playground that would have attracted all the worst elements of humanity."

Cindi raised her eyebrows. "Whoa. That's a bit harsh."

"They could have just voted no to changing the clause in the Plan," Melanie said. "Without their official consent, Jason North-wood would have had to give up the idea."

"You obviously didn't know Northwood." Josh looked grim.

"He had a reputation for getting what he wanted. Besides, word is that Paul Sullivan was planning on voting for the arcade, and probably his wife as well, since they would get a lot more money from the arcade lease than Foster pays them for the bakery."

"Exactly what Doug said," Liza murmured.

"That's still only two votes," Cindi said, speaking with her mouth full and earning another reproving look from Liza. "What about the other six?"

Josh swallowed another mouthful of his breakfast. "I heard that Amanda what's-her-name was thinking of voting for it, too. It wouldn't surprise me if Warren and Jim were leaning that way as well. After all, it would bring money into the town."

Liza growled. "Trust them to go for the big bucks and to hell with anyone else."

"Well, we don't know for sure they would have voted for the arcade," Melanie said, unwilling to believe that Jim Farmer, the city planner, and Warren Pierce would have wanted to change anything about Sully's Landing. Warren had been manager of the bank for years and was always crowing about the town's virtues.

"We don't know they wouldn't have," Josh said, "which put the vote up in the air. It could have gone either way. Someone must have been desperate to stop Jason Northwood from ruining Sully's Landing."

"And you think that's why he was killed?" Liza looked worried as she stared at Josh.

Melanie knew her grandmother had to be remembering Doug's words the day before.

Jason Northwood is the scum of the earth and belongs in the depths of hell.

In the next instant she scolded herself for even thinking that Doug could commit cold-blooded murder. He was loud and sometimes a little too assertive, but he was no killer.

"The police seem to think so," Josh said, reaching for a helping of French toast. "Eleanor is supposed to make a statement this evening on the news. You know it's big news if our mayor makes an announcement on TV."

"She must be devastated." Liza picked up her tea and drained the cup before adding, "Eleanor Knight might be the mayor of Sully's Landing, but she does tend to overreact whenever there's a crisis in the town. Remember that tree that came down in the storm last month and took out the mailbox on the corner of Willow Avenue, and how she came on TV to reassure everyone that it was an isolated incident? The way she was talking, you'd have thought we'd been attacked by aliens."

Cindi snorted, spraying crumbs from her mouth. "Sorry." She grabbed her napkin and dabbed at the table. "You shouldn't make me laugh when my mouth's full."

Liza shook her head, but before she could say anything, Josh got up from his chair.

"Gotta run." He checked his watch. "I've got an interview with a desk clerk at the Windshore in fifteen minutes."

Liza's eyes gleamed. "You will tell us if you find out anything else?"

Josh grinned. "Don't worry. You'll hear it before it goes live. It will give me an excuse to come for another fantastic breakfast. You two have to be the best cooks in the entire state of Oregon."

"Go on with you," Liza murmured. "Flattery will get you everywhere."

"I know." Josh winked at Melanie and dug his fist into Cindi's shoulder. "I'll let myself out. See you guys later." He walked past Max's bed, giving the dog a pat on the head before disappearing through the door.

"Cheeky bugger," Cindi muttered.

Melanie laughed at the young woman's perfect imitation of Liza's English accent. She couldn't help noticing the faint pink glow in Cindi's cheeks. In spite of the assistant's adamant claims that she had eyes only for Nick Hazelton, a somewhat stern young man who seemed far too rigid to be the vibrant young woman's boyfriend, it seemed Cindi wasn't entirely unfazed by Josh's attention.

"I'd better get going, too," Cindi said, getting to her feet. "I've got beds to make and bathrooms to clean."

"Yes, you do." Liza got up, too, and started picking up the empty dishes. "And we have dishes to wash and a kitchen to clean. There's never a dull moment at the Merry Ghost Inn."

"At least," Melanie said later as she stacked mugs into the dishwasher, "this time the murder doesn't involve us or anyone at the inn."

Liza stopped scrubbing the top of the stove and turned to look at her. "At least we hope it doesn't."

Prospect Free Library

0001500104748